THE UNITED FEDERATION MARINE CORPS

BOOK 7: COLONEL

Colonel Jonathan P. Brazee
USMC (Ret)

Copyright © 2015 Jonathan Brazee

Semper Fi Press

Acknowledgements:

I want to thank all those who took the time to pre-read this book, catching my mistakes in both content and typing. I want to thank Christina Cutting, my editor, for her help in the book and for catching my many typos and mistakes. Any remaining typos and inaccuracies are solely my fault. Finally, I want to thank those in my mailing list who gave me invaluable advice and insight concerning *Lieutenant Colonel*, this book and the upcoming final book in the series.

Original Cover Art by Almaz Sharipov

TARAWA

Chapter 1

"Staff, present, ARMS!" Major Maurice "Mary" Abd Elmonim, the battalion operations officer and the commander of troops for the ceremony shouted out as all six officers brought their swords up in a crisp salute.

Ryck returned the salute in his best drill field manner.

"Staff, order, ARMS," Mary said before doing an about face, and in a much louder command, shouted out, "Battalion, order, ARMS!"

Looking over the COT's shoulder, Ryck saw the entire battalion, all five companies, complete the order seemlessly.

It seemed like only a week ago, not almost three years, that he'd proudly taken command of Second Battalion, Third Marines, the "Fuzos." Now, it was over.

"Sergeant Major, deliver the colors to the commanding officer!" the COT shouted out.

Sergeant Major Hector "Hecs" Phantawisangtong immediately stepped off and marched to the color guard. Ryck kept his eyes locked forward, but he could still see Hecs take the battalion colors from the bearer. Hecs stepped off to the right, left hand at the base of the pole, right hand half-way up, and marched directly to Ryck.

As he marched, Sergeant Timko Pleasance, the narrator, with his deep, resonant voice, spoke over the microphone:

Ladies and gentlemen, we now come to the most solemn moment of the ceremony, that actual passing of command. The battle colors of a Marine Corps unit symbolize both the storied history of the unit as well as the authority and accountability of command. Transferring the colors during the ceremony symbolizes the relinquishing of command by Lieutenant Colonel Ryck Lysander. By accepting the colors, Major Sandy Haunish Peltier-Aswad accepts command and confirms his total commitment to the Marines and sailors that he will command. Sergeant Major Hector Amarin Phantawisangtong is delivering the colors to the commanding officer.

Hecs had crossed the field to reach Ryck and stopped in front of him. The two men looked each other in the eye, showing no emotion.

"Ladies and gentlemen, please rise for the transfer of the colors," Sgt Pleasance said.

First the staff, then the battalion, were called to attention as Pleasance read the orders:

From: Commanding General, First Marine Division
To: Lieutenant Colonel Ryck Lysander, United Federation Marine Corps
Subj: Division Special Order 3-19
Effective 0001 GMT, 19 May 359, you stand detached as the commanding officer, Second Battalion, Third Marines, and are transferred to the Fleet Retired List.
Signed, Norris K. Meintenbach, Major General, United Federation Marine Corps, Commanding General.

Hecs pushed out his arms, presenting the battalion colors to Ryck.

"Sir . . ." he whispered.

"It's OK, Hecs. Really," Ryck whispered back as he took the colors.

The wind picked up, and the colors flew out, battle streamers fluttering. Ryck felt the presence of the long line of previous commanders watching over him. If they were watching him, Ryck hoped they were at peace with Ryck's time in command.

Pleasance immediately launched into the second set of orders:

From: Commanding General, First Marine Division
To: Major Sandy Haunish Peltier-Aswad, United
Federation Marine Corps
Subj: Division Special Order 3-20
Effective 0001 GMT, 19 May 359, you are ordered to report
for duty to Second Battalion, Third Marines, as the
commanding officer.
Signed, Norris K. Meintenbach, Major General, United
Federation Marine Corps, Commanding General.

Still holding the colors, Ryck whispered, "Ready, Two!" On the command, he executed a left face while Sandy executed a right face. For someone taking a command, and as a major at that, Sandy looked miserable.

"I told you to stick with me, Sandy, and you'd go far," Ryck whispered as he thrust out the colors.

"This isn't how I wanted, it, sir," Sandy whispered back as he accepted them.

Both men faced the front again where Hecs was waiting. Hecs saluted, and then accepted the colors as Sandy handed them to him. As Hecs marched off to return the colors to the color guard, the two commanders, outgoing and incoming, turned to face each other again. Sandy saluted, and Ryck returned it before taking Sandy's hand and shaking it.

"Sir, I—"

"We've already discussed it, Sandy. Let it go. Just take in the moment for yourself. You've got the battalion for three months before Lieutenant Colonel Lu Wan gets here to take over, but until then, command! We may not have done much since getting back from Freemantle, but you've been there before. A mission can pop up in a moment's notice. And if I have to leave the battalion to anyone, there's nobody that I would trust more to take it than you."

"Ladies and gentlemen, be seated," Pleasance passed over the sound system.

The rest of the ceremony was somewhat of a blur. Brigadier General Eternal Light made the remarks, which was somewhat a slap in the face in and of itself. General Meintenbach evidently didn't want any of the shit to splash onto him, Ryck figured.

One thing stuck out in Ryck's mind, though. The pass in review was inspiring. Ryck had originally planned for a small change of command in his office. The men, however, had a different agenda and had insisted on a full ceremony, and they stood tall and proud as they marched by, pointedly delaying their present arms until it was obvious that they were saluting Ryck, not the general.

General Eternal Light gave flowers to Hannah and Esther and certificates to both of them and the boys as well. He gave a short speech lauding Ryck's career, which although Ryck didn't listen, he appreciated. He might not have wanted to be the reviewing officer, but the general was making a good show of it.

Finally, it was over. Sergeant Pleasance thanked the audience and invited them to the O-club for Sandy's reception.

Ryck stepped back, and before Sandy could say anything else, he simply shook the new CO's hand.

"Go see to Popper," Ryck told him, nodding his head at Sandy's young wife who was proudly making her way from the bleachers to them. "Be happy for her, OK?"

Ryck turned away to leave the two. He didn't want to put a damper on what was a great moment in Sandy's professional career. For three months or not, he was a Marine battalion commanding officer.

As Ryck started walking to his family, he was intercepted by a contingent of Marines, retired and still on active duty. Colonel Bert Nidischii', his best friend, Colonel Fearless uKhiwa, his former commander, Colonel (ret) Moses Ketter, Master Gunnery Sergeant Bobbi Samuleson, and General (ret) Praeter came up in a group to shake his hand. Ryck could see others from his career hanging back, not wanting to interfere with this illustrious group.

"You OK?" Bert asked, hand out.

"Sure, I'm copacetic. Fine," Ryck answered. "I'm about to be a free man."

"I . . . I," Bert started.

"I know. But really, it's all good."

"I should say so," Sams said. "Hitting the course every day, a man of leisure. I'll be joining you soon, and me and you can play together sometimes, right?"

"Golf? You haven't played a day in your life, Sams," Ryck said with a laugh.

"Sure, but that don't mean I can't start, right? I mean, how hard can it be, just hitting a little ole ball around?"

Leave it to Sams to lighten the mood, Ryck thought, surprisingly feeling better.

"Sorry it had to end this way," Colonel uKhiwa said, shaking his hand.

Ryck had been surprised but honored to see the colonel at the ceremony. The rest of the guests were stationed on Tarawa, but the colonel had come all the way from Alexander, and on short notice. Ryck and the colonel had not started out on good terms when Ryck was one of his company commanders, but the man had become a mentor for Ryck, and by resigning his commission, Ryck felt he'd let the colonel down. He'd let a lot of people down.

"Hey, you've got a lot of well-wishers here, and I can see Hannah over there waiting with your kids. We'll catch up with you at the reception, OK?" Bert asked.

"Sure thing. I'll see you there," Ryck said, shaking each hand again before stepping off to where his family waited for him.

Except that the intervening separation was filled with 60 or 70 people, mostly Marines and a few corpsmen, men who had served with him. A few he didn't recognize or couldn't put a name to the face. He faked it, shaking hands, saying thanks to the men for showing up. Most, though, he knew. Prince Jellico. Jorge Simone. Frank Lim. Cleo Davidson. Naranbaatar "Genghis" Bayarsaikhan and Mike "Hog" McAult, two of his company commanders who had peeled out of formation from the pass in review to join the small mob. And many more, from Ryck's past, from recruit training to men from 2/3.

"This sucks, colonel!" a voice called out.

Ryck turned from the hand he was shaking to see Shart, Staff Sergeant Clarence Gutierrez, standing in back of a few Marines. Shart had served with him twice, on GKA Nutrition and in the Cygni B system,

"That fucking asshole deserved it," Shart insisted.

The Marines around him nodded.

And that was the crux of the matter. "That fucking asshole deserved it" was probably true, but it hadn't been up to Ryck to take matters into his own hands.

It had only been seven days ago that Ryck single-handedly destroyed his career. He'd been at the annual Military Outlook and Beyond Conference in Lisbon on Earth. As was customary, the battalion commander for 2/3, whose patron was the old Portuguese *Corpo de Fuzileiros*, was invited. He'd already attended the last conference and been feted like a star. The Portuguese organizers were thrilled that "their" battalion was commanded by one of four Marine Federation Nova holders and perhaps the best-known Marine on active duty.

Normally, Ryck was just a member of the audience, but one of the breakouts was on the use of the Raider Battalion, and as Ryck was a former company commander and briefly the acting commanding officer of the Raiders, he was asked to sit on the panel. Unfortunately, the Commandant of the Marine Corps, General Devon Papadakis, the man whose pet project had been the formation of the Raiders when he was the Director of Marine Corps Personnel, was also on the panel.

Ryck had always held that the mission on Acquisition was the wrong mission for the Raiders. They had gone in light against a larger, more heavily armed SOG home base. A standard infantry battalion, with its PICS Marines and attachments, would have had a far easier mission, but the lightly-armed Raiders faced an armored enemy. The Raiders had prevailed, but at a heavy cost.

During the panel discussion, Ryck pointed this out several times, but the commandant had flatly disagreed with Ryck, stating that a quick, hard-hitting elite unit was what was needed, and the Raiders' success in the mission had proven his point. A number of questions during the Q & A were directed at the fight between the Marines and the SOG, and the general and Ryck were mostly on opposite sides of the issue.

The breakout was the last of the day, and Ryck quickly retired to the hotel bar where he downed a few quick drinks to calm down his festering anger. Their so-called "success," while technically true, had been too expensive. Ryck had been damned proud of his Marines, but he knew even one platoon of PICS Marines could have handled the SOG Nizzies with little, if any casualties. Marines had died just to validate then LtGen Papadakis' work.

He switched to gin after two beers, needing something a bit stronger. Ryck didn't drink much, but he thought he could use the soporific effect of the gin to help calm him down. Unfortunately, the general, probably equally as angry, was also into the booze. As he came back into the lobby, he spotted Ryck at his bar stool and made a beeline for him.

"You were out of line there, Colonel," he said, his breath heavy with alcohol.

Ryck turned to look at his commandant, the head of the Corps, sneered, and turned back to his drink, ignoring the man.

"I'm talking to you, Colonel," the commandant said, his voice rising.

"I hear you jabbering, but I'm not listening. I'm off duty and enjoying my drink," Ryck told him, still facing away.

The commandant grabbed Ryck's chair, spinning him around to face him.

"You will do as I say, Colonel, and I say you will listen to me! You may be the great Ryck Lysander, but you're really just a punk. And I am, I am the fucking Commandant of Marine Corps. You don't mean shit to me. I made you. Me. It was my mission, my idea, that put you there on Acquisition. The mission succeeded because of me!" he yelled, spittle flying out of his mouth to land on Ryck's chest.

Ryck looked down at the glistening spit, slowly put his drink down, then stood up and leaned forward until his chest was almost touching the commandant's.

"Your precious mission cost us 312 Marines and sailors, all good men, the best. They all died because of your grubbing pride, *sir!*"

"That was your fault, Lysander! If you'd been even half-way competent, they'd be alive today. You should have been court-martialed, Colonel, instead of protected," he screamed as an aide tried to pull him back. "You killed them! You killed them with your incompetence, just like you killed your men on Freemantle!"

With that, something inside of Ryck broke. He didn't consciously decide anything. His body just reacted. With every essence in his body, he put all his anger, all his frustration, into the swing, his fist catching the general right at the left side of his jaw. Ryck's fist kept traveling, almost tearing the general's jaw off and knocking him cold.

A sense of calm swept over him and he looked down at the commandant, lying face down and motionless. Ryck didn't know if the man was alive or dead, and he didn't care. The aide, a major whose name Ryck had never gotten, stared in shock, then ran out to get help. The 20 people or so in the bar stared silently, not sure what to do. Ryck knew what to do, though. He turned back and sat down, picking up his drink. He had just finished it when the local police arrived on the scene. They stood around at first, not sure what to do as the rescue squad took away the general, who had just started to come around. They looked at Ryck, well aware of who he was, and the senior police officer hesitantly asked Ryck what had happened.

"The general forgot himself, and I reminded him of who he was," Ryck simply said.

At that moment, a Navy staff judge advocate, a full captain, rushed in and took over. He assured the police that the military would handle the matter, and with an obvious sense of relief, they left.

Captain Grissom, the Navy lawyer, asked Ryck to follow him to his hotel room where several Marines and sailors waited. He asked Ryck what had happened, and Ryck told him flat out and with no excuses. General Papadakis had insulted him and he'd hit his commandant, knocking the man out and breaking his jaw. Captain

Grisson recorded Ryck's statement and then ordered him to his room where Ryck took a shower and fell into a deep and peaceful sleep.

In the morning, Ryck called Hannah, and then after telling her what he was going to do, he tendered his resignation from the Corps. To his surprise, his resignation was immediately accepted and orders cut for his return to Tarawa. He would not be facing a court-martial. Six days later, he was turning over the battalion to Sandy and retiring from the Corps.

Ryck posed for a few holos with the men as he made his way to his family. Nine-year-old Benjamin was in hog heaven, seeing the entire battalion lined up for his dad. Of Ryck and Hannah's three children, he was the one most enthralled with the Marines. He even had a child-sized set of skins with fake bone inserts that he proudly wore while playing. Ryck thought Ben had not quite grasped the situation, that his dad was leaving the Marines and under less than laudable conditions.

The twins, as young teens, understood though, and they stood soberly with Hannah, who seemed to be trying to hold back from breaking out in tears.

Ryck gave Hannah a hug and a kiss on the cheek before saying, "Why don't you head on home. No reason to go to the reception."

"You sure? What about Sandy?" she asked.

"Yeah, I'm sure. Sandy'll understand. I think the kids need to get back home."

Ryck was more worried about Hannah. His strong wife was taking this hard, and he didn't want her to lose it in public.

"OK, then, if you're sure. When will you be back?"

"Oh, not long. I just need to show my face."

Esther took a step forward and shoved her head between his arm and his side, her "snugglebunny" moment that she normally reserved for home and hadn't done for at least a year as she had started to mature. Ryck was in uniform, but what were they going to do? Shave his head and send him to Waystation? He pulled her in tight and hugged her with more force than he'd intended.

"It's going to be OK, daddy. And we're all proud of you," she mumbled into his side.

They stood like that for a few more moments before Hannah gathered up the kids and led them away. More well-wishers came up to him with his family gone, and it was a good twenty minutes before he could get into his Hyundai and drive over to the club. He got out of his hover, took a deep breath, and marched up the entry steps and into the venerable old building where the reception was in full-swing. Sandy was the center of attention, as it should be. It was his moment.

Ryck went up to the bar and ordered a beer, then changed it to a panderfruit juice at the last moment. It had been a few too many drinks that had gotten him into this situation, and he thought something non-alcoholic would be a better choice.

With Ryck in the club, though, some of the crowd started to drift over to him to offer, well, condolences would be the most accurate description. Before too long, there were a dozen or more Marines standing around him, telling him it wasn't fair, that he should fight back, that he could go to the press. It all got to be too much for him. He couldn't take their comments anymore, even as heart-felt as they were. And this day was for Sandy, not for someone with only a few hours left in the Corps. He finally made an abrupt excuse, breaking contact and fleeing out the side door of the club. From the looks on their faces, he'd just hurt a few of them, but he just couldn't take it anymore.

He walked under a huge old alder that he'd always admired and sat on the bench, looking out over the small koi pond that graced the club grounds. The koi, sensing his presence, came to gather at his feet, waiting for food to be tossed down to them. Ryck watched the swirling oranges, yellows, blacks, and whites as the eager fish tried to maneuver into position. They were like the Corps, eager bodies wanting more from him, the hero. But just like with the Corps, Ryck had nothing more to give.

Suddenly, he knew where he wanted to be. He got up and made his way to the hover. The big car lifted up and he drove it slowly out of the camp, the last time he would be driving off a base as a Marine. The gate guard saluted him as he passed through. The guard was a civilian jimmylegs,[1] but Ryck returned the salute as crisply as he could.

Twenty minutes later, Ryck pulled up in front of the Globe and Laurel. He sat in his hover for ten minutes, lost in his thoughts before getting out and making his way to the entrance. For a moment, he was taken back to when he was about to become a new lieutenant, and three young recruits had made a small scene right there at the entrance, barging into him and calling him an "oldster." They'd been so proud of their making it through boot camp that they'd felt invincible. Ryck had "corrected" them of that notion, but in the end had given them 12 credits for a drink on him.

What was that young Marine's name? Rage something. Rage MacManus or McHarris, Ryck wondered, surprised that he'd even remembered that much.

He wondered where they were now, if they were still Marines, if they had gotten out, or if they'd been killed on some far-off world somewhere. He shook his head and pushed into the dark pub, his eyes taking a moment to adjust.

"Welcome, Colonel," Mr. Geiland, the manager said as Ryck came in.

Ryck didn't even know Mr. Geiland's first name, but he'd been a part of the pub since before Ryck had even been born. Yet he seemed to remember every Marine who had ever graced the pub.

"A Corona?" he asked, knowing that was Ryck's favorite drink.

"Um, I, I don't think so. Not now, at least. I think I want to check the back room, if that's OK," Ryck said.

"Of course. I'll keep it closed off to anyone else," Mr. Geiland said.

Ryck thanked him and walked to the back of the pub, opening the door to the separate dining room behind a wall mounted with signed holos of famous and high-ranking Marines. A small amount of light made it into the room from two small, curtained windows, but that was enough for Ryck. He knew what he wanted to see. Class 2-59's box was on the right wall, third row, four

---

[1] Jimmylegs: Slang for a civilian security guard.

up from the bottom. It was missing the bottle of port, drunk six years before after Donte had been killed. It was not light enough to read the labels on the remaining two bottles, but he knew which one was the champagne and which was the sherry.

Ryck looked around the room at the other boxes mounted on the walls. Most were empty, the last members of their class long gone. Others were missing the port, and some only had the sherry left. A few had only the champagne in them, representing classes in which no one had made general, either because no one had been selected or as with 1-122, no one had survived past captain, all having been killed during the War of the Far Reaches. The boxes represented centuries of Marine officers: Marines no longer alive, no longer serving. And while Ryck was still alive, he would no longer wear the uniform that had become symbolic of who he was. If he wasn't a serving Marine anymore, then just who was he? He didn't know anything else.

He took a seat at one of the tables and lost himself in thought. He tried not to feel sorry for himself. His loss was nothing when compared to others, those for whom hundreds of bottles of port had already been drunk. And, Ryck knew, whatever happened to him was his own damned fault.

An hour or so later, the door creaked open. Mr. Geiland had promised to keep the room closed, but Ryck didn't turn around to see who had invaded his privacy. He heard a clink of a bottle and finally looked up to see Jorge Simone holding two Coronas.

"I thought you might be here when you disappeared from the reception. And Mr. Geiland said this is your brew," the short, broad-shouldered heavy-worlder said, holding one bottle out.

Ryck hesitated a moment before reaching out and taking the ice-cold bottle in his hand. He raised it and took a long swallow before using the top of the bottle as a pointer and indicating the seat beside him. Jorge pulled the chair back and sat down.

The two sat in silence for a while before Jorge said, "We all thought the next one would be for you."

Ryck harrumphed. Jorge was telling him that the champagne would have been opened for him when he made general, the first star in the class.

"It's always been for you, Jorge. We all knew that back at NOTC."[2]

"Could be, now, at least," Jorge said without false modesty.

Jorge Simone was a genius, a capable Marine who was rising through the ranks based on his unmatched abilities. He hadn't seen the combat that Ryck had as he kept getting pulled from line units and put on staffs. Commanders who wanted to be promoted themselves knew to pull Jorge and get him to improve their units and performance. In many ways, Jorge was a prisoner of his talent. But that talent was going to carry him a long ways.

"It always was going to be you. We all knew that," Ryck lied.

The reality was that Ryck thought he had a chance. Jorge might have more inherent talent, but Ryck had more accomplishments, and he had a public persona, in part thanks to the two flicks that portrayed him in a very positive light. According to *The Alien's Are Here*, Ryck pretty much single-handedly won the Trinocular War, which upset the Navy and more than a few Marines to no end.

And Ryck wanted that magnum of champagne with every fiber of his being. It had become the center of his dreams, one he had been more and more sure was within his reach. And now it wasn't.

The two Marines sat in silence, sipping their beers. Ryck appreciated that. Jorge's presence was comforting, but too much talk would have been annoying. Silence was better.

Finally, Jorge got up, stretched, and said, "Well, I've got to get going. You going to stay here long?"

"No, just a little while longer."

"OK, then. Well, needless to say, if you need anything, give me a shout. I'm here for at least another two years," Jorge said before shaking Ryck's hand and making his way out of the room.

With the sun going down, the room was getting darker, but Ryck didn't get up to turn on the old-fashioned incandescent lights. Darkness was fine with him. He sat in silence, an empty beer bottle in his hand, checking his Mountbane watch, a gift from Hannah.

---

[2] NOTC: Naval Officers Training Course

As the time approached 1900, his pulse started racing. The seconds ticked off too quickly. He had thoughts of trying to change his mind, to put a stop to things. But it was too late, he knew.

As his watch hit 1901 local, or 0001 GMT, 29 May 359, Mr. Ryck Lysander, civilian, sat in the darkness as tears began to roll down his face.

Chapter 2

"Honey, have you seen the yellow?" Hannah asked, as she opened the cabinets, trying to find the GKA Base 33.

"Oh, yeah. I sort of did some rearranging of things. I put all the flavor bases in this drawer here," he said, pulling out the bottom drawer by the oven.

"Why did you do that?" she asked, trying to find the yellow. "I can't tell which is which from just the tops."

"It makes more sense this way. All the flavor bases are here, right by the oven and stove. I've got fiber and bulk bases up over here in the pantry, and the oils over here. The raw organics are here by the cooler."

"But I can't even tell what is what," Hannah complained.

"No, no, it makes sense, Hannah. See? Yellow is Number 33, so it is right after 30, which is after 22, 23, and 24. Just count up the numbers," Ryck told her.

"I don't want to count up the numbers. I use yellow all the time, so I keep it here with porky and . . . where's the porky?" she asked as she looked in the cabinet over the stove.

"I told you, baby, the raw organics are all over here. See? Porky, GF 42." Ryck said, pulling a white container of the base out of the cabinet. "Isn't this more organized?"

Hannah took the porky out of his hand, placed it on the counter, and then took his hands in hers.

She looked him in the eyes and said, "Look, Ryck. I know you're bored here, but this is my kitchen. I've had things organized my way for 17 years now while you were deployed to everywhere in the known galaxy, and I like it this way. I know where things are. So please, just leave things alone."

"But—"

"No 'buts.' I want things my way. It may not be according to Marine standards, but this is a family home, not a Marine company. And I want things back to my way. Understood?"

Ryck swallowed twice, wondering why she seemed upset, but he knew enough to simply answer, "Understood."

****

"Bye, dad!" Esther said, leaning over the back of the couch to give him a kiss on the cheek.

"Have a good time," Ryck started before looking up at his daughter—and stopping dead.

"What do you have on?" he asked her incredulously.

"What do you mean?" she asked, trying hard to sound innocent while using the back of the couch to block his view of her.

Ryck's daughter, his 14-year-old daughter, was wearing tight hot pink shorts, with emphasis on the "tight" and "short." They left nothing to the imagination. On top, she had on a silkie sleeve that clung to her budding figure. The silkies, which wrapped tightly around the torso, had come into fashion months before, and Ryck had even appreciated seeing women walking around in them. But those were grown women, not his daughter! To top it off, she had deep blue eye "patches" makeup to match the blue of the silkie, patches that ran from around her eyes all the way to her hairline at the top of her ears.

"What do I mean? You know what I mean! You are not going out dressed like that!" he thundered.

"Told you," Noah said in a smug tone from where he was lying on the floor watching the holo.

"But dad!" she started, her face screwed up in frustration.

"'But dad' nothing! You are not going out in public dressed like that!"

"All the girls do. And besides, Mom lets me dress like this!" she insisted.

She does? Ryck wondered, unsure of himself.

Hannah, despite her very religious upbringing, was more liberal in many ways than Ryck was, but this seemed a little far even for her. Ryck looked down to where his son was lying for confirmation if his wife actually let Esther wear the silkie or not, but Noah kept his head turned away, staying out of the confrontation.

Esther reached over and took Ryck's hand in hers.

"Please, daddy? Everyone dresses like this. It is no big deal."

"You are not 'everyone.' And no, you are not going outside our house looking like that," Ryck said, extracting his hand from hers.

"Daddy! I can't believe you are ruining my life like this! It's not my fault you got kicked out of the Corps, but I'm the one getting punished!"

Ryck's mouth dropped open, and even Noah turned back to look at the two in shock as Esther stomped her foot and ran upstairs in tears.

Esther was upset, but it was Ryck's heart that was breaking into pieces.

****

"But you promised me that when I got out, you'd have a place for me on the board," Ryck said.

"Yes, that's true, Colonel. And don't worry. We still want you, but maybe not for a while. Your, uh, departure from the Marines, or rather, your actions that preceded it are not the kind of image we want for our board members."

"But the public, they don't really know about that, right? I'm still me, you know, from *The Alien's Are Here*. I've still got my Nova and all of that. That was why you wanted me, you said."

"I know what I said when we approached you, but . . . Colonel, can I be blunt here?" the Trieste Industries VP asked.

"Sure, of course."

"We at Trieste don't really give a rat's ass for the public. We are a defense contractor, pure and simple, and we need to be on good terms with the brass in both the Navy and Marines. You taking out the commandant like that, well, that's not really the kind of thing that's going to help us in getting contracts. The commandant won't think too highly of us if we bring you onboard."

"He won't be commandant for long," Ryck protested.

"And we still want you. Just not now. So please, Colonel, have some patience. We'll revisit this after things have calmed down and some people have moved on to the retired list."

Ryck looked back with a resigned expression at the VP, the same man who'd been heavily courting him for the last seven years, ever since he'd been awarded the Nova, and asked, "How long do you think that will be?"

"Oh, not long. Five, maybe ten years or so."

Ten grubbing years? What the hell am I supposed to do until then? My retirement pay isn't enough to pay the bills, and I can't rely on Hannah to keep getting raises. I've got to get something going!

"OK, Mr. Dunlop, I understand. Please keep me in mind, though, and let me know when you might want me."

"Of course, Colonel Lysander, of course. You'll be the first to know."

****

"You call that a shot?" Ryck asked Sams. "What was that drive, all of 70 meters? Want to use the blue tees?"

"Hey, I've got better things to do," Sams said. "Some of us don't have all day just to loaf around."

He looked up at Ryck after that last comment, a grimace on his face.

Ryck laughed off the unintended reminder that he was now a civilian, and not by his own choice. Sams looked mortified, and Ryck's laugh didn't seem to do much to alleviate that.

Sams had always been an irreverent smart-ass. It was part of who he was. But he was like all of Ryck's old friends in the Corps who were walking on egg-shells around him, afraid to say anything that could point back to Ryck's resignation.

"Hey, it's about time you did some work. Here, get out of the way and let a pro show you how it's done, my man."

He pulled out his new Rancer driver, an extravagant beauty that he really couldn't afford. It wasn't as if he really loved golf that much. This was only the third time he'd been on the course since getting out. But it had made him feel better, even if he knew it would do nothing to lower his handicap.

He raised the iridescent blue club high with his left arm as an offering to the gods, before he stepped up to the tee. The club was made from one solidly fabricated piece of tolumethalyne, the latest and greatest from Monsanto. It wasn't approved by the ancient PGA, but the upstart—well, if 60-plus years could be still considered an upstart—UPGA[3] allowed for its use, and the club had flown off the shelves since its release a year ago. It was still pretty hard to get, but availability was a little better at the military exchanges, and Ryck had grabbed one the day before his release from active duty. He was pretty sure Hannah knew how much the club cost, but she hadn't said a word about that.

It was a beautiful morning, the sun just beginning to burn off the dew on the first hole. Even with Sams' complete lack of experience, Ryck knew they could get through 18 with more than enough time to catch Esther's 1230 game. He'd made every practice and game since resigning, and he wasn't going to miss this one.

He teed up, then made an exaggerated effort to look down the fairway, shielding his eyes as if trying to see. He addressed the ball and started to make his backswing, stopping halfway and looking back.

---

[3] UPGA: Universal Professional Golf Association

"Look now, Sams, 'cause in a moment, this ball is going to be so far down the fairway that your feeble eyes won't be able to see it anymore."

Sams just huffed and rolled his eyes.

Ryck finished his backswing, and with a herculean effort, brought his club down—hitting the ground just in front of the tee and screaming in pain as his right shoulder seemed to explode.

"Mother-grubbing son of a bitch!" he yelled, dropping his precious driver and twirling around like a dervish.

"Yeah, I guess you showed me. I'm looking down the fairway, and I can't see your ball," Sams said sarcastically. "Oh, wait a minute, there it is. I think you went, uh, all of five meters?"

Ryck stopped his twirling, then held out his right arm. His shoulder burned.

"Fuck, fuck, fuck, that fucking hurts!" he said as he flexed and twisted the arm.

"Well, I may not be an expert, but I think you're supposed to hit the ball, not the ground. I think that divot went farther than your ball, there, Colonel," Sams said.

"Yeah, thanks for that," Ryck said, glowering at his friend.

He walked over to where he dropped his club and picked it up, inspecting it. It didn't look damaged, to his relief. He took an easy practice swing and almost dropped the club again, his shoulder adamantly protesting. He'd done something to it, that was for sure.

Golf? A big bad Marine, and I hurt myself playing Golf? Esther's playing soccer in a few hours, and that's a much tougher sport, and I bet she gets through unscathed!

He swung once more, and he knew he had to stop. He needed a couple of days of nanos cleaning up whatever he'd done to the shoulder.

"Uh, Sams. I don't think I can continue," he admitted.

"No shit? You serious, Colonel?" Sams said.

"Yeah, I'm serious. I think I tore something," Ryck said, waiting for some smart-ass remark.

"Shit, tough break. Well, I'm guessing that clubhouse has got some cold beer, huh? Let's say I buy you one, you know, for medical purposes, to deaden the pain."

Ryck widened his eyes slightly, surprised that Sams hadn't smacked-talked him.

Sams has a heart?

"OK, I think I'll take you up on that. Sorry to mess up your day."

"Shit happens. Even to you," Sams said.

Using his left hand, he placed his club back in the caddy, ordering "Clubhouse."

He watched the caddy raise up on its gimbaled tracks and move to the walkway where it picked up speed and was on its way.

"OK, let's go," he told Sams as the two men started back.

He gingerly rotated his shoulder, feeling the sharp stabs of pain.

Halfway back, Sams said, "You know, if you were so embarrassed that you were going to lose to me, I could have played blindfolded. You didn't have to go to all that trouble just to get out of playing."

A slight smile turned the corners of Ryck's mouth. Yes, Sams was Sams, and he couldn't resist who he was. All was right in the world

****

"Are you grubbing blind?" Ryck shouted at the ref as he ran out onto the field. "She purposely took out my daughter!"

"Sir, I'm going to have to ask you to get off the field," the ref told him.

"Not until you red card her. That was a blatant foul. I can't believe you didn't see it!"

"Sir, I'm not going to ask you again. Get off the field, now!"

"Dad, stop it. You've got to go, now," Esther said grabbing his right arm and trying to pull him off the field.

Ryck winced at the pain from his morning injury, but his anger overcame that.

"But she fouled you," Ryck protested. "On purpose. Look, your leg's bleeding!"

"Yeah, I know, and I'll get her back. But you're going to make us forfeit the match if you don't get off the field."

Ryck looked up at the ref, who now had a bemused expression on his face, watching the slender daughter holding back the bigger father while trying to reason with him. Ryck wanted to march over and punch his condescending face, but the looks on the faces of the girls, from both teams, and most of all, Esther's quiet but forceful pleadings, stopped him. He shook off Esther's hold on him and turned around.

"I'm going to file a report on this, mark my words!" he shouted as he marched off the field.

Mr. Jamison, the coach, stared daggers at him as he came off the field. Ryck's presence at every practice and game was probably not appreciated by the coach, Ryck knew. Well, maybe not the presence so much as Ryck's constant suggestions on how to make the team better.

But this was his daughter, and he'd be damned if he'd sit by when someone hurt his little girl!

****

Ryck stepped back with a critical eye and evaluated the corner stand.

Not too bad, he thought. *At least it looks like it'll fit.*

The first one he'd made had not been quite square, and when he'd hung it on the wall, it wobbled, not laying flush. The Masterwood was really pretty easy to work with, but it still took the woodworker to input the correct dimensions. But Ryck was learning.

Hannah had been right, Ryck realized, when she suggested he take up a hobby. There was a calming effect as he rubbed in the oils that highlighted the Masterwood's grain.

Heck, maybe I'll get some natural wood, and try that next, he thought as he worked the stand.

His PA brought him back from wherever his mind had wandered. He glanced at it and saw it was Sandy calling. He wiped his hands free of the oil, then picked his PA up.

"Hey, Sandy, good to hear from you. What's up?"

"I just wanted to let you know we can't come over Friday."

"Oh, sorry to hear that. Hannah will be disappointed," he said, even if he realized Hannah would be fine with it—it was Ryck who was disappointed.

"What about Sunday then? I'm going to try a porchetta I saw on *The Home Cook*. Not fabricated, but the real deal. Can you imagine it? Me, a freaking chef?"

"Uh, I don't think so. I'm not going to be around for a while," Sandy said hesitantly.

"Why? I mean. . .oh!" Ryck said as he realized what was happening. "Can you tell me where?"

If anything, Sandy looked even more uncomfortable as he replied, "Not really, sir. You know the drill."

Ryck did know the drill. The battalion was being called out, and Ryck didn't have the "need to know." He was out of the loop. If he'd felt the severance of his ties to the Corps before, this just cemented it.

For the close to two years after getting back from the mission on Freemantle, the battalion had not deployed again in response to a mission. Everything had been simple training and routine mini-deployments. Now, after he'd relinquished command, the Fuzos were marching to the sound of guns once more. Without him.

To say Ryck was jealous was a severe understatement. He'd seen more than enough combat in his career, but still, he knew he wanted more. Combat was the only time he felt truly alive, and he knew he was addicted to the adrenaline high. And now he was going through withdrawals cold turkey.

"Yeah, I know it. OK, we'll see you when we see you," Ryck said. "Keep your head down, Sandy."

"Sure will. Well, I've got to run now. I'll touch base when I get back," Sandy said, cutting the connection.

Ryck stared at his PA for a moment before putting it down. He picked up his corner stand and started to slowly rub the linseed oil into the wood.

****

"General Papadakis is stepping down," Hannah told him as she walked in the door.

"Oh, that actually smells good, Ryck," she added as she hung up her coat and walked up to the table. "What is it?"

"Pork adobo and garlic rice," Ryck said automatically before he reacted to her statement.

"He's resigning? But he's only got seven months left anyway. Why resign now?" he asked.

"He has to. No choice," she said, taking her seat. "What's adobo?"

"It's an old Filipino dish. But what do you mean, he has to?"

"Regen, of course. He's got no choice."

That took Ryck aback. He'd heard that the commandant had not done well with the normal nano-therapy to repair his shattered jaw, something about a reaction to the treatment itself. But regen? The pain had to be pretty severe for him to resort to regen given the consequences.

The position of Commandant of the Marine Corps was a Prime 1 billet, and as such, could not be held by someone undergoing regen. That was what Hannah meant by he "has to." By choosing to accept regen, by Federation law he had to step down. And with only seven months left in his tour, there wasn't any way he'd come back and take over the billet again. No, he was done. Ryck had knocked the bastard out of the Corps!

"If you keep cooking like this, we may just have to retire our fabricator!" she exclaimed as she took a bite of the savory stew. "Isn't that right, kids?"

"Dad's the best chef!" Ben said proudly while the other two nodded their agreement while stuffing their faces.

"Really, Ryck, this be delicious."

A smile spread over Ryck's face, and if Hannah thought that smile had anything to do with her compliment, all the better.

****

Ryck sat on the couch in just his underwear, sipping a Corona. His jeans and shirt were in a pile on the floor where he'd dropped them. He had an end table in the garage that needed to get a second coat of oil (he was trying tung oil this time, not linseed), but he just couldn't build up an interest in getting to it, and with the kids at school and Hannah at work, he had the house to himself.

Ryck let out a satisfactorily loud burp. The second burp was more of a misfire, barely registering. He took another swallow of beer to ammo up for another try. He gave it another shot, and this time, while not as loud as the first, it was acceptable.

My accomplishment for the day, he thought to himself as he lifted his bottle for an imaginary toast.

He'd gone on base earlier in the morning to make a PX[4] run. The base had been eerily quiet. The exchange itself was busy with dependents and retirees, but there were very few Marines in uniforms anywhere on base. It wasn't just Sandy and 2/3 that had been called out, but most of the units. Whatever had instigated all of this was big. And Ryck had no idea what was going on. Hannah,

---

[4] PX: Post Exchange, a store for military personnel, retirees, and dependents.

with her position in R & D, would know, but Ryck hadn't pressed her. He didn't want to put her in the position of choosing between telling Ryck or maintaining security procedures. And maybe Ryck didn't want to know which way she would go: duty or her husband.

He took the last swallow of his Corona and contemplated getting another, but decided he was comfortable just sitting there as he was for a while. He had all the time in the world, after all.

When his PA buzzed, he contemplated just leaving it be. But habits are hard to break, and answering a buzzing PA was an ingrained reaction. He didn't bother to get up but simply yelled out "Connect," putting it on speaker mode.

"Ryck, I'm glad I caught you. Can you come into Headquarters now?" Bert asked.

What?

"Uh, I'm kinda busy here," Ryck said, scratching his balls while wondering what Bert wanted.

"It's pretty important, Ryck. Where are you, anyway? I can't see you."

"I've got my hands full," he said, removing his hand from its scratching. "My PA's on the coffee table."

"No matter. Can you get here by 11:45? At my office?" Bert asked.

Ryck hadn't been inside Headquarters since he'd retired, and he wasn't sure he really wanted to go there.

"Like I said, I'm pretty busy. I've got a full schedule today. Why do you want to see me anyway?"

"I can't really say that here. But you really need to come in. I'll expect you by 11:45, OK?"

He can't tell me over the PA? Ryck wondered, his curiosity beginning to overcome his lack of motivation. *What the heck is this?*

Ryck cupped his hand over his mouth and breathed out. He had the beer on his breath, but he didn't think it was too strong. A quick NoBuzz should take care of that, and no one would know he'd been drinking.

That was when he realized he would comply with Bert's request.

"OK, I'm on my way. I'll get there as soon as I can."

"Great. See you in a few."

Whatever's going on, at least I'll find out what it is, Ryck thought as he jumped up to get ready.

Chapter 3

At 11:42, Ryck entered Bert's outer office, a visitor's badge hanging from his shirt pocket. Bert's secretary looked up as Ryck came in and immediately buzzed the colonel. A moment later, Bert came out of his office and shook Ryck's hand.

"Glad you made it in so quick. Come on," Bert said, ushering Ryck out of the door as he told his secretary, "Danya, let them know we're on our way."

"What, we're not meeting in your office?" Ryck asked.

"No, not here."

"Bert, what's going on?" Ryck asked as Bert took off at a quick clip.

"Not here. You'll find out more soon enough," Bert said, speeding up even more so that Ryck had to struggle to keep up.

Curiouser and curiouser! Ryck thought to himself, but willing to stop questioning for the moment. *What rabbit hole am I about to fall into?*

They went down, not up, into the bowels of the building. This was where all the high-level secured spaces were. Twice, they had to stop and get retinal scans to prove they were who they were and that they were authorized to be there. Finally, on the CC deck, Bert led Ryck past an armed Marine guard and into one of the secure conference rooms. Ryck had never been below the BB deck before, so he couldn't help but to look forward to seeing what this conference room would look like.

The room looked just like the ones on the higher decks, but what was different was the men who were in it. Ryck was surprised to see so many Navy officers there, but more surprising was the rank level of them. Admiral Eaton, the quadrant commander himself, was there, along with four other flag officers that Ryck could see. For the Marines, General Mbanefo, the incoming commandant, led an equally impressive collection of star ranks, Ryck's previous godfather, Lieutenant General Ukiah among them. Several civilians were also in attendance, including the Federation Liaison to Tarawa—who from the seating, was not even the senior civilian present.

What the grubbing hell is going on here, and why do they want me?

"Ah, Colonel Lysander, I'm glad you're here. Please, take a seat," General Mbanefo said, indicating an empty chair across from him.

Ryck sat down and sat silently while all eyes were on him. He didn't ask anything; he'd find out soon enough why he'd been called in.

"Well, Colonel, I imagine you want to know why you're here, am I right?" the general ask.

"Yes, sir."

"A man of few words," Admiral Eaton said, whether approvingly or disapprovingly, Ryck didn't know.

"We have a development here, and you're involved. The Trinoculars have initiated contact with us out on the Blue Line. They had a very specific request, and that is where you come in."

"The Trinoculars, sir?" Ryck asked, breaking his intent to remain silent until he understood what was going on.

"Yes, the Trinoculars. As you know, we have had an uneasy truce with them, which is more by inference than any direct communications. They stay on their side of the line, humans stay on our side of the line. Recently, there has been, well, activity on their side, which has resulted in most of the governments putting our forces on alert. But last night, our time, a single ship came forward and crossed the line. It came close to being blasted out of space, but cooler heads prevailed, and a message, of sorts, was delivered."

"I don't understand, sir. A message 'of sorts?'"

"Well, we still don't have a reliable translation capability with them. But this message is very clear. They want to meet with us. More importantly, with you."

Ryck stared at the general stupidly.

What the. . .?

The general nodded and said, "Exactly. Our thoughts exactly," even if Ryck hadn't said a word.

None of this made any sense to Ryck. Why would the capys want to meet, and more importantly, meet with him? He wasn't a Marine anymore, and even if he were, he would just be a lowly lieutenant colonel.

"We don't have much time, Colonel. At 2000 this evening, you will be on your way to that meeting, so we have a lot to get done. We didn't get the go-ahead from the chairman until an hour ago; otherwise we would have pulled you in earlier. Now we have to make up for lost time," the general said.

The chairman approved this? The Chairman of the United Federation himself?

"Sir, I, uh, I don't quite get all of this. And leaving tonight? I have to ask my wife about it. I'm a civilian now, not a Marine," he said, his mind in a jumble.

"Not quite there, Colonel," the Director of Marine Corps Personnel said. "As of, well, a whole 32 minutes ago," he continued after looking down at his watch, "you have been recalled back into the Marine Corps."

"Sir?" Ryck said, realizing that he was sounding like a complete idiot, but he was simply overwhelmed and that was about the best response he could give.

"When you retired, you were placed on the Fleet Retired List, to stay there until your 70th birthday or until the Chairman of the Federation desired your service again. And the chairman has so desired. Welcome back, Colonel."

"But the commandant. . ."

"General Papadikas is fully aware of your re-instatement and is happy to give you and your mission his full support both now and after next week when he himself retires," General Mbanefo said, interrupting Ryck. "General Nguyen, I believe there was that one other thing?"

"Oh, yes, of course. An emergency selection board was convened, and you have been selected for promotion to full bird. Congratulations."

Once again, all Ryck had was, "Sir?"

"We have to clear the present list as per Code 92, so your expected date of promotion will be July 1. However, you are authorized to be frocked[5] as of today, so once again, congrats."

I'm a colonel? A full bird?

"Do you have any questions before we push on?" General Mbanefo asked.

"Sir, why me?" he asked, to him the most important question.

"They asked for you and the *FS Justin Mathis*," the general told him.

"The *Mathis*, but that's not—"

"Exactly, Colonel. You got it in one."

"*The Aliens Are Here*," Ryck said under his breath.

The flick, which had enjoyed considerable commercial, if not critical, success, had told a somewhat fanciful version of the Trinocular War. Ryck had been heavily featured, as had the destroyer the *FS Justin Mathis*. Except, there never was a *Justin Mathis*. Over a spat of some kind, the Navy had withdrawn support from the flick, so the producers had simply created a composite ship that incorporated a number of heroic battles as fought by several other ships. And not just Federation ships. The climatic naval battle in the flick was based on the exploits of a very real Greater France ship, the *GF Georges Leygues*.

If the Trinoculars were asking for both Ryck and the *Mathis*, then they'd somehow pulled the names from the flick. This was all too surreal for Ryck. A momentous occasion for human kind, and it was being predicated on a grubbing flick?

"I'm here, but what about the *Mathis*?" Ryck asked.

"Please, Colonel, give us some credit," Admiral Eaton said. "As we speak, the *FS Antelope* is being re-designated as the *FS Justin Mathis*."

"Is it just us? I mean, the flick focused only the Federation, not any of the allies," Ryck asked while trying to marshal his thoughts.

---

[5] Frocked: a practice where someone selected for promotion is allowed to put on the rank insignia and enjoy all the benefits of that promotion except for pay. Officially, the Marine still has his old rank, but unofficially, he has his new rank.

"We have Vice-Bishop Donato here from the Brotherhood," the general said, indicating one of the civilians, "but until we know more about this supposed threat, we are keeping this classified at the highest levels. Only our two governments are aware of it for now.

"I know you must have more questions, but we really have to push on. We're running out of time.

"Where are you, Colonel Nidischii'? Oh, over there. Why don't you get Colonel Lysander's uniforms and kit together? He's going to need to be here for the duration until he leaves. And let his family know he's working on a project for us."

Bert acknowledged and left, but not before giving Ryck a wink. That had a surprisingly strong effect on Ryck in grounding him. It was all OBE[6] anyway. If he was already recalled, he had no choice in the matter, and he had to buckle down and get ready.

Not that he would change anything even if the choice had been his. He was back in the Corps!

---

[6] OBE: Overcome By Events

FS JUSTIN MATHIS

Chapter 4

The newly designated *FS Justin Mathis* floated motionless in space, right at the edge of the Blue Line. Ryck stood on the bridge with the crew, waiting for the signal to proceed.

The *Mathis* was a *Wildebeest-class* destroyer, one of the older classes still in service. It normally carried a crew of 80. For this trip, the crew had been stripped to the bare minimum of 31. Fifteen other men had been added to the party, though, to include almost a dozen civilian experts of various stripes, three Brotherhood reps, and Rear Admiral Hancock Baris, the senior man and overall mission commander.

Ryck was already in his vacsuit, the helmet unsealed and pushed back over his shoulders. They'd been on station for over three hours, but the Trinoculars had not made a move. Ryck was glad for the diaper gels in his vacsuit. Without a head on the bridge (who was the genius who omitted that?) the admiral himself had had to make a hasty withdrawal to answer the call of nature. He'd rushed back after only a few minutes, but nothing had happened in his absence. There was no change in the line of capy ships.

A vacsuit is not too conducive to sitting in gravity, so after another two hours, Ryck had wedged himself against a bank of monitors in the back of the bridge and was half-drifting off when the bridge came to life. A single Trinocular ship was slowly moving forward, coming to a stop right on the Blue Line.

"Bring her forward," the *Mathis'* captain told the helm. "I want her exactly 30 meters from that ship and oriented on it."

Thirty meters was nothing in the vast reaches of space. It was tight even at a station with ships docked next to each other. Ryck had never heard of such close quarters in open space, and he had visions of collisions that would put the best flick special effects to shame. But the helmsman did his thing, and with help from the nav AI, managed to bring the *Mathis* to a halt just off the Trinocular ship.

"Are you ready, Colonel?" the admiral asked.

"Yes, sir."

"I don't have any memorable things to say, so just do your job," the admiral added. "I don't have to remind you to keep your recorder running and broadcasting at all times, and as soon as you can, get our experts over there so they can take over."

Ryck nodded and left the bridge, followed by a Navy rating. The *Mathis* was a fairly small ship, so it only took a minute or so to reach Airlock 1-C. Ryck pulled up his helmet as the sailor checked its seal and gave Ryck a thumb's up.

The next step was still a little unclear. Ryck was to make a ship-to-ship transfer, but the specific details were lacking. The Trinoculars had sent an animation of some sort that showed the ships adjacent to each other. A human figure—representing Ryck, they assumed—made a crossing along an illuminated path. A hatch on the capy ship opened, and the figure moved inside.

"You are reading all greens," the ship's captain announced over Ryck's comms. "If you're ready, I'm going to give the order to cycle the lock, sir."

"Roger that," Ryck responded.

The red light over the lock turned green, and another sailor opened the inner hatch. Ryck stepped inside, and the sailor handed him his vacsac. The inner hatch then closed, isolating him. Thought had been given as to having someone or someones join him. The Brotherhood had wanted a rep, as did the Navy. A xenobiologist who specialized in the Trinoculars was considered, an option that Ryck preferred. But in the end, it was just Ryck. The animation had shown only one human, so one person it was until Ryck could clear it with the Trinoculars for the others to come across.

A moment later, the air in the lock was pumped out, and Ryck was in a vacuum. The outer hatch began to open, but instead of Ryck just stepping out, he was pushed back as air rushed in—from open space.

It only took a second for the air to equalize, and Ryck immediately checked his readout to see what was going on. He was in a breathable atmosphere, with about a 22% O2 content. There were some weird trace gasses, but nothing harmful. The bottom line was that Ryck could breathe the air if he were out of his vacsuit.

The scientist-types had assured Ryck that he would be able to breathe aboard the capy ship. But this was in open space. It should be a vacuum out there.

"Colonel Lysander, are you OK?" a voice came over his comms.

"Uh, yeah. I'm fine. Are you reading the atmosphere here?"

"Yes, we are. Wait one."

Ryck, still in the airlock, moved forward to where he could see the capy ship, only 30 meters away. It looked huge, but what caught Ryck's attention was the shimmering tunnel that stretched between the two ships. He could see through the walls of the tunnel, but it was as if he was looking through heat waves in the desert training area back on Tarawa. Evidently, the "illuminated path" in the capy animation was more than just an indicator of the route he was supposed to take. It was some sort of pressurized connecting tunnel. Such a force-field tunnel was theoretically possible and had been achieved in labs, but no one, to Ryck's knowledge, had ever been able to devise a practical application of such a tunnel. No *human,* that was. Evidently, the Trinoculars had managed it.

"You are to proceed, Colonel" the voice came back over his comms.

Ryck idly wondered who it was passing the word to him. It would have been nice to have met the man first, to be able to put a face and name to his connection back to the ship—and to humanity.

He gave his thrusters a short blast, and he was out of the *Mathis.* With only 30 meters, it took him less than a minute, even at 1% thrust, to cross over. Just before he arrived, a hatch opened up on the side of the capy ship. Inside the ship, a capy stood waiting, his head jutting off to Ryck's lower left. Ryck adjusted his yaw thruster, spinning him around so that he and the capy were oriented together. With one more tiny puff, Ryck crossed the threshold and was in the ship—a Trinocular ship. A week ago, he was worrying about getting the kids to practice in time. Now he was the first human envoy in a Trinocular vessel. The hatch closed behind him with a degree of finality.

To Ryck's surprise, there was no artificial gravity in the ship. The capy hadn't been standing but rather floating in Zero G. The capy turned and started to pull itself out of the compartment.

"Wait!" Ryck shouted, breaking open his vacsuit helmet.

The capy came to the inner hatch to the compartment, ignoring Ryck, so he lunged out and grabbed the capy's foot, stopping him.

"Wait. I've got to do something!" he said, pulling up his vacsac and opening it.

The capy merely watched Ryck with no change of expression that Ryck could see. Ryck wiggled out of his vacsuit and pulled out his blues. Within a minute or two, Ryck was smoothing out his uniform. Wearing the blues hadn't been his idea, but someone on high had decided that the uniform would infer a higher degree of authority. This was probably the same person who had decided Ryck should be a full colonel as well. Ryck wasn't sure that the Trinoculars had any concept of uniforms or rank, but orders were orders.

There were several weapons in the vacsac, but Ryck left them there. Alone on the capy ship, if they wanted to do him harm, they would, and his Ruger was not going to make much difference to that.

"OK, buddy, let's go," Ryck said, pointing at the open hatch.

The capy said nothing, but Ryck could smell something like cinnamon that seemed to waft over to him. It tickled the back of his nostrils, threatening to make him sneeze. Ryck floated there for close to 30 seconds before the capy turned and pulled itself through the hatch.

Leaving his vacsuit behind but towing his vacsac, Ryck followed. He expected a long corridor, so he was surprised to immediately enter a huge open space, possible 70 meters wide and even longer, possibly 100 meters long. This had to be the entire interior of the ship aside from the propulsion unit. All around him, a couple of hundred capys bustled about, doing whatever capys did to run a ship. Ryck had a moment of vertigo as he looked around. Where humans liked to orient themselves together, heads all in one direction, feet in the other, the Trinoculars evidently didn't care much about that. They moved about and worked haphazardly without any discernible "up" or "down." Ryck didn't like it at all and had to take a moment to swallow down his discomfort. Mankind's first envoy to an alien species did not need to be marked by him losing his lunch.

"I'm inside the, well, not the bridge, but it looks like the whole ship," Ryck whispered into his throat mic.

There was no response.

"*Mathis*, this is Colonel Lysander, do you read me?"

Silence.

Grubbing great. No comms!

On both GKA Nutrition and HAC-440, the capys had been able to block Marine comms. Even if there were no hostilities at the moment, it seemed as if that capability was in play. Ryck hoped that wasn't an indication of something sinister in the works.

Inside the big open space, small balls seemed to be hanging fixed in place. Ryck's guide was crossing the open area by grabbing the balls and pulling itself along. Ryck shrugged and followed, if not quite as smoothly as the capy.

To his surprise, none of the others seem to pay him much attention. If Ryck were escorting a capy to the *Mathis'* bridge, every swinging dick on the ship would be jockeying to get a good look.

Ryck's guide led him to a position no different than any other.

It turned to Ryck and said, "Query?" as an image of Ryck, or the actor who played Ryck in the flick appeared in front of them.

"Rycklysander," the capy said, its voice a low monotone.

"Uh, yeah, I mean yes. I am Colonel Ryck Lysander, United Federation Marine Corps."

"Query? Rycklysander?" it said again, only now Ryck could see the voice was emanating from a small sphere attached to the capy's utility belt.

A strong smell of mown grass hit Ryck.

"Yes. Ryck Lysander," he said.

The capy seemed to consider that. It turned to three other capys, all who seemed to be in the same "class," as the xenobiologists termed the different body types of Trinoculars.

A few whistling sounds were evident, and Ryck's scalp felt itchy, but there was no speaking as Ryck would term it. Several warring smells hovered just at the edge of what Ryck could discern.

From the dissection of what turned out to be Trinocular young, Ryck knew that the capys could see well into wavelengths too low for humans, and that they could sense vibrations, but Ryck came to the conclusion that there might be an olfactory component of capy communications.

"Query? Effessjustinmathis?" the capy asked as it turned back to Ryck.

"Yes, there," Ryck said, pointing back to where the airlock was.

His (what, his interpreter? Guide?) turned back to the others. Ryck heartedly wished the other three would move to some semblance of order. Two of them were almost aligned with each other, but the third was off by at least 100 degrees, and all three were off of Ryck and his guide.

"Query? Effessjustinmathis? Location?" his capy said through the sphere.

This time, as it said "Effessjustinmathis," a human-sounding voice said, *"FS Justin Mathis."*

Shit! They've recorded the sound of the flick! he suddenly realized.

He pulled out his PA. As he expected, it was blocked from the net, but its internal memory was intact. He entered *"F.S. Justin Mathis,"* and got an image of the ship from the movie. Except the ship 30 meters away from the capy ship was not a match. He quickly pulled up *"F.S. Antelope"* and got an image of the new *Mathis*.

"Here, the *F.S. Justin Mathis*."

The capys crowded forward and looked at his PA. The creatures had never shown any emotion that Ryck could recognize as such, but he could almost feel the confusion coming from it.

"Query?" it started, then forgoing its own "Effessjustinmathis," only the recording from the flick played.

"Yes, *FS Justin Mathis*. Here!" Ryck said, using his finger to poke the image on the PA screen.

The four capys held another conference as more smells, one of them a nasty, acrid scent that almost got Ryck to coughing, seemed to war with each other.

If they really do use smells to communicate, how the hell do they keep them from interfering with each other, especially here in this big, frigging compartment? Ryck wondered.

His capy turned back to him and touched the image of the Mathis on his PA. "Image equal ship. Negative equal Effessjustinmathis. Query? Effessjustinmathis location."

Then it hit him. They thought the *FS Justin Mathis* was a person, an individual.

"The *F S Justin Mathis* is the ship! Uh, Effessjustinmathis," he said, trying to run the words together, "equals ship. Is ship."

The four put their heads together, literally. With their feet spread in various directions, they locked hands and held their heads within centimeters from each other. There were some whistles, and once again, some subsonics seemed to vibrate at the base of his skull. More scents reached Ryck, one surprisingly like lavender. Back on Tarawa, Hannah sometimes soaked in a lavender bath. She said it had a calming effect. Ryck hoped that meant it had a calming effect here, too.

His capy, as he was beginning to consider it, let go of the others and turned back to him.

"Query? Confirm. Effessjustinmathis negative equal human," the voice from the sphere asked.

An image of a human, no one that Ryck recognized, appeared in the air between them.

The recorded voice from the flick said *"FS Justin Mathis"* while the sphere said "negative" as the human image seemed to explode into fragments.

"Yes. Affirmative. The *FS Justin Mathis* is a ship, not a human," Ryck said, relieved to have gotten the point across.

"We go," his guide said as the other three capys turned and left.

"To the ship? The *Mathis*?" Ryck asked. "We have more humans there to meet with you."

His capy said nothing and grabbed one of the little floating balls to spin himself about.

Is he getting any of this? Ryck wondered.

"Stop! I need to report back to my command," Ryck said, grabbing its leg once again.

"We go," it said again.

"What? Uh, query? Go where?" Ryck asked.

"We go," the capy repeated, followed by a cross between a grunt and a whistle as lavender flooded the space around Ryck.

An image appeared in the space between them. It took only a moment to realize it was a representation of the Blue Line with the human and Trinocular ships arrayed facing each other. One ship, and with a sinking heart, Ryck knew exactly what ship that was, was moving away from the line, away from the human side of space.

"We go," the capy repeated.

Ryck was supposed to make contact, then get the capys to accept the experts waiting on the *Mathis* to take over from him. It looked like that was going to have to wait. Ryck was going for a ride into Trinocular space whether he wanted to or not.

For Ryck, that was decidedly a "not."

TRINOCULAR SPACE

Chapter 5

"Well, Carl, how much longer? How much time?" Ryck asked.

"Carl" was his capy. Ryck had been tired of calling him the equivalent of "Hey you!" He understood that the capys did have personal designators, if not names in the human sense, but Ryck couldn't yet grasp the rules of naming, which seemed to shift depending on too many factors for him to remember. So, Carl it was.

As outwardly emotionless as always, Carl said, "Sixteen hours to the destination."

As usual when they discussed their destination, the smell of lavender wafted over Ryck. Ryck frankly was getting a kick out of it all, and kept asking just to get his hit of the flowery aroma. Ryck had no idea what awaited him there. Once or twice, Carl had tried to explain, but the translators couldn't seem to handle that yet.

Over the last three days, his Sony Lingua 3000 and Carl's translation sphere had made amazing progress. With the Sony hooked up to the AI in his PA, the almost impossible-to-understand dialog they'd had when he first arrived had matured into an almost reasonable conversation ability. There were still gaps, but at least they were communicating. All the time human scientists had spent with the Trinocular juveniles had not produced anything like this. Of course, that was because the juveniles, as Ryck found out, couldn't really speak and could only understand rudimentary commands.

It wasn't just the Sony and his AI, though. The capy translator sphere was a marvelous piece of gear. Working with some sort of liquid molecular array that Ryck knew the corporate R & D departments would give their left nuts for, it had tremendous capabilities, and with both his AI and the sphere communicating, they had formed an interface that exponentially increased the ability to translate from one language to the other.

If the capys used only sounds to communicate, the translators would be even more accurate, Ryck knew. But the capys relied very little on sounds in the frequencies that humans could detect. They also used subsonics that were picked up through the skin and even controlled bioelectrical impulses that were picked up by the third "eye" in the middle of their foreheads, which worked something along the lines of an Earth shark's ampullae of Lorenzini. They were also heavily dependent on aromas to understand the capy equivalent of emotions.

Still, there were fundamental differences in how both species thought. It had taken Ryck over four hours to convey the idea that a ship could be named. Carl could not grasp that. He (with "Carl" as a name, Ryck had started to think of him as a "he") understood that the *Mathis* was not a human, but he thought that the ship must be an organic construct of some kind and sentient. The concept of a machine having a name was so foreign to him that he evidently thought their translators were faulty.

Ryck still couldn't believe his situation. A short week ago, he was home, out of the Corps. Now he was humankind's envoy to the Trinoculars. With his personal decorations from Greater France and the Confederation, he used to joke with Bert that all he needed was one each from the SOG and the Trinoculars, and he'd have a clean sweep of his former enemies. He didn't know exactly what his position was with them, and he could be on his way for a ceremonial execution for all he knew, but he didn't get that feeling. He thought good things were ahead of him.

"Sixteen hours? Then may I have some more glop to eat?" he said, using a simple sentence construction as his AI recommended.

"Yes, Ryck," Carl said, only recently dropping the full "Rycklysander." "You may every eat glop to your utmost contentment."

The "glop" was one of his juvenile jokes, but it was an accurate description of the white gel that the Trinoculars fed him.

Carl assured him it would take care of his nutritional needs, and it didn't taste half bad, but it looked like someone took Elmer's and squirted a pile of it on a plate. He'd probably catch shit from the scientist types when all of this was over. "Glop" though, was not as bad as his "taking a Papadakis."

He hoped that one would stick.

Chapter 6

Two hours from their destination, wherever that was, the ship's lights dimmed inside the huge compartment. Ryck had almost gotten use to the seemingly haphazard turmoil inside the ship, but the dimming of the lights raised his anxiety more than a bit. If it weren't for the small wisps of lavender that reached him amongst all the other smells, he'd probably be more anxious, but Hannah had been right. Lavender did calm the nerves.

"Ryck, we are transfer now," Carl said as he pulled himself to the front of the little cubbyhole Ryck had constructed.

Like the majority of human interstellar vessels, the capy ship did not enter a planet's atmosphere, so when Carl told him they would be transferring to another ship, he was not surprised. He wondered where they were, though. His best guess was that it was the capy home world.

Ryck straightened out his blues. He'd taken off the blouse and trou shortly after settling in. The capys did not wear clothing and did not seem to be dutifully impressed with his blues, and with his unexpected departure, he had nothing else to wear. So he'd stripped down to his skivvies to keep his uniform as clean as possible. Now, he'd make his appearance looking the best he could, even if it made no difference to his hosts. He could report to the capy high muckety-mucks stark naked, and he didn't think they would blink.

His rank made no difference either, not that he was going to offer to revert when he got back. The concept of rank was just one more thing Carl didn't seem to grasp. The best that Ryck could understand was that the capys served in the position for which they were best suited or "designed," as his translator offered. There was no higher or lower status as humans understood it, more of a "belonging" as a certain cog in the big capy machine. Ryck didn't get the feeling that any one position was considered more important than another.

As Ryck pulled himself out of his compartment, Carl said, "Your weapon with you is good."

That took Ryck by surprise, but he had no idea as to Trinocular protocol. There were plenty of human cultures where a weapon was the societal norm. On Kellerman, government officials wore swords at their waists for all official functions, for example. Perhaps this was a similar thing. Ryck bent back, pulled out his Sam Browne belt and put it on, and grabbed his Ruger and holster. Carl didn't say anything else, so Ryck figured he didn't need a long arm.

Without gravity, Ryck was glad he had gone with his bravos, that is, his blues with ribbons instead of medals. He didn't want them to float around as he navigated in Zero G. He pulled down on the base of his blouse, though, as an act of habit, as he left the cubby hole and followed Carl across the compartment. He focused on the little floating balls that acted as anchors from which he could pull himself. The balls reacted to the capys, shifting position to put them within reach of any capy who needed them, but they did not react to Ryck at all. He had to make sure his aim was on in order to grab and direct his route. On a couple of earlier occasions, he'd missed and kept floating off on a tangent until he bumped into a capy or a bulkhead and could get himself oriented in the right direction again.

This time, he made it across to where Carl was leading him. It was a compartment like the one he'd used to enter the ship. Carl waved his hand over a small box, and the outer hatch opened to the stars. Ryck's heart jumped—he was in his blues, after all, not a vacsuit. But Carl wasn't in a vacsuit either, and he launched himself through the hatch. Ryck had no choice but to follow suit.

When he'd made the crossing from the *Mathis* to the ship, he'd had the propulsion jets from the vacsuit. In his blues, he had nothing, and his initial jump was slightly off target. He started angling to the edge of the tunnel, and he had images of piercing it and finding himself in the vacuum of open space. He tried to twist his body, cycling his legs to straighten out, but that was more instinctual than effective. As he reached the edge of the tunnel, he put out one hand as if to ward it off. Instead of piercing the tunnel wall, however, he was softly bounced back inside, his forward momentum unabated. Within moments, he had arrived at the nondescript, round vessel at the end of the tunnel. Cables ringed the hatch, and Ryck grabbed one, pulling himself into the small craft. Carl was already inside, and if he had noticed Ryck's gyrations out in the tunnel, he didn't mention it.

During the crossing, he'd caught a glimpse of a planet in the distance. He didn't know how big the planet was, so he couldn't estimate how far away it was, but he had the impression that it was farther than he would have expected for normal planetary shuttling. Once again, though, he had no idea just where they were going. His destination could be a station and not a planet.

Four of the soldier capys were already in the small shuttle. They ignored Carl and Ryck, but Ryck had to wonder why they were the only other capys in the shuttle. He hoped they were just hitching a ride. Surreptitiously, he checked the safety on his Ruger, shifting his weight on the bench seat so he could draw the handgun quickly if necessary.

Ryck barely felt the shuttle move as it broke away from the crossing tunnel and started to their destination. Carl didn't say a word, and Ryck kept his attention on the four soldiers. He'd killed another soldier on GenAg 13 in hand-to-hand combat, but he was under no impression that he could take out four of them. He eyed their jai alai *xistera*-like weapons hanging from their utility belts, wondering if he could get the jump on all of them before they could draw.

Probably not, he realized.

The compartment was small, so the odors of the capys became more pronounced. There was the underlying wet dog and cinnamon, the two more common aromas Ryck could detect around the capys, but the waft of lavender was getting a little stronger. That relaxed Ryck a tiny bit, but he still kept up his vigil. He glanced back at Carl, who as usual, showed no signs of emotion. If something was up, Carl was hiding it well.

Ryck sat in silence, ready for anything, but hoping that his anxiety was unwarranted. To his surprise, he almost nodded off when a tingle washed over him. With his AI, he'd concluded the tingle was when the capys were using either their subsonics or their bioelectrics to communicate. This had been a heavy jolt, so Ryck wondered if this was the capy equivalent to shouting.

Two of the soldiers shifted their weight, and Ryck let his hand fall to cover the Ruger's grip. Nothing else obviously happened, and it took a few minutes for him to realize that the smells were gone. It was as if someone had sprayed unscented air freshener all around him.

What the heck does that mean? he wondered.

That was about all the time he had to contemplate before gravity suddenly took a hold of him. Ryck sighed with relief. He hadn't liked being in Zero G for such a long stretch of time. He could feel forces on his body as the shuttle maneuvered in the atmosphere of wherever they'd arrived. It still took some time, but finally, a gentle bump signaled that the shuttle had landed.

Immediately, the blue glow of personal shields surrounded the soldiers as they stood up and moved to the door. Carl followed, so Ryck joined him, ready to debark. The hatch swung open, letting in too-bright sunlight, far into the upper spectrums. Ryck closed his eyes and turned his head away as cold, biting air rushed in. Belatedly, Ryck wondered if the air was safe for him. If he had a taster as on his vacsuit, his AI could analyze it, but in his blues, he just had to trust that he wasn't inhaling poisons that were going to kill him.

He opened his eyes to just slits and looked out, but he couldn't see much. He wished he had some sunglasses with him, but those were not authorized for wear when in uniform, so he'd never thought to bring any on the initial contact. His vacsuit face shield would automatically darken in such intense light, but that wasn't doing him much good here.

He stumbled out after Carl and his eyes adjusted. It was still too bright for him, but at least he could see the four soldiers take position surrounding Carl and him.

Am I a prisoner? he wondered as the small group stepped off.

It was then that he noticed his surroundings. This was obviously a town of some sort, with emphasis on the "was."

On either side of Ryck round, igloo-shaped buildings, or what was left of them, lined the path forward. Something had happened here, something big. The obvious signs of destruction—the scorched walls, the rubble, the destroyed scrap of metal that had to have once been a vehicle, the acrid tang of ferrous metal that had been hit by energy weapons—were all Ryck needed to know that he'd stepped into a war zone. But who or what was fighting, Ryck didn't have a clue.

Ryck glanced at his escort. Neither Carl nor his guard seemed to show any sign of anxiety.

After only 200 meters or so, the buildings petered out. A precious few seemed untouched. The igloo comparison was even more apparent if Ryck ignored the fact that the buildings were made of some sort of brown material and not ice. With the open compartment aboard their ship, Ryck would have guessed their buildings would be large and open, too. The igloos could only hold a handful of capys at a time, and they were nothing like the buildings he and Sams had observed being built on Hac-440.

As the buildings opened up, more vegetation was visible. Ryck had been to the Alien Horticulture Gardens on Venus, so he knew that not all of the alien vegetation discovered by man was grass and trees. This was pretty far out there, though. Looking like big, cloud ear funguses, but in shades of magentas and reds, this was an alien world in the best Hollybolly tradition. Despite the situation, Ryck had to look around in amazement. Every other planet and moon he'd been on was either sterile or had been terraformed, so this was something totally new to him. He was being led by the hand on this tour, but still, he felt akin to the Federation Navy's Deep Space Scouts, seeing things that no human had ever seen before.

The sound of distant firing caught Ryck's attention as if he'd been lassoed. He dropped all thoughts of alien explorations and weird plants and focused on what he was hearing.

"Carl, what's going on?" he asked after closing the distance with his guide.

"To see, to see for you soon," Carl said hurriedly, a departure from his normal plodding rhythm.

A whiff of lavender seemed to escape from him, and almost immediately, Ryck felt the tingle of subsonics again like a slap in the face. It was like a door being shut, and the lavender was cut off.

"You will wait five, after you will see," Carl said, back to his normal slow rhythm.

A thought surfaced, and Ryck looked back at Carl as the capy turned away from him.

Could the lavender mean something else? he wondered.

Ryck knew the capys were not actually emitting lavender, but that was the closest his brain could classify the smell. He wasn't sure it was even that close to the Earth flower, but it was his new baseline. He'd assumed the aroma indicated calmness or happiness, given how lavender affected people.

What if in capy-smell, it's different? What if it means anxiety or fear? And what if the soldier-boys don't like that and are telling Carl to man up?

Ryck was no scientist, and his AI was no help, but he was pretty sure he was onto something. If he was, though, then what was making Carl so concerned?

He'd find out in five, he guessed. But he didn't know five what? Human minutes? Capy days? Dinner times?

It was minutes. The front two soldiers simply halted. Carl kept moving forward, with Ryck following, until the two were even with the two soldiers. Five klicks or so ahead of Ryck, down a gentle slope covered with purples and magentas, a battle was raging. There were no aircraft buzzing the battlefield, no huge explosions, but Ryck's combat instincts kicked in, his nerves abuzz. He couldn't quite make out what was happening with his naked eyes. It looked like there might be capys in the shit with larger combat-suited beings of some sort.

Ryck didn't have binos. Once again, why bring binos to a meet and greet aboard a capy ship?

He took out his PA's iris and clipped it to his collar. He then tried to record what was happening down below him, intending to blow it up so he could better make sense of things. Of course, as in the capy ship, the PA was shielded. All his readouts remained green, but nothing was being recorded.

Without a word, Ryck angled off to the left, leaving the capys behind. They didn't follow him. From his fights on both Livingston and G.K.A. Nutrition Six, Ryck knew he had to get about 200 meters away to get out from under the Trinocular cloak so his PA could work again. He trudged through the fungus-like vegetation, briefly wondering what animal life might be scurrying around his ankles, ready and able to defend its territory from him.

He paced off 126 steps, which for him, was 200 meters. He glanced back at Carl and the four soldiers, but it looked like they hadn't moved. He faced the battle and turned on his PA's recorder. The green light came on, and to Ryck's relief, the stupid thing was working.

Ryck turned on the screen and zoomed in on the battle which seemed to be petering out. Hundreds of capys littered the ground. While he watched, a last few were cut down, and Ryck could see no more. With his recorder on manual, he controlled what was in the PA iris' field of view. He turned his body slightly, and his iris picked up the combat suited-opponents.

Except they were not in combat suits, the best Ryck could tell. They were birds, huge birds, each easily three times the size of a capy.

Ryck knew they were not really birds, but as with the lavender, his brain adjusted to what he was comprehending. Possibly five meters tall, they were bipedal, but with four upper limbs. The upper two were small, the bottom two were heavily muscled and carried weapons. Ryck zoomed in on the weapons. One was something Ryck didn't recognize, but the other was a sword.

A freaking sword? Really? Going into battle like an old-timey pirate?

The more he looked at the creature, the less bird-like it looked. It did have a beak of sorts, and it had what looked like feathers fanned up around its neck like a strutting turkey and hanging from the smaller upper arms. The fan was a bright yellow and red, as were the ones on the arms, but as Ryck watched, the fan seemed to fold and collapse against the thing's back. Ryck panned out, and he could see about four of the things, and in front of them had to be a hundred dead capys.

Whatever these things were, they were deadly.

And suddenly Ryck knew why he was here. The Trinoculars were in a war and they needed allies.

EARTH

Chapter 7

The hatch to the shuttle whispered open and Ryck, RADM Baris, and Conner Therault, the Federation chief xenobiologist, stepped out to an armed cordon of FCDC guards. A Marine captain and a Navy lieutenant commander watched the three men anxiously as they waited by the open door of a Kestrel limo.

Ryck had been under what he described as house arrest since his return to the *Mathis*, never leaving his stateroom, which was guarded 24/7 by rotating two-man teams of large, tough-looking sailors. The admiral said this was simply isolation for security reasons, and Ryck understood that, but he hadn't liked it. Other than his guards, his only face-to-face contact had been with the admiral, a brief encounter with the ship's captain, Conner, and two of his team. Conner told him the Brotherhood reps were fit to be tied, but the official word was that Ryck was under medical quarantine. Even when the Federation personnel came into his stateroom, they went through the façade of putting on environmental suits.

Immediately after reaching human space, Ryck had uploaded his report along with the recording of the fight between the capys and the bird-things, so the powers that be knew what the capys wanted and what was facing them. Ryck hadn't been kept in the loop as to how this was received, but he imagined he'd kicked open an anthill.

"You ready for this?" Conner asked him as the three men stepped off between the FCDC guards.

"I've given them everything already, but yeah, let's get it over with," Ryck answered.

Conner, and even the admiral, had proven to be good companions during the transit to Earth. Conner and his team had wanted as much information about the Trinoculars as possible, and Ryck had dredged up everything he could remember. His AI had been vampired, and Conner's linguistics expert, a huge bear of a man named Alger Prose, had been ecstatic to receive that data. The linguist had kept to himself after that, but the rest of the team along with the admiral had spent hours discussing the ramifications of what had transpired. Not that what they thought would have any bearings on what was to be done. That would be decided at the highest level of the governments that were involved. But still, Ryck had been glad to have the conversations. He'd been the sole representative of man to the capys for over a week, and he was glad to bring the others into the picture.

"Gentlemen, if we can?" the lieutenant commander asked after saluting. "They're waiting for you."

The three men got into the limo and settled in for the ride to the Center. Ryck had been in Brussels for his diplomatic training, so he was familiar with the city. It had kept most of its old charm, he thought, and he rather liked it. Driving past the Cinquantenaire arch, the Basilica of the Sacred Heart, even the rows of old Flemish townhouses, their familiarity was almost homelike, and that helped calm him.

And he needed to be calmed, he realized ruefully. He wasn't in any trouble. In fact, the early indications he'd received from Admiral Baris was that the council was more than pleased with his mission, even if they were deeply divided as to the capy request. For once, the messenger was not being shot. Still, he was going to be meeting with the chairman and the entire council from the Federation along with the heads of states and representatives of the Brotherhood, the Confederation, Greater France, and half a dozen other governments. The *Mathis* had even been kept in a far-system orbit out in the Kuiper Belt for two extra days to allow for the arrival of the other worthies.

The three men sat in silence as the limo pulled into the VIP arrival tunnel at the Center. The huge glass and steel building that served as the capital of the Federation was completely at odds with the architectural style of the rest of the city center. However, much as the pyramid in the courtyard of the Louvre in Paris initially seemed so out-of-place, so had the Center become part of the city's very essence. Ryck could almost feel the power emanating from it.

None of the three men had any input as to the response from mankind to the capys, but this was all part of the show, they knew. The chairman would parade them around, a reminder that the capys had requested a Federation officer to meet with them. Not a Brotherhood citizen, not a Confed, an Advocacy member, or a New Budapest soldier, but a Federation Marine. Ryck doubted that the connection between the movie and the request had been disseminated. That would give away their advantage, and the chairman had not made it to the top by throwing away advantages in the past. He would not be about to start now.

A young man in a blue pinstripe suit met the limo as it came to a stop and sank down to the ground.

"Please, we need to hurry. They've been assembled for half an hour already," he told them, taking Admiral Baris by the upper arm as if to pull him along.

The admiral shook his arm free, but picked up the pace, followed by Ryck and Conner. They entered the building through a well-fortified gate—and scanned to the millimeter, Ryck knew. In the private areas where the tourists were not allowed, security was constant, tight, and invasive. They could probably tell him when he'd have to take his next shit.

After only a few twists and turns, their guide led them through a small door, down a few steps, and out into the assembly hall where several hundred of the leaders of humanity had gathered.

"Ladies and gentlemen, Rear Admiral Hancock Baris, commander of the Trinocular mission, Dr. Conner Therault, chief xenobiologist, and Colonel Ryck Lysander, the liaison to the Trinoculars," a voice boomed out over the speakers.

A few people started to clap, followed by more, and then still more, until the entire hall was awash in sound. It was better than people screaming for his scalp, but Ryck felt uncomfortable. These were the leaders of humanity, the people who steered the human race to the future. Ryck had just been a messenger boy, relaying a request for help. It was certainly historical, but it hadn't taken much of anything on his part.

Ryck and the other two were ushered to their seats at the side of the dais. The three men stood there, acknowledging the crowd until the applause started to peter out and their pinstriped guide motioned for them to sit.

The chairman himself was the first to speak. It was evident to Ryck that the man realized this was going down in history, and every word, every gesture, looked rehearsed. Even the continual breaking out of applause from the audience seemed part of the performance. It was a rah-rah speech, first identifying the danger of the Klethos, as the capys called the bird-like creatures fighting them, then rallying around the idea that humanity, led by the Federation, could rise up to meet this threat.

The president of the Confederation and a few of the representatives from other governments sat stone-faced during the speech. Ryck didn't think they were too pleased with the "led by the Federation" tone to the chairman's words.

"Your expression, Colonel," the admiral whispered beside Ryck.

Ryck had let his guard down while looking at the envoys. He quickly switched to an attentive, and he hoped admiring expression frozen on his face.

The chairman droned on for close to 45 minutes. He tended to the verbose, but this was a little long even for him, especially as he really said nothing.

Finally, he sat down, turning the mic over to Admiral Wadden, the Chief of Naval Operations. Admiral Wadden looked like a sly fox with something to hide—which was pretty much a case of looks reflecting the person. He was the penultimate politician and was an oddsmaker favorite for becoming chairman someday.

Admiral Wadden was there to brief the threat. He went into detail that surprised Ryck. He wasn't sure how the Navy had determined so much from so little data. Conner, sitting beside him, seemed equally surprised. Ryck tried to keep that from showing as he kept the same interested expression he'd used for the chairman glued to his face.

The more the admiral talked, the more evident the response to the capy request would be. The admiral was prepping the audience, nothing more, and if he replaced facts with conjecture, so be it if that served the cause.

When the admiral turned the podium back to the chairman, Ryck already knew the decision.

The chairman took the podium, then looked deliberately through the audience, a great man thinking great thoughts.

Just say it and forget the theatrics, Ryck thought.

When the so-called great men spoke, it was the lowly sailor and Marine who had to act on it.

"Ladies and gentlemen, it comes down to this. A race of beings is in danger of being exterminated. True, we were at war with this race not too long ago, but humanity is not one to hold grudges from the past. And as human beings, we cannot allow an entire race, the first intelligent race we've encountered, to be wiped out. We must act. And so, with the full agreement of the Brotherhood, the Confederation of Free States, and other governments as they come onboard with us, we will honor the Trinocular request. We will not ignore the threat but move with all the resources and power we have. We will rise to the challenge and defend not only the Trinoculars, but all of humanity, so help us God!"

The entire audience rose as one in thunderous applause, Ryck included. Outwardly, he was the enthusiastic Marine, ready to march into battle. Inwardly, he hoped they understood what they were getting into.

TARAWA

Chapter 8

"I'm used to them," Ryck said, trying to keep his voice calm. "There won't be any feeling out process."

Colonel Jasper Nelson, the division personnel officer protested, "But we've gone over this. Three-Six is ready to go, and as far as 2/3, LtCol Lu Wan will not report in for another week, and then he's got to get snapped in. No, 3/6 is ready."

"Major Peltier-Aswad is more than capable of leading the battalion, Colonel. I know that for a fact."

"But a major? For a mission of this magnitude?" Nelson asked.

Colonel Nelson was a long-time O6[7] on his twilight tour. Ryck got the feeling that the man resented Ryck's sudden resurrection and quick promotion to colonel. He seemed determined to stifle Ryck's priorities and instigate his own. Everyone realized that this was a historic mission, one with extremely high visibility, and Ryck suspected the colonel thought he might be able to parlay his part in the mission into a promotion. Ryck didn't have time for that, and he didn't give a rat's ass for the other colonel's career aspirations.

He realized that requesting 2/3 was getting back to his old habits of gathering men he knew around him, but his point about being familiar with the battalion was none-the-less valid. This was a fact-finding mission, true, but one that could easily result in at least some fighting. With representational units from five other

---

[7] O6: Colonel

militaries, the confusion was going to be bad enough, so Ryck wanted as much familiarity as possible.

"I do believe the chairman himself said I get who I want, no questions asked, right?"

"Well, yes, but within reason—" Nelson started.

"I never heard that caveat. It's 2/3, pure and simple. Next item?" he asked, looking around the table.

He'd been in this meeting for over three hours already, and he was getting antsy. He had very little time before they embarked, not enough time to do this right.

He looked over to the chairs alongside the wall and caught Hannah's eye. As the director of theoretical research, she didn't rate a seat at the table itself, but at least she was in the room, and if Ryck couldn't be home, this was something positive. Most of all, she would know what was going on. He didn't have to worry about opsec[8] with her, either.

Hannah gave him a very slow, deliberate wink, then pursed her lips in a tiny ghost kiss. It was nothing, but it was everything. Ryck held back a smile as he focused on Nelson's next bitch, something about the proposed chain of command of the joint force.

Having won the battle over 2/3, Ryck could afford to let the man blather on. Ryck may only be a colonel, and a frocked one at that, and he knew quite a few flag officers thought a mere colonel was too junior for the mission, but the capys had wanted him, and the combined leadership of the various human governments had agreed to that. The bottom line was that the Brotherhood Admiral Ethan Parks was the overall mission commander, and Rear Admiral Baris was the Federation commander, but for the ground forces, the one that could possibly see action, Ryck was in command. Once on a planet, Ryck was in charge of humanity's first potential contact with the Klethos. No one, not even the Federation Third Vice Minister, who was a four-star equivalent and the senior civilian in the task force, could overrule him.

It might sound melodramatic, but in some ways, the future of humanity could rest squarely on Ryck's shoulders.

---

[8] Opsec: Operational Security

Chapter 9

"Hey, congrats on the promotion, Ryck, I mean sir," Lieutenant Colonel Jorge Simone said as he entered Ryck's office.

"Thanks, Jorge, but I'm still officially a lieutenant colonel. I've only been frocked," Ryck told him. "You know, for political reasons."

"Doesn't matter, sir. I see the eagles on your collar, and that trumps any official date of rank. *Quid visum accipias est.*"

"Uh, what was that?" Ryck asked.

"Oh, sorry. I guess it means what you see is what it is. I see the eagles, so you're a colonel as far as I'm concerned."

Ryck tried to hold back a smile. Jorge Simone looked like a thug. A very stupid, rock of a man. Short at about 1.5 meters, he had the typical broad-shouldered, no-neck, stocky build of other heavy worlders. His deep-set beady eyes added to the impression of a brainless hunk of muscle. Well, *quid visum*-whatever he just said certainly was not appropriate to describe him. Ryck didn't know if he'd ever met anyone as smart as Jorge.

"OK, whatever. I know, if it quacks like a duck and all of that," Ryck said, using a phrase a little less high-brow. "Please, take a seat."

"So, sir, I guess you're pretty busy about now," Jorge said, looking at the mess that was Ryck's office.

"That's a grubbing understatement. I get one thing done and two more land on my lap. Make that three more."

Jorge chuckled, then said, "I would imagine that to be the case. But then again, that's what you get paid the big bucks for."

"Hah! I'm only frocked. I'm still at an O-5's pay!" Ryck said as both men broke into laughter.

"You've got me there, sir."

"I bet you're wondering why I asked you to come see me," Ryck said.

"The question has crossed my mind, sir. I'd have to postulate that I can be of some assistance to you, but that might be somewhat presumptuous."

Ryck thought he detected a hint of eagerness in Jorge's voice. Ryck had been inundated with offers of assistance as Marines came out of the woodwork; Marines he knew and Marines he didn't. This was a historic mission, and depending on what transpired, it could be a career maker for those connected to it. It could be a career killer, too, but Marines were not noted for being overly cautious.

"No, you're not being presumptuous. I do need your assistance."

Jorge smiled and said, "Then let me know. I told General Caruthers that you had asked me to come over, and he's preemptively cut me loose until you embark. I am at your disposal."

"Uh, that's not quite what I mean, Jorge," Ryck started as Jorge's eyes clouded over ever-so-slightly.

"What I mean is that I want you to join me for the duration. I know you're in a plum billet now, and General Caruthers is going places. But I'm overwhelmed here, and time is getting short. I'm not ashamed to admit that I'm in over my head, and I need help. I can't offer you the battalion. Major Peltier-Aswad's got that. We don't have a set T/O for this hybrid brigade, but what I really need is sort of a chief of staff. And I want you for that. Not just for a couple of days, but until we get back."

Jorge sat back, obviously taken by surprise.

"Why me, sir? I don't have that much operational experience, and we've never worked together. You sort of, well, I mean, your reputation—"

"My reputation is that I surround myself with my posse," Ryck interrupted. "And I do. But we have worked together, at NOTC. I know your capabilities. And I know why you don't have much in the way of operational experience. It's because you keep getting snapped up by all the brass to keep things organized, to keep things running. And don't sell yourself short on your tactical ability. I still remember the staff all pissed off when you beat the system on the RCET[9] back at Annapolis."

"But that was just a training exercise. It wasn't real," Jorge protested.

"But you figured it out.

"Look, I know I'm not some general, and Caruthers can do more for you. And I realize that it might be awkward for you with me in command. But I want to offer you the position, if you would accept it."

Please accept it, Ryck silently implored, trying to will Jorge to say yes. *I need your help!*

Jorge looked at Ryck for a few moments, his face expressionless. Ryck felt his heart drop. He had to find someone, and Jorge had been his first choice.

"Sir, I'm at a loss for words, something very rare for me. I'm honored that you are asking, and, well, excuse my language, but fucking-A yeah I accept! Are you kidding me, sir? I'd give my left nut for this, maybe my right one, too!"

Relief swept over Ryck as Jorge jumped to his feet, hand outstretched. Ryck took it and almost regretted it as the excited Marine almost crushed it. Almost, but not really. This was a huge benefit, one Ryck knew he needed.

"Welcome aboard, Colonel," Ryck said. "I wish I could give you some time to get oriented, but you have to jump right in the fire. Starting in," he paused, looking at his watch, "12 minutes with the J4's staff. If you need anyone to build a staff, just let the master guns know, and we'll try and get him. Speaking of which, do I need to call the general?"

"No, sir. That's my job now, to run interference and take care of the routine. I've got a couple of Marines I'd like to bring over, and I'll get up with the master guns later. But if the meeting with the J4 is at Headquarters, I need to fly. Afterward, if you have time, I'd like a short sit-down with you to get your commanders' guidance and run a few ideas by you. If that's OK, sir."

Ryck had to keep a straight face as the excited new chief of staff positively beamed with energy.

---

[9] Realistic Combat Environment Trainer. This is a huge simulator used to train Marines and sailors how to fight.

"That sounds good; just let me know when. The J4 meeting is in our conference room, so that will save some time. Top Sunawata from my staff and Captain Libre from the battalion will be there, but I want you to get saddled up as soon as possible. You'd better get going," Ryck said.

"Roger that, sir," he said, turning to go out the hatch.

Just before he left the office, Jorge turned around and said, "Thank you, sir, thank you for the opportunity. I really appreciate it."

"No problem. I'm really counting on you."

He felt a load lift off his shoulders, and for a moment, he just leaned back in satisfaction. Then his PA beeped, reminding him that having a chief of staff was just one finger in the dyke, and the ocean was still threatening to flood in.

He glanced at the PA readout and quickly snatched up the device.

"General Mbanefo, what can I do for you, sir?" he asked.

It just never stopped. He'd be glad to finally get on the ship and be able to catch his breath.

Chapter 10

"Yes, sir, I'll keep that in mind," Ryck said, shaking the general's hand and leading him out of his office.

"We're all counting on you, Ryck, and I'm going to need your input if and when this Quail Hunt kicks off," Lieutenant General Ernesto Bolivar said. "Well, I'm going to leave you now. I know you're up to your ass in alligators, so I'll get out of your hair."

The alligators were well past Ryck's ass and closing in on his throat, but a colonel did not turn away a three-star, especially one who could be his commanding general soon. LtGen Bolivar was slated to take command of the ground element of the Joint Human Defense Fleet, which was being readied in case the combined governments decided to actively intervene on the side of the capys. The general had more time to prepare his force, but it was also much larger and more complex. And it could be all for naught if mankind decided to leave the Trinoculars and the Klethos to each other. But the general had to prepare as if war was imminent, and Ryck's Task Force Hannah would be part of his future force, but a part that was leaving in less than a day. What Ryck did could affect the entire fleet operation, and the general was trying to both keep tabs and offer guidance without getting too much in the way. Ryck hated it, but he understood it and didn't blame the general, who had a good reputation among the fleet.

Actually, he'd been left pretty much alone by the brass, with only General Bolivar, General Mbanefo, who was already acting as the commandant even if he still had a couple of days before the actual change of command, and Admiral Baris spending any degree of time with him.

Ryck watched the general leave before turning around and getting to his desk. The issue of his different ground components being on their own ships was still taking too much of his time and efforts. Ryck would have liaisons from the other units with him on the mission, but the Confederation century would be on a Confed ship, the Brotherhood minor host on the fleet flagship, the Greater France company on the old *Jeanne d'Arc,* and so on. There could be a threat to humanity coming, if the capys were telling the truth, but until that was confirmed, the various forces of man didn't want foreign units having free reign to wander about their respective ships.

Even the Federation had chosen to send an older ship as the troop carrier for the task force. Instead of an *Inchon*-class, the Federation flagship was the *FS Brandenburg*, which was not nearly as capable of a troop transport. New at the time of the War of the Far Reaches, and with a notable combat record, the *Brandenburg* was never-the-less older technology now, though, so any foreign observers would not be able to ferret out much that would be of any use.

Ryck thought that choosing an older ship was ridiculous. He was under the philosophy that you took the biggest stick you could find into a fight. Granted, this was technically an info-gathering mission, not a combat mission, but getting close to any fight going on could draw them in. And while he felt in his gut that the capys were sincere, this could be some sort of trap. The capys and humanity had been in an all-out war not too long ago, after all.

"Sir, you got a minute?" Sandy asked, sticking his head in the hatch.

Ryck didn't have a minute, but Sandy was his battalion commander, so he sighed and asked, "What is it?"

"There's someone here to see you," Sandy said.

Ryck looked up, hoping it wasn't some other brass trying to impart his fingerprint on the op. To his surprise, Sergeant Hans Çağlar walked into the office.

"Hans! Great to see you. I thought you were on Alexander now. What are you doing here?" Ryck asked the big Marine.

"I had to come see you sir, you know, to see if I could join up with you."

"But you're at the Leadership Course now. You can't be done yet, right?"

"Well, sir, no, I'm not done," the sergeant said quietly. "But I had to come. You need me with you."

"Our sergeant is sort of UA[10] now," Sandy said from where he still stood in the doorway.

"You're UA?" Ryck asked stunned.

As far as he knew, Çağlar hadn't broken a regulation during his entire career.

"Yes, sir, I'm UA. But if you're going into a fight, I need to be there. That's where I belong. If you went out there and anything happened to you, I don't know if I could live with myself, thinking maybe I could have changed something. I've been with you thick and thin, sir, in some real shit, and my place is with you."

Ryck listened, even more stunned. That had to be the longest speech he'd ever heard Çağlar make. The guy would barely string ten words together.

"I . . . I don't know what to say, Hans. I mean, of course I would welcome you in any unit with me. I told you that before you went to the course. But now, now you're UA. You just took off from your place of duty? What about that?"

"Well, sir, I'm thinking you can make that an authorized absence."

"What? I don't get you," Ryck said.

"I think what the good sergeant means is that you've got carte blanche to pull in just about anyone you want. So if you put him on your wish list, his absence would be authorized," Sandy said.

"Is that what you mean?" Ryck asked.

"Yes, sir, begging the colonel's pardon. I'm sorry to ask, but I didn't know what else to do," Çağlar said, looking like a whipped puppy. A big, strapping whipped puppy, but a puppy just the same.

Ryck was touched. Hans was not the sharpest crayon in the box, but he was loyal and trustworthy. He'd put his career on the line to try and join Ryck, risking prison time and a dishonorable discharge. He couldn't let that happen.

"Well, Major, I think you better ask Top Sunawata to cut the sergeant here some orders. And you, Sergeant Çağlar, you're cutting it pretty close. We leave in the morning, so you'd better draw your kit. I want you here at the office at 0600 sharp."

---

[10] UA: Unauthorized absence

Relief flowed over Çağlar's face.

"Yes, sir! Thank you, sir!"

"I mean it. Time's a-wastin'," Ryck told him.

"Well, what was I supposed to do?" Ryck asked Sandy as the sergeant took off to get ready.

"Not much. I think you're pretty much stuck with him. If you had said no, I think he would have found a way to stow away on the *Brandenburg*."

"You're probably right."

"Colonel Simone's called a staff meeting. Are you going to be there?" Sandy asked.

"Nope. I've got too much to do, and that's why I have a chief of staff. I'll let him worry about all of that," Ryck answered.

"Roger that, sir. Well, I need to take off. He doesn't brook well with latecomers."

"I can't imagine he does," Ryck said with a laugh.

Asking Jorge Simone to join him might have been the best decision he'd made to date. Ryck hated to think how far behind they'd be without the man. He sat back down at his desk and pulled up his to-do list. Not all of it was going to get done, and he'd come to terms with that. He just hoped he'd be able to get the most vital tasks accomplished before embarking.

His PA beeped with yet another incoming message. He glanced at it, intending to relegate it to the end of the to-do queue, but the return address caught his eye. He opened it and read the message, a smile turning the corners of his mouth up ever-so-slightly, not that he'd ever admit that to anyone.

It was from Major Titus Pohlmeyer, Confederation of Free States Army. The good major was informing him that he'd just arrived on planet to take up the duties as the liaison to the task force ground command. He would be on the *Brandenburg* with Ryck. Ryck still had the major's contact number on his PA, encrypted for security. He'd never taken Titus up on his offer to, well, whatever had been offered at the spaceport back at New Mumbai, but as ordered by his seniors, he had kept the number. And now, his old babysitter was back with him, at least for the meantime.

And he was still a major? Either the Confederation was much slower with its promotions or Titus' job was better accomplished with enough rank to get things done, but not enough to draw any attention to him. Ryck was pretty sure it was the latter reason. Still, that wouldn't stop Ryck from razzing on the major if he had the chance.

He closed the message and had just started on the armor report when he heard someone enter his office unannounced.

What the fuck now? he wondered as he looked up.

His frown shifted to a smile as he saw Hannah come in. With her in the loop, while he hadn't seen her enough, at least they'd been able to share a few meals together.

She sat down on one of the two chairs centered in front of his desk.

"I take it you won't be coming home tonight?" she asked.

"I don't think I can, baby. You should see what I've got left to do. I just don't see it happening. I'm sorry."

"No, don't be sorry, Ryck. The kids want to see you, but they're so proud of you, especially after, well, you know . . ."

"Especially after all the other kids gave them so much shit for me being kicked out," Ryck said.

A sanitized version of Ryck's liaison with the capys had been given to the media, as had his present command billet. Sandy had said he'd gained a sort of cult hero status. That status could be fleeting, Ryck knew, but after what his kids had gone through, he didn't care.

"Look, I'll try to come by and pick up my gear around seven," Ryck said.

"I can bring it."

"No, I want to get it. I'll confirm around six, but if I can, I want to tell the kids goodbye."

"But nothing tonight, right?" she asked.

"No, I'm afraid not. You should see my to-do list," he said, pointing at his PA on his desk.

"I'm not complaining. Just verifying," she said, rising from the chair and going to the door.

Ryck was a little disappointed that she didn't even say goodbye. It wasn't his fault, and she should realize that.

He was surprised, though, that she didn't leave but closed the door instead. And locked it.

"This isn't the most romantic spot, but with Jorge Simone keeping everyone at his meeting, it will have to do," she said, turning with that look in her eyes. A look Ryck knew well.

This was an official Marine Corps office, and Ryck was on duty. It was so wrong, but still, the thought excited him. Still, he took a quick glance back at his PA.

"The rest of your to-do list will wait, Mr. Lysander. I've just put one more thing on the top of the list, and we be about to cross that off," she said, unbuttoning her blouse.

She was right. The rest of the list could wait.

FS BRANDENBURG

Chapter 11

Ryck closed the connection with Colonel Rommers. The ground element commander of the Brotherhood forces had an aggressive personality, to say the least, and he was most evidently not happy to be answering to Ryck. Several times each cycle, he was contacting Ryck over the task force command circuit to discuss his ideas on ground operations. While not expressly stating them as ultimatums, Ryck got the message. The Brotherhood minor host (comparable to a Federation battalion) would cooperate with the rest of the joint task force, but they would not be subject to Federation orders. This was expressly at odds with the joint memorandum of understanding signed by the Brotherhood government, and Ryck wasn't sure if he should inform Rear Admiral Baris of this or not. So far, Ryck had been keeping this to himself. Rommers hadn't exactly stated that the Brotherhood host would be acting independently, after all, only implied it.

Ryck had worked with Brotherhood forces several times in training over the years, and he'd always been impressed with their professionalism. With Rommers' constant maneuvering, it was almost a relief to know that petty personalities and power-grabbing was a factor with them just as with about every other force. Their religious foundation didn't change this basic aspect of human nature.

The other commanders did not seem to be as confrontational or power-grabbing. The Confederation century, commanded by LTC Rosario Hennesey—who Ryck had met during the Telchines operation, and whose assignment could not have been coincidence—had been much more cooperative, as had the companies from

Greater France, Outback, New Budapest, the Advocacy, Purgatory, and even the company from the Alliance of Free States.

Cooperative or not, this was still a hodge-podge of a force that had never trained together. Ryck had liaisons from each of the ground units with him aboard the *Brandenburg*, but he knew if the task force were committed to ground combat, chaos would be the most likely result. Ryck had gone through coordination pains before with 2/3 when it was designated as one of the new integrated assault battalions, but that had been child's play in comparison to this cluster fuck.

Ryck understood the political nature of the military make-up of the task force. As a commander, though, he'd rather have had strictly Marines in the ground task force and let the Navy deal with making every government happy that they were represented.

He didn't even have a full command staff. Ryck had managed to pull a few Marines to create a skeleton staff, to include Lieutenant Colonel Story Hanh-de Friese as his operations officer, but they were still woefully under-staffed for what was the equivalent to a rather robust brigade.

Ryck had always eagerly marched to the sound of guns, but for perhaps the first time in his career, he was half-way hoping that any potential combat would wait for the formation of the Expeditionary force and Operation Quail Hunt. Let General Bolivar worry about dealing with all the other forces.

His hatch chime sounded, and Jorge Simone's voice came over the speaker inside his stateroom, "CO, do you have a moment?"

Ryck buzzed open the hatch and his harried chief-of-staff came in and gratefully collapsed into the chair to which Ryck pointed.

"What do you got?" Ryck asked.

Jorge held up his PA and said, "Major Gerold. He's got a Brotherhood ops order that he insists you see. It's well, it's interesting, to say the least."

"What does Story think?" Ryck asked.

Ryck had never met LtCol Hanh-de Friese before his assignment to the task force and was still trying to get a feel for the Marine. Story had been Jorge's recommendation, and he had been immediately available, so he had concurred with his chief of staff's recommendation.

"He hates it and will not incorporate it into any ops order he has to develop," Jorge admitted.

"I thought you told me that Story said Major Gerold was an OK guy," Ryck said.

"He did. I think so, too. But *corvus oculum corvi non eruit*, you know," Jorge told him.

Ryck was glad he had Jorge on board, but he was getting a little tired of his continual use of Latin phrases as if he expected Ryck to understand them all. First Liam Stilicho, and now Jorge. Ryck was a grubbing commander, not a scholar of ancient languages. He raised one eyebrow at Jorge.

"Uh, it means 'a raven will not pick out the eye of another raven,'" Jorge told him.

"Like honor among thieves?" Ryck asked.

"Yes, same meaning. The Brotherhood is sticking together. Gerold's just the messenger."

"And we don't kill the messenger, I know," Ryck stated quickly before Jorge could come up with the Latin phrase for that.

"If Story doesn't like it, why bring it to me?" Ryck asked. "You should be short-stopping this kind of thing."

"Because Vice Bishop Flannery accompanied Gerold with it, and he insisted that you have to see it with your own eyes."

The vice bishop was the Brotherhood liaison to the Federation and second highest-ranking Brotherhood civilian in the task force.

"Is that it on your PA," Ryck asked.

"Yes, sir."

"Turn your PA around so I can see it," Ryck told him.

Jorge nodded, then twisted his wrist so his PA's display screen faced Ryck.

Ryck glanced up at the lit screen for a second, then said, "OK, I saw it with my own eyes. Tell the honorable vice bishop he can now keep his nose out of our business.

"No," he added hurriedly, "you know what I mean. Tell him thank you and that I will take it into serious consideration should the need arise for a mission."

"Roger that, sir," Jorge said with a smile as he turned off his PA's display. "Done."

"How is Story doing? Are you monitoring him?" Ryck asked, changing the subject.

"He's doing fine. He should have five rough contingency plans to you in a couple of hours. "Mary" Abd Elmonim and the rest of the battalion Three shop are giving him support, but Story is on it. This delay has been somewhat of a godsend, though, giving him more time to hammer these out."

For all the rush to get the task force together, the capys had delayed the actual crossover past the Blue Line and into their space. It had given the military side of the task force time to collect its breath and settle things down, but the civilian side was chomping at their bits and in a state of, if not near panic, then at least strong apprehension as they tried to figure out what the delay meant.

"OK, but keep an eye on him. Not too close, but, well—"

"But you don't know him and are not sure of what he can do, sir," Jorge interrupted.

Which was spot on. Ryck had always made an effort to surround himself with tried and true Marines, Marines he knew. Story had been Jorge's choice. But he had chosen Jorge, so he knew he should give the man the benefit of the doubt.

Ryck smiled and started to say, "Well, yeah, but—"

"No reason *not* to be concerned, sir, until after he proves himself, at least. I know he's not in your posse, but even a staff puke like me can have a posse of my own," Jorge said, a broad smile on his face. "You'll be more than pleased with his work."

"OK, I'm sure I will," Ryck said before his PA's chime for attention cut him off again.

Ryck had turned off the vocals, as usual, so he had to turn his PA over to see who was calling. A message was flashing that he had Brigadier General Nuncy on the meson comms in the comms shack. General Nuncy was the J1 for the follow-on Task Force, so the message would be more along the lines of admin rather than ops, but still, a colonel did not keep a flag officer waiting.

"OK, that's the J1. I've got to go take it," he told his chief of staff. "I still don't have a warm-and-fuzzy about the command circuit with all the players. Have Gunner Barnhouse give me a brief at 1600."

"I'll pass that to Sandy," Jorge told him.

Ryck held back a rueful grimace. He'd just spent close to three years as the 2/3 commanding officer, and with them onboard the *Brandenburg* with him, he was still tending to reach down and touch the Marines in the battalion. But Sandy was the CO now, and Jorge had gently reminded him of that—as a good chief of staff should do. Even without a full staff of his own and his need to poach assistance from the battalion, Ryck still needed to follow the chain-of-command.

"Roger that. Ask Sandy to set that up. OK, I've got to go take that call," he told Jorge.

He left his stateroom and hurried down the passage to the comms shack, which was located just past the ship's CO's stateroom.

A smile crossed his face as he recalled that as a private, he'd always assumed that those Marines at the highest levels were somehow gods, answering to no one. Yet here he was, a full-bird colonel, just now politely reminded that he couldn't just bypass the battalion command to get something done as he rushed to answer the call from a general.

Both uphill and down, he was still just a cog in the big green machine.

Chapter 12

"Crossing the Blue Line and into Trinocular space," the helmsman informed the bridge.

"Very well. Continue to the rendezvous," Captain Lester Linney ordered.

After close to two weeks, the capys had requested that the task force enter their space and conduct a rendezvous with several capy ships just beyond the picket line.

Ryck and Jorge stood in the back of the bridge, out of the crew's way. Rear Admiral Baris and Vice Bishop Flannery had been subtly jockeying for position near the captain, but the *Bradnenburg's* bridge was not set up for guests, even high-ranking guests. Linney sat in the command chair, and the guests had to make do with milling about while looking like they belonged.

The capy picket line of several thousand ships had parted like the Red Sea, or more aptly, like a giant iris opening up, leaving a tube-like corridor through which the 15 ships of the task forces were now entering. All the ships, capy and human, were actually spread out over quite a distance, but in the ship's display, it looked like a big mouth had opened to swallow the task force. Ryck had been in capy space before, and he thought the capys were earnest in their requests, but still, he could imagine the mouth closing in on them as a small appetizer.

The rendezvous point was only 500,000 km past the Blue Line, but the task force proceeded slowly. So it took almost a full hour to ease into position where 22 capy ships waited for them, one ship out in front of the rest. The *Brandenburg,* the *Mathis,* and the Brotherhood *Jericho* left the formation and edged forward to meet the leading ship.

The *Mathis* was not a major capital ship, but the capys had insisted on her presence. The humans had hemmed and hawed among themselves—the navies of each of the participating governments tended to be rather traditionally bent, and by all rights, the *Brandenburg* should have been the prime vessel, not some converted frigate. But the home governments had intervened, and the *Mathis* it was—accompanied by the *Brandenburg* and the *Jericho*. Some talk had been made that Ryck should cross-deck back to the *Mathis*, but Admiral Parks had nixed that. Ryck would stay on the *Brandenburg*, and if the capys wanted him, they would have to adjust. It was the capys, after all, who were the seeking assistance, not the other way around.

Ryck didn't think that the capys understood the human rules of military hierarchy, and Dr. Reslin Waterford, the new Federation chief xenobiologist for the task force agreed. But the military had a long tradition of ignoring civilian experts, and the general consensus among the brass was that the capys would have to bend to human traditions. Ryck had some long talks with Dr. Waterford about this, but despite Ryck's central position with the capys, he was still a frocked colonel, outranked by more than a few military and civilians in the task force.

The capy ship edged up to the *Mathis*. Ryck had expected that, but he didn't offer an I-told-you-so—even if he felt it inside. It took some serious communications for the capys to understand that their party was to board the *Brandenburg*. Almost two hours had passed before the capy ship left the *Mathis* and approached the Joint Task Force flagship. The fact that the *Brandenburg* was to be the liaison ship had not been an easy decision in and of itself. With Admiral Parks on the *Jericho*, that had been the initial choice, but some slick maneuvering by the Federation politicos had convinced the Brotherhood that the risk was too great, and that with the capys' connection with Ryck, that would mean Ryck should be on the *Jericho* as well—and with the rest of his Marines. Admiral Parks quickly ordered that the meeting take place on the *Brandenburg*.

Ryck could see some tense faces as the two ships came together. Forty meters left no degree of a cushion between two huge ships. Captain Linney actually broke out into a sweat, the back of his shirt dark and wet.

"Why don't they use shuttles?" Jorge asked. "You rode one down to the planet surface before, right?"

"Who the hell knows? Yes, I got into a shuttle, but even for that, I had to take one of their space tunnels from the ship to it," Ryck answered.

"It's not like it's a particularly difficult concept," Jorge continued.

"Not for us. But don't let the teddy bear appearance fool you. These are really alien creatures, and they are hard to figure out," Ryck said.

"I know, I know," Jorge said. "But physics is physics, and this tunnel is not a reasonable progression from a scientific standpoint."

Ryck let it go. He had more experience with the capys than any human, and he'd given up trying to figure out how the capy mind worked.

"Greeting party, to L4," Admiral Baris said as the capy ship eased into place.

L4 was one of the ship's larger airlocks. Initially, the plan had been for the capy delegation to enter right into the main hangar deck, but no one was sure if the capy space tunnel would provide protection from the force field that kept space out and air inside the hangar. It probably would not be good if the capy delegation fell over dead as they entered the ship.

Ryck and Jorge followed the admiral, the vice bishop, and several other luminaries out of the bridge. He glanced back to see Captain Linney give an obvious sigh of relief now that he had the bridge back to himself. Ryck fully empathized with the ship's CO and had to chuckle out loud. Jorge looked at him, eyebrows raised in a question, but Ryck waved him off.

The "greeting party" had to cool their heels for almost 20 minutes before the announcement was passed that three capys were on their way to the ship. The honor guard snapped back up to attention, weapons at present arms. They held that for over a minute while the lock cycled. The inner hatch opened, and three capys stepped out.

Admiral Baris stepped forward to meet them, hand out to shake, of all things, and said, "Welcome to the *FS Brandenburg*. I am Rear Admiral . . . Baris . . . and, I uh . . . in the name of humanity . . . I'm the senior—"

His prepared speech petered out as the three capys neatly sidestepped the admiral and walked directly up to Ryck. Ryck was no expert—no human was—but he was pretty sure that the lead capy was his former guide.

"Hi Carl," he said. "Good to see you again."

"Greetings, Ryck Lysander. Agree, this is a good meeting between us. Here is our destination," Carl said, holding out a small black box. "Your systems should be able to decipher it. So we should go now. Where should we locate ourselves?"

Damn! Right to the point, Ryck thought, looking over Carl's shoulder at Admiral Baris.

The man's mouth gaped open as he tried to process what had happened.

Ryck held back a smile. Admiral Baris was a pretty good guy, all told. But no one, not even Ryck, could foresee how the capys would react. Still, Ryck had been sure the capys would not comprehend military honors, and he had been right. Capys and humans were simply on different wavelengths. Ryck was amazed that they could even communicate, much less be culturally attuned to each other.

Ryck took the black box and handed it to Commander Dodson, the ship's XO.

"We have a stateroom for you and your, um . . ." he started indicating the other two capys. When Carl said nothing, Ryck went on, "and we can take you there now. We'd also like to know just where we are heading. Your communications have not been to clear on that."

"Please take us to this place," Carl said.

Ryck was confused. Was "this place" the stateroom or the task force's destination? He looked up at Dr. Waterford who shrugged his shoulders.

Great help that, Ryck thought without rancor.

"Please follow me," Ryck said, deciding that the stateroom was the best choice.

The stateroom had been the Flag Stateroom B, the second largest stateroom on the ship, and one that had been wired with enough surveillance to spy on a planet. It was not exactly a jail for the capys, but the intent was to keep them isolated there as much as possible.

Both the admiral and the vice bishop seemed to have recovered from the unintended (at least Ryck thought it was unintended) slight and were stepping up to follow Ryck and the three capys. With two Navy gunners mates leading, the party made its way up three decks and over to the stateroom.

"Ask them again where is our destination," Admiral Baris whispered into Ryck's ear.

Ryck nodded, then asked, "Carl, can you tell me where we are going?"

"To our destination. I gave that to you previously," Carl said through his translator, his voice flat and toneless.

"But what is there?" Ryck asked.

"Our destination," Carl answered.

A faint whiff of something like linseed oil reached Ryck. He wasn't sure what emotion that signified, but he was sure it had to do with what they would find when they arrived.

Ryck looked back at the admiral and shrugged. He hoped Carl had been correct and they would be able to read the coordinates of their destination. Even if they could, though, he'd really like to know now just what awaited them there.

Celestial Coordinates 153, 712, -109

Chapter 13

Captain Lawrence Yun snorted with frustration before turning to look to Ryck. "Ask them again about the Klethos' ships. I want to know why we can't just interdict them in space before they land."

Ryck stared at the task force J3 for a moment, contemplating telling the captain that he was not there as the capy translator. Carl could understand any of them just as well as he could understand Ryck. Somehow, though, the other people seem to assume that Ryck had some sort of special bond with the capys, that his Standard could somehow be understood better than theirs. But Yun was Federation, and Ryck knew the admiral would not appreciate showing any disunity in the ranks to the various liaisons and reps from the other forces.

He looked over the captain's shoulder for a moment, where he caught Titus Pohlmeyer's eyes. The Confederation major winked at Ryck, but whether from the crazy notion that Ryck's Standard was better understood or from some other tangent, Ryck didn't know.

Ryck turned back to Carl, who stood with the other two capys. Trinoculars did not sit, so the three of them stood silently at one end of the conference table. No one had quite figured out yet just what the three represented. Carl had done all the communicating since their arrival, but Ryck was pretty sure he was not the big dog of the group. The other two might be silent and express no discernible emotion, but most of the humans thought they were a sort of ambassadorial triumvirate. Just how much power they had in representing the Trinoculars as a whole was something that had the task force command (and their governments back home) arguing back and forth. What was known was that at least as far as the task force could detect, the three were not in communications with the 22 capy ships that had accompanied them to the system.

Yun's question was actually valid. The task force had dropped out of bubble space (thank God that the capys used the same science to navigate between the stars, one of the few things that seemed to be the same between them and humanity) at the outreaches of an unnamed solar system some 240 parsecs from Earth. Carl had finally conveyed the information that the planet, for which the capys evidently had no name, was a Trinocular colony planet currently under attack by the Klethos. Forward-reaching surveillance had clear indications of combat on the planet's surface, but there were no signs of naval vessels other than a few dead capy hulks floating in orbit.

If the Klethos fighters had invaded the planet, how had they arrived? Were they just debarked and left to their own devices? That would make a huge difference in tactics should there be a clash.

Ryck sighed, then turned to Carl. "How did the Klethos attack force land on the planet?"

Carl looked at Ryck with his unblinking gaze for several moments before saying, "By their ships."

"Where are the ships now?" Ryck asked.

"The ships are there," Carl intoned.

"Bullshit," someone said from behind Ryck. "Unless the ships have some amazing cloaking capability, they just weren't there."

The Trinocular ships had their own cloaking capabilities that had stymied human acquisition technology when they first clashed, so Ryck wouldn't be too sure that the Klethos couldn't have something even better. But his gut told him that wasn't the issue. It was communication. The translators, human and capy, ran smoothly now and with barely any hesitation. The words were understandable, both alone and in context. But Ryck thought there was still a miss somewhere. What Carl was saying was true, Ryck was sure. It was just that no one could quite grasp his exact meaning. As Conner Therault pointed out at almost every staff meeting, the translators worked well with spoken words, but the capys used more than sounds to communicate, and so a good portion of what the capys were "saying," so-to-speak, was simply lost.

Anthropomorphizing was a natural tendency, and familiarity made that worse. But Ryck had to remind himself that for all the capys looked like three-eyed, six-foot-tall toy capybaras, they were alien creatures, totally different than humans. Assuming anything about them could prove dangerous if push came to shove and fighting broke out.

Chapter 14

Ryck watched the recording one more time. It had been taken by the *CS Petra*, a small aviso that evidently had far more intelligence-gathering capabilities than any normal ship of that class. The Federation did not have avisos but often used the slightly larger (and faster) corvettes for the same purpose, although Ryck had to admit that, based on the quality of the recording, the Confederation ship might put the corvettes to shame.

Ryck pushed that thought aside. While he didn't like to think that the Federation Navy had any equals, much less superiors, in any area of combat, the important thing for now, at least to him, was the recording itself. While the governments clashed on whether to grant the capys' request to land combat troops, Ryck had to be ready if and when the call came, and the recordings and analytics were his best look to date at how the Klethos operated.

The scene on his display was the snow-swept planet's surface and an array of 513 capys, all of them warrior class. The capys were in a buffalo horn formation, essentially in line with the ends curved forward. Facing them were 51 Klethos, each about 20 meters or so apart.

To Ryck, two klicks was a pretty broad frontage for only 51 soldiers, especially as there was no sign of anything other than the soldiers, capy and Kletho alike. That fact alone was another factor that was under intense human debate. Both species were spacefaring, and the capys, at least, had some technologies that were superior to that of human kind. Yet for all intents and purposes, this particular battle on the planet's surface seemed to be *mano y mano*, or *capy y kletho*. There was no sign of air, armor, arty, or any other means of combat. This was infantry at its base level. It just didn't make sense.

When put to the question, Carl had simply said that this was "total combat." But it wasn't that, at least to the human point of view. It was limited combat.

As the capy formation ponderously moved forward to contact, a lone Klethos stepped forward and went into gyrations, almost a dance, that lasted several minutes before stepping back into their loose line. It was as if it was challenging the advancing Trinoculars.

Back at NOTC, Ryck had watched an old 2D film, either 20th or 21st century, Old Reckoning, about the Zulu forces fighting the British Army at the Battle of Rorke's Drift. The old-timey flick was shot from the perspective of the British soldiers, and their bravery and ingenuity was discussed by the class, but many of the midshipmen, Ryck included, were enthralled by the Zulu *udibi*, or warriors. Before the battle was commenced, various *udibi* conducted ceremonial dances, shaking their *assengai* and *iklwa*, or their longer throwing spears and short stabbing spears, at the waiting British soldiers. To Ryck, what the Klethos soldier had done had a degree of similarity with the Zulu *udibi*, something perhaps heightened as each Kletho soldier had a sword in one hand.

This connection with the ancient Zulu *udibi* was probably why Ryck was describing the capy formation as a buffalo horn formation, which was invented by Shaka kaSenzangakhona, the great (if ultimately destructive) Zulu king. It was not lost on Ryck, though, that from the perspective of the flick as an analogy, the Klethos, outnumbered, would be the British, and the capys would be the advancing Zulu.

Ryck shook his head clear. He knew that those who forgot history were doomed to repeat it, but this was not human history. This was a clash between two non-human races, and to ascribe too much humanity to either side would be a huge mistake.

He sped up the recording to where the capy force closed in on the Klethos. He could see the capys firing their jai alai cesta-like personal weapons, the balls of energy shooting to envelope the Klethos. A few of the Klethos fired back, but most stood there, personal shields glowing as they rebuffed the capy guns. The data streaming on the recording verified the release of both energy and kinetic weapons, but the total energy release was lower than what would have been released in a similar human vs. human fight.

A few capys faltered and fell, but not many as the "marching teddy bears" kept advancing. They closed to 700 meters, 600 meters, 500 meters, and still, they kept coming.

It was all so surreal. This was the 4th Century, New Reckoning, where naval battles took place at almost 100,000 klicks and land battles could take place at 20 or more klicks apart. Yet the two sides were closing in like the Romans and Visigoths at Pollentia or the Swedes and Danes at the Battle of Brávellir.

Both species have technology, so why not use it? he wondered.

His fleeting analogy to Romans and Visigoths was being too generous, Ryck thought. This wasn't a military operation. It was a street brawl without any discernible tactics, like in the final scene *The Gang* when the Vultures and the Bad Boyz rushed together for the flick's climactic melee scene. That was Hollybolly, though, while this was real life—alien life, but real, none-the-less. To Ryck, someone weaned on the teat of military tactics, this lack of order was more foreign than the fact that marching teddy bears were fighting giant toothed birds. How could any military force fight successfully without tactics?

Ryck had to get to the bottom of that, and somewhere, deep inside of his warrior's consciousness, he knew this was an important piece of information.

Still, while the professional officer in him demeaned the lack of any type of tactical organization, the warrior in him felt a flicker if visceral admiration, even jealousy. The fighting did not seem to rely on technology, and there were no evident tactical brains maneuvering the armies for a victory. This was almost hand-to-hand, capy against Klethos. The capys had their type of lock-step coordination even if they didn't have any other maneuvering that Ryck could observe, but the Klethos were individual fighters, each living or dying as a direct result of its own actions. There was almost a degree of purity to that, one in which the ancient gods of war could revel.

At less than 100 meters, the Klethos broke their line and charged—literally charged, like WWI soldiers going over the top.

Capys fell beneath the Klethos' rifles, but to Ryck's continual astonishment, the Klethos seemed to favor their swords.

Fucking swords!

Ryck had watched the recording at least 30 times, both with the rest of the command staff and alone in his stateroom, and it still astonished him each time he watched. From the perspective of looking down from above, Ryck watched the bigger Klethos move incredibly fast as they reached the capys, who in turn surrounded and closed in around each Klethos soldier. The Klethos left lower arms, the ones holding the swords, rose and fell in huge, distance-covering scythes, felling multiple capys with each sweep. The battlefield became a butcher's shop as the capys' blue-tinged blood stained the snow while body parts formed small heaps.

Every now and again—too few from the capys' perspective—a Klethos fell, taken down by a writhing mound of the furry Trinoculars. But the fight was lopsided, the outcome obvious within the first few moments of battle. Within ten minutes, it was over. Each capy was down. Only 23 showed any signs of life, although the *Petra's* sensors were either not sensitive enough or not enough was known about the capy physiology to determine how badly those 23 were hurt and if they would survive their wounds.

Five Klethos had fallen, three of them torn apart by the capy soldiers. The broken Klethos bodies bled a bright red blood, more to the scarlet than human blood, but still more familiar to Ryck. Of the remaining 46 Klethos, at least six seemed to be in some distress, but once again, the *Petra's* sensors could only show the visuals but not how badly any of the Klethos might be hurt.

At least they can be hurt, Ryck thought, once again with a feeling of relief. *They aren't invincible.*

The surviving Klethos ignored the wounded capys, picked up their fallen comrades, and instead of retreating back, continued forward, toward more capy forces some 50 klicks away. It seemed that they intended to carry on the fight.

None of the humans even knew what this fight was about, and Carl couldn't illuminate them adequately. The capys colonized new worlds, seeking land and resources to raise their young. What the Klethos wanted remained a mystery. From what Carl told them, it seemed as if the Klethos did not colonize the worlds they took from the capys but left them once taken. But if the capys came back to re-colonize, so did the Klethos.

To date, the Klethos had reportedly taken over 80% of Trinocular space, including their home world. Why, no one was sure. When asked, Carl had said that the Klethos came because "that is what they are."

More data was coming in on the Klethos from numerous space-borne sources. Ryck's initial recordings hadn't been much more than visuals. But with far more sophisticated instruments on board the human spacecraft, a more detailed picture was coalescing. The Klethos stood close to four meters tall and massed about 1400 kg, or a good 50% more than a Marine in a PICS. They were oxygen-breathers, had a high metabolism, and their bodies seem to run about three degrees higher than human norm. Analysis of their exhalations indicated that they might be vegetarians. They were also significantly quicker than humans despite their greater bulk.

Their main weapon was still being analyzed, but it seemed to be somewhat similar to a meson-beam rifle. It was described as the "main" weapon in the briefs, but while watching the recordings, Ryck thought their main weapon, or at least their weapon of choice, might be their swords. The sword excited the mechanical engineers and physicists in the task force. It was unbelievably thin, from all available data, and it shimmered with a hereto unknown energy field of some sort. To Ryck, though, the important fact was how easily it sliced through capys. He wasn't sure it would be as effective against a PICS, if it came to that, but he wasn't sure a PICS could stand up to it, either, and he wasn't sure he wanted to find out.

Ryck rebooted the recording back to the beginning of the fight. He wanted to slow-mo the hand-to-hand to try and decipher a weakness in the big warriors. The capys were bad enough, as Ryck well knew. He was confident that humans were now better fighters than the capys, and the Trinocular's initial gains in the war were simply because humans didn't yet know how to fight them, but that didn't make them pushovers. But the Klethos were destroying the capys, and that didn't bode well for the task force. If Ryck could glean any weakness at all in them, that might well mean the difference between victory and defeat.

He looked at his watch and contemplated calling Jorge back. Two sets of eyes were better than one. But Jorge had only left him an hour before to get some needed sleep. He could summon Sandy, Story, or Hecs, he knew, but decided to let them rest, too. Ryck needed sleep as well, but maybe once more watching the fight, and then he could catch some z's.

He hit play and leaned forward as that first Klethos started its dance one more time.

Chapter 15

"Let's go," Ryck said, poking his head into the Bravo wardroom where his chief of staff, Sandy, the ship's engineer, and the command master chief were playing Vizzim. "We've got a brief."

"Our mission?" Jorge asked, dropping his player console and standing up.

"I'm guessing, but yeah, I think so."

"What do you think it'll be?" Sandy asked as he slipped his blouse back on from where he'd hung it over the back of his chair.

"Don't know. But we'll find out soon enough," Ryck said.

He could guess, though. The stream of messages coming from most of the involved governments had a distinctly hawkish tone, and Ryck thought the powers-that-be wanted to test themselves against this potential threat. Ryck had taken a stand against any rash decisions. He didn't like the idea of putting his men against an unknown enemy, but yet again, he *did* like the idea of putting his men against an unknown enemy, if that made sense. Wearing his commander's hat, a little caution might be in order. Wearing his warrior's headdress, though, he could feel the call to battle making stirrings in his soul.

His hesitation had more to do with the ad hoc and hodgepodge nature of the task force than anything else, though. He was the ground force commander, but his force was far from an integrated unit. It was a mishmash from all the governments who wanted to be involved for their own reasons.

Back in the 20th Century, Old Reckoning, the most militarily and economically powerful country on Earth, the United States of America, had gotten slapped in the face when Iran took over their embassy and kept American citizens hostage. When the decision was made to go after the hostages, each of the services had to be part of the mission for pride's sake, if nothing else. The various components had no experience working together, and some of the components could not even directly communicate with others. As a result, out there in the Iranian desert, there was a collision on the ground between a Marine helicopter and an Air Force transport plane. Americans died, and the mission was scrubbed. This case study was taught at NOTC and most advanced schools as well. A single well-trained unit might have succeeded in the mission, but with everyone wanting to be part of it, and without enough combined training, the mission was doomed. Politics, even if they were inter-service politics, trumped tactical doctrine.

Ryck was confident of the abilities of his Marines. He knew that the other forces involved were professional, capable units. But what they hadn't done, to any great degree, was to operate together. In the recent Trinocular War, combined operations had been almost unheard of. Each government had essentially been given sectors, their own AORs[11] and had then operated independently within them.

Ryck feared that in this case, the sum was less than the parts. The warrior in him might want to test himself against the Klethos, but as a commander, he understood the task force's major weakness.

And now he was going to find out which way the bigwigs decided as they made their way to the meeting. Each of the other four men was cleared for the conference room, so they followed Ryck down the passage to where a chief gunners mate, flanked by two armed gunners mates, performed a retinal scan on each of them. Ryck held back as smile as he submitted to the scan.

What? Do they think some unauthorized spy sneaked in through open space?

The five of them parted as they entered the already half-filled room. Ryck, due to his position, had a prime seat at the head table. The others had to make due finding a seat at the other two tables. Those coming in much later would be standing. Still each of the 60 or so men was at least in the room. Most of the combined staffs would be attending via a cam link, the same link as would be going to each of the other ships in the task force.

"So, do we get to play?" Major Titus Pohlmeyer asked Ryck as he slid by him to take his seat. Titus was the junior man at the

---

[11] AOR: Area of Operations

head table—his position as the Confed liaison, not his rank, earned him that place.

"I think you might know before anyone else," Ryck said as Titus squeezed past him. "So you tell me."

The Confederation major rolled his eyes and made an exaggerated shrug of his shoulders. Ryck noticed that he didn't deny Ryck's statement, however.

Titus took his seat, and Ryck sat quietly, waiting for the big man. They would all know soon enough. Ryck started fiddling with his stylus, rapping it on the table until he realized what he was doing and pocketed it before sitting on his hands to keep them silent. He wasn't sure what he wanted, not that that made any difference to things. He knew starting a fight with his disparate force was probably a bad idea, and he was wary of the monsters he had seen. And if it came to a fight, there was no doubt in his mind that Marines (and soldiers, guardsmen, and the rest) would die. Still, part of him wanted to challenge the Klethos. He was pretty sure modern tactics, using combined arms, could carry the day. He understood the argument, too, that if the Klethos did invade human space, then humanity had to know how to fight the creatures.

The conference room filled. Anxious men tried to hide their emotions by chatting about anything, the more inane the better. Ryck just sat there, not meeting anyone's eyes.

Finally, Rear Admiral Baris, flanked by Vice Bishop Flannery and Lester Linney, entered the conference room. The assembled men came to attention and stood there until the admiral and the vice bishop took their seats.

"Gentlemen," the admiral began. "I am sure you are all ready to finally know what we are going to be doing here."

There was a quiet undercurrent mumbling of agreement from the rest.

"I can't tell you right at this moment, though. Chief, if you please?"

One of the ship's chiefs standing up alongside a control box, hit a switch, and the holo base powered up. The green indicator light came on, indicating that it was waiting for a transmission. It took another four minutes, but finally a shape appeared, coalescing into the face of Admiral Parks, the overall mission commander.

The face turned to the side and asked someone out of range, "Am I with everyone?"

"Yes, sir. Every ship," a voice could be heard.

"OK, then. Let's get this going," the admiral said, facing back to the front holocam.

"Men and women of humanity, our governments have come to an agreement on a course of action. As you can imagine, this was not easy, and that is why we've been sitting here in far orbit in this system. Our Trinocular allies have waited patiently as well, even while their comrades have suffered grievously on the planet's surface."

The admiral's use of the word "allies," was telling, Ryck thought.

"Mankind is a varied race, and we have many different viewpoints. Not all of our governments have agreed as to the proper course of action. So we have come to a compromise. The task force will be splitting up."

A loud murmur filled the *Brandenburg's* conference room.

"The forces of the Federation, the Confederation of Free States, Greater France, Outback, New Budapest, Purgatory, and Wayward Station will land ground forces on the planet, which we have now designated Tri-30. These forces will put themselves in a position to block the Klethos from attacking the Trinoculars. They will not initiate offensive operations but may defend themselves if attacked. Rear Admiral Baris, on the *FS Brandenburg*, will assume command of Task Force Dauntless Shield-Bravo. All liaison personnel will remain with your current assigned positions for the nonce. The remainder of the task force will pull out of the system and provide naval cover should the need arise. Upon the conclusion of TF Dauntless Shield-Bravo's mission, the complete task force will be prepared to act upon further orders of our respective governments.

"With that, I leave Admiral Baris to further brief those affected while we conduct our own preparations. This is a pivotal moment in human history, in the history of the galaxy. Before we break, I charge all of you to remember the unfortunate results of hasty actions the last time humans met our galactic neighbors."

The admiral seemed to want to say something else, but he evidently changed his mind and simply said, "Go with God. Parks, out."

So, the Brotherhood didn't want to play, Ryck thought.

It wasn't a surprise to Ryck. After joining with the Federation to interdict the initial homeworld of the SOG, the Brotherhood had vowed to never interdict another world again and had taken a decidedly dovish stance since then. The Trinocular War, in which they had participated, had served to push them further from active conflict.

As for how the rest fell out, both those taking part in the landing and those joining the Brotherhood out of the system, the diplomats would have to figure out what that all indicated.

"Gentlemen—and ladies—" Admiral Baris added quickly to include the women serving on other ships in the new task force, "we'll be landing in 22 hours, so we have a lot to cover. This is going to be a long one, so grab the stimulant of your choice. Recon and Exploratores are launching as we speak, so there is no turning back now. With that, I'll turn it over to Captain Yun for the initial brief now."

Ryck felt a thrill sweep through him. He'd been against any potential confrontation, he'd tried to think cautiously, but this was what he wanted in his heart of hearts. It wasn't his choice to put humans on the surface in the path of danger, but now that the decision was made, he was glad that he would be the one leading the men—and women, in two of the units—on the mission. And it would be combat, he was sure. There was no way the Klethos would allow for anything else.

TRI-30

Chapter 16

"Let's take a walkabout, Hans," Ryck said, looking out over the mass of men in the *Brandenburg's* huge Hangar C where they had been gathering for the last hour. Lines of Marines had just started filing into the four adjacent armories to get into their PICS. Even with four lines, however, it was going to take a while for the brigade staff's turn.

Unlike officers going last for chow, in this case, going last was a good deal. With at least another hour to go, Ryck could feel the air on his skin for a while longer yet and more importantly, take one last piss and shit before it was recycling tubes and gel diapers for the duration. Going last was a good deal, for once.

With Çağlar in tow, Ryck walked up to a group of Golf Company Marines.

"Ooh-rah, sir," several of the Marines chorused as Ryck joined them.

"Sergeant Winston, long time. How's Eugenia?" Ryck asked.

"Great sir. I mean, I don't know right now, of course, but she was keeping up her mom and dad when I left. At least now I can get a good night's sleep," the sergeant said as the Marines around him broke out into laughter.

A month before Ryck's little incident in Portugal, Ryck had attended Eugenia's christening. He got invited to many such family events, and he tried his hardest to make it to each one. Some officers thought it was a bad idea, but to Ryck, if one of his Marines or sailors thought enough to invite him to something they felt was that important, then Ryck should make every effort to honor that request.

"Don't worry, we'll get you back soon enough to you can enjoy having your sleep interrupted every night," Ryck said to more laughter.

Ryck spotted Captain Derrick St. Armis hurrying up, eyes locked on him. St. Armis was the new Golf Company commander, and he was kind of a kiss ass, to be blunt. Ryck wanted to have a little time away from staff and just mix and mingle with the men without their officers around. Although he was a colonel, in his mind, Ryck still thought of himself as a sergeant, and he missed that time in his career. He'd felt a close, personal connection with his Marines then, something that had trickled away a little more with each promotion. He knew that was probably why he'd collected his posse, to try and keep as many of those relationships as he could.

"Reverse, march," he whispered to Çağlar, as he parted with, "You'll have to bring her around the CP when we get back, Sergeant. You gents keep your heads down, you hear?"

Deftly avoiding St. Armis, Ryck and Çağlar moved into the line of Armadillos. Ryck still wasn't a fan of the big tracs, but that wasn't the fault of their crews. The Marines were proud their vehicles, and Ryck let them know he was counting on them.

For the next hour, Ryck and Çağlar made the rounds. Hecs was doing the same thing, and they met up together with the Echo Company Marines, all of whom were already in their PICS. Unlike when St. Armis tried to join him, Ryck welcomed a few words with Captain Bayarsaikhan when the company commander joined them. It might not have been fair, but he'd known Genghis longer than any other Marine excepting for Hecs. They'd been recruits together, and that was a special bond.

Ryck spotted newly pinned Captain Delbert looking lost as he watched the Marines prepare to debark.

"Talk to you later," he told Hecs and Genghis.

"Whitney, you ready for this?" he asked Delbert.

The captain hurriedly said, "Yes, sir! I've got it."

Ryck wasn't too sure. Delbert had on his railroad tracks for less than a month, and now, as the battalion assistant operations officer, he was tasked with being the liaison back aboard the ship. It might seem like a thankless job, but it was vital to the Marines planetside.

"I know you want to be with us, but Major Peltier-Aswad and I agree that you're the man for the job. We need you to keep those squids in shape, right?"

Delbert barely cracked a smile, but he dutifully nodded and said, "Yes, sir."

"Look, in all seriousness, the Navy's our brothers-in-arms, but, and this is a big but, their first priority is to their ships. If a threat comes up, protecting the ships will outweigh a measly brigade on the surface. I've been there before when the Navy bugged out, and I don't want to do that again. If the shit hits the fan somehow, you need to make sure we're covered, understand?"

"Yes, sir. I understand. But I'm just a captain—" he started.

"*Just* a captain? What the fuck, Whitney? I don't care what your rank is, you're a Marine, and that's what matters. And I expect you to perform your duties as a Marine, private, captain, or grubbing commandant," Ryck said, a speck of spit flying out of his mouth as his emotions got the best of him.

"I'm only a captain?" Saint Pete's ass! Is he really up to the task? Ryck wondered.

"Of course, sir. I mean, yes, sir. I'll do what needs to be done," Delbert sputtered out.

"I think we're up," Çağlar told Ryck, interrupting the two Marines.

"What? Oh, yeah, sure. We'd better get going then," he answered. "Pay attention to what I told you, Captain. I know we can count on you."

Ryck slapped Delbert on the shoulder, then he and Çağlar joined the back of the line at the mounting station, and within moments, entered their respective on-decks.

Staff Sergeant David Kyser didn't take Ryck's scan, even if it was still SOP[12] to scan each Marine's implant, and instead merely punched Ryck's code into the retriever. Within moments, Ryck's PICS came up from the bowels of the ship somewhere and was

---

[12] SOP: Standard Operating Procedure

hooked up to the rack. Kyser eyeballed the readouts before putting his thumb on the accept button.

Kyser was an Ellison native, where Ryck's parents had been born and from where they had emigrated to Prosperity. Very, very few Ellison natives ever enlisted into the service. The population had pretty long memories, and the massacre during the strikes 50-plus years earlier had left the Ellisonians carrying a long grudge.

"Here you go, sir," Kyser said, bending Ryck's PICS slightly at the waist.

Getting into a PICS had always been somewhat of a circus contortion. Each Marine had to bend down, raise his arms, and then slide up into the chrysalis, twisting in a 180 to squirm into position. Ryck gave Çağlar, who was standing in the next on-deck, a thumbs up as he raised his arms and started to slide in—and gasped as a lance of fire shot down from his right shoulder.

What the fuck?

"Shit, Kyser, what did you do to my PICS?" Ryck said, looking back and down over his shoulder, half in and half out of his combat suit.

"What do you mean, sir?" the staff sergeant asked, bending down to peer up past Ryck's legs and up to his face.

"Oh, nothing. Forget it," Ryck said sourly as he gingerly lowered the arm slightly and started to worm his way into position.

It wasn't Kyser or his PICS, Ryck knew. His shoulder was still giving him problems ever since his stupid golf injury. He'd taken two nano-boosts, and the shoulder would be OK for a couple of days, but then the pain would come back. It was normally more of an ache, but the awkward position required to mount his PICS had probably torn something loose again.

Ryck ignored the throbbing as he slid into position and ran his check. His suit was at 100%, not that he'd expected anything different. Kyser was good at his job, perhaps even better than CWO3 Yalur, the armory chief. The staff sergeant, who had been awarded a BC3 at the battle for the fort on Freemantle, had a way with the suits. Sams said the guy was born with a direct cranial interface and didn't need the PICS' synaptic probes to access a suit's data.

"Battle Pack 1, check," Ryck said. "Readouts, check."

It would have been strange if Kyser had given him anything other and a BP1, but procedures were procedures, and Ryck went down his checklist with power, combat load, and comms.

The entire check took less than 15 seconds, and Kyser gave him a slap on the chest and a "System confirmed. You are green, sir."

Ryck turned just as Çağlar lumbered up. A PICS was a PICS, and they all had the same external dimensions, but somehow, even mounted up, the sergeant gave the impression of bulk.

Ryck motioned for Çağlar to follow as they returned to the hangar, passing the Combat Cargo Manifest Petty Officer who had scanned them in. Ryck pulled up a quick data dump; only nine men had not yet been manifested, five of them being the four armorers and CWO3 Yalur. They would be the last five men to get into their PICS and be certified as combat ready.

Getting men in their PICS was only one small part of a Ship-to-Surface operation. Captain Knowles, with Top Egan as his Combat Control SNCO, were in charge of the myriad of aspects of getting the brigade off the ship and safely on the ground, something Ryck didn't envy. But still, Ryck was the commander and responsible for all aspects of the operation, so he pulled up the AWSAT, or Assault Wave and Serial Assignment Table one more time and married it with the Debarkation Timeline Checklist. The AWSAT designated when and on which craft all personnel and equipment would be embarked and was the plan on what was *supposed* to happen, while the DTC was what was actually taking place. Miraculously, the two were marrying up so far. Knowles, Egan, and Lieutenant Commander Hyunh, the ship's Embarkation Officer, seemed to have their shit together.

Things were a little more organized than they had been earlier as the initial wave of Marines were now being directed to their debark stations. Ten storks were already positioned, and each one would take 20 PICS Marines from Fox Company in the "dangle" mode, with an open cargo bay. Ryck loved doing the dangle, his PICS' shoulders clamped into the harness and nothing but open space "beneath" his feet. But that was for the combat Marines, those who were to secure the LZ. Ryck would follow like most of rest in the ship's shuttles.

It was going to take at least four hours to get the Marines on the ground where they would marry up with the Outback and New Budapest companies. Ryck had 2/3, along with its tanks and Armadillos, a full arty company, and a platoon of engineers as the core of the Federation force. With the Brotherhood not playing, the Marines were by far the most robust unit in the task force. Both the Outback and New Budapest companies were light infantry, although the New Budapest company had their wicked little Kígyó anti-armor missiles, which might prove to be handy.

Kígyó meant "snake" in Hungarian, the planet's ancestral language, and Ryck had been a company commander in 1/11, whose patron was Mexico's *Fuerza de Infantería de Marina*. The battalion's logo had the Mexican eagle with a snake in its claws, and Ryck hoped that the symbology would not hold true, and if it came to it, the Kígyó would defeat the bird-like Klethos.

The Confederation century, the Greater France and Purgatory companies, and the Wayward Station detachment would land some 80 klicks to the north. Jorge, who had cross-decked five hours before, would be acting as Ryck's representative with that group. He wouldn't technically be in command given the political maneuverings going on, but for all intents and purposes, he was running the show up north. He'd never commanded Marines in combat, and now, if push came to shove, his first "command" would be with foreign troops.

Both landings would be a good 200 kilometers from the existing front lines between the Klethos and the Trinoculars. No one knew how close was too close before drawing a possible reaction, but as the Klethos had shown no sign of having transportation assets (disregarding their getting to the planet in the first place), Ryck was fairly confident that both forces would be able to land unopposed.

Despite the very conservative distance, in Ryck's mind, the first wave of the assault would consist of Fox company and a single Davis (a single tank maxed out a Stork's lifting capability in Earth-range atmospheres). The initial landing force would be covered by Navy Experion fighters, Marine Ospreys, and both a monitor and the *FS Smithfield*, a cruiser. The second wave would not be released until the LZ was secured. Carl has assured Ryck that the LZ was still safely in capy hands, but Ryck wanted human confirmation for that before the shuttles crossed the LOD and commenced their descent.

Ryck made his way behind the line of Davises. The nine tanks were a welcome security blanket. Ryck was even glad for the Armadillos. He'd hated them on Gaziantep and Freemantle, but the Klethos had shown no signs of having anything that could stand up to them.

As he and Çağlar approached their shuttle, ten Marines in the Golf Company marshaling station were on line doing the "Surrey Slide." The PICS Marine on the far right was the "director," moving his PICS in a sliding step, bending at the knees and rising back up, his arms moving in set patterns. Before he stopped, the Marine next to him repeated the same move, and so on down the line. All ten Marines were moving in the same pattern, but one after the other, like a physical version of a singing round.

A new-join from 3/12 had brought the dance to the battalion, and it had taken off over the last two months. Some of the officers and SNCOs, including Hecs, didn't approve, but to Ryck, anything that expanded a Marine's ability to maneuver in his PICS was a good idea. Sandy agreed with Ryck, and it was ultimately Sandy's call.

Ryck and Sandy angled off to go around the end of the line to get to their embark station. The tenth Marine was just starting his steps as the two passed him, and Ryck couldn't help it. He spun around with one foot as a pivot, the other outstretched, something he'd worked on after watching the Drum Corps PICS Marines do that back on Sierra Dorado during 1/11's Patron Day celebration. He came down a little heavily with a resounding crash, now the 11th Marine in line. He immediately started the same series of moves he'd seen the others do. Slide, bend, head down, push up with arms to the right before snapping them to the left and coming into a muscle beach pose. He held the pose before spinning around, almost hitting Çağlar before continuing.

There had been a moment of silence before the watching Marines burst into cheers over their externals. All of them had their displays, and all knew that it was him who had joined the line. His speakers muted the burst of noise, but Ryck saw one of the unprotected sailors raise his hands to his ears in an attempt to block off the amplified cheers.

"Not bad," Sams said on the P2P. "You been practicing that?"

Ryck isolated Sams on his display, saw he was 15 meters to his seven o'clock, and raised a mechanical middle finger behind him in Sam's direction.

"Ah, you wound me, sir!" Sams said with a laugh.

"You just wish you had moves like me," Ryck replied.

His little display had been fun, and the Marines had seemed to enjoy it, but it aggravated his shoulder again.

Hell, it was worth it, he thought, a smile creeping over his face.

A few moments later, he and Çağlar were moving into their marshalling station. Çağlar checked them in with the stick leader as Marines from Fox started hooking into their Storks. Ryck connected with Jorge for an update. The *CS Duluth* was not as big as the *Brandenburg*, nor did any of those forces have a Stork equivalent, so the entire force would land via shuttles. The initial drop for the two forces would be coordinated, but it would take them two hours longer to get all the men and women on the planet.

Ryck felt the familiar rise of excitement as his display counted down to L-Hour. He didn't need to pull up his bioreadouts to know his pulse had quickened, his blood pressure had risen. Idly, he wondered who was monitoring him and what they would think of his vitals. He'd never considered something like that early in his career, but if he, as the task force commander could pull up the vitals of any Federation Marine or sailor in his command, he'd slowly come to the realization that he would also be monitored by someone. It didn't bother him, though—mostly. He sometimes wondered if that unknown watcher deemed him lacking, what would they do? Not that he expected that.

A Navy gunners mate escorted Carl and his two shadows to the marshalling station. The three capys simply stood there, not just the two normally silent ones, but Carl as well.

They can't tell who I am in a PICS, Ryck realized.

He didn't know if that little piece of knowledge would ever come in handy, but it was worth noting.

"Carl, are you ready for this," Ryck asked.

The Trinocular liaison turned to Ryck and said, "Yes, Ryck Lysander. We are ready."

With the Marines in their PICS, they dwarfed the shorter, stouter capys. Ryck had asked if they had any sort of armor or combat suits, but he was told they didn't. Ryck got the feeling that the concept was strange to the capys. Which was strange to Ryck in and of itself. Surely combat armor was a natural progression, and if the capys had space-going ships and energy-generated personal shielding, the idea of physical shielding or armor was no great leap.

Well, the human forces had a varied range of combat suits. LtCol Lefevre, the Greater France liaison, stood out with his smooth, almost white suit, and Major Pohlmeyer's Confederation combat suit was a bristling mass of protuberances and weapons. The New Budapest company didn't even come to the party with combat suits. The New Budapest Army had a poor-man's combat suit in their inventory, but the company attached to the task force was one of their elite but lightly-armed Ranger companies.

"First wave, launch," the ship's launch officer ordered the Storks as Ryck's display hit zero, breaking him out of his reverie.

One-by-one, each of the first ten Storks lifted up and started forward, their sides shimmering as they pierced the hangar bay shield. Navy deck hands used their little mules to lift the next ten Storks, each already loaded with Marines, to their respective lift points. If necessary, a Stork could have taken off from their previous spots, but the Navy, ever safety conscious, preferred to move craft within crowded cargo bays. The deck hands were pretty quick, too. Ryck had never gotten over how odd it looked to see a single blue-clad sailor simply lifting an entire Stork and quickly walking it across the deck. Within two minutes, the second wave was ready, and the launch officer started to send them out.

With two waves of Storks gone, there was more room to maneuver. The deck hands moved the first wave of shuttles. Five would carry Marines, five would carry tanks.

"Bravo-2, move to the embark point," Lieutenant Vincent passed on the frequency assigned the stick. The lieutenant, Sandy's adjutant, was the stick leader, and even a task force commander was under his direction with regards to embarking.

"Carl, that's us. Follow Sergeant Çağlar, please."

"Hans, wave your hand. They don't know who you are in your PICS," he ordered Çağlar on the P2P.

In single file, the Marines, liaisons, and capys made their way within the lit green lines that designated their path to their embark point. The deck officer could program the lines at will, but to the grunts, it was just stay between the lines. Other sticks had other colors, so that made it even easier. It may have been pandering to the lowest common denominator, but it worked. And with 60-ton tanks moving forward just a few meters away, it was probably a good idea.

The hangar bay was chaos, but a controlled chaos. Within a minute, the first Marine in Ryck's stick was being directed onboard the shuttle. Within another minute, all 62 men—well, 59 and three capys—were onboard. Thirty seconds later, the shuttle lifted off the deck, and as it pierced the gate, left the ship's artificial gravity field.

The Federation Marines and sailors were locked into their stations, standing but backs in the cradle frames. The shuttle recognized LtCol Lefevre's Rigaudeau-3 combat suit and Major Pohlmeyer's CAS-20, but the rest of the liaisons had to hold on to remain in place. The capys, no surprise to Ryck, easily stood in place, not moving. After the time spent in Zero G on the capy ship, he'd rather expected that.

Ryck turned his attention away from those in the cargo hold of the shuttle as he pulled up Jorge and his force. They were on track as well. For a task force with a huge potential to become a complete cluster-fuck, things were running smoothly. Too smoothly. Ryck wasn't superstitious, but he knew the sayings concerning when things were going too well.

Twenty minutes after leaving the ship, the shuttles reached the LOD.[13] The third wave was already debarking the ship, but until

---

[13] LOD: Line of Departure

the LZ[14] was secured by humans, they would just sit there. No one knew the Klethos' capabilities, and they could easily have the weapons to knock shuttles out of the sky.

Ryck switched over to Sandy's PICS, feeling only slightly guilty that he was listening in. The first line of Storks had dropped their Marines, and the second wave was inbound. There were over 300 capys around the LZ, but no sign of Klethos. Sandy, or rather Hog McAult, pushed his Marines out, expanding the security. The second wave of Storks dropped its Marines, still to no resistance.

Ryck slaved to Lieutenant Pallenbatter, Hog's Second Platoon commander. Pallenbatter was out on the edges of the security. In his sight, capys were on the move, none paying attention to the Marines. Warriors were moving to the lieutenant's right, and a few of the huge worker-types were moving in the opposite direction. They were as naked as they had been in the warm air of HAC-440, but they didn't seem fazed by the cold temperatures and wind-blown snow.

A steady stream of data flicked through Ryck's display. He asked his AI to pull up Klethos intel, and none of the surveillance showed any change in the Klethos march across the planet.

"Sandy, are you secure?" Ryck asked.

"I was about to report to you, but yes. We've got no sign of belligerents," Sandy said.

He could have said "Klethos," Ryck knew, but not everyone on the human side completely trusted the Trinoculars, and the humans had to be ready for any sign that this was a well-choreographed trap by their erstwhile allies.

"OK, then, I'm declaring the LZ secure," Ryck said.

"Landing Control Officer, commence Phase Two," he told the Navy ship-to-surface controller.

The Navy controlled the airspace in the TAOR[15], and that included the area between the ships and the planet. But that was only for coordination. Once the first Marine landed on Tri-30, command was Ryck's. It was his call on when to proceed.

---

[14] LZ: Landing Zone
[15] TAOR: Tactical Area of Responsibility.

Within seconds, the first wave of shuttles passed the LOD and ten minutes later, entered the planet's atmosphere. The intense heat of re-entry ionized the air with bright flashes of yellow, pink, and white light. Ryck's comms faltered as the AI tried to filter the snippets of transmission. Within moments, though, the shuttle was in smoother air and commencing its gentle descent. Where the Storks had screamed down to the surface, the shuttles took a more economical route down. Ryck was busy with his comms and data inflow for the next 25 minutes as the shuttles looped around, staying away from the known Klethos positions as they navigated to the LZ. Ryck was on the P2P with Jorge when the shuttle slowed down and came to a gentle landing on the ground.

Ryck was on his second capy world. And this time, he might have to lead a combined force in battle.

Chapter 17

"Roger, understood, sir," Squadron Leader Hollyer, the New Budapest company commander said. "We'll be on it."

Ryck watched the commander pull his scarf closer as he turned to trudge off in the snow. The task force had been on the Trinocular planet for two days already, and while Ryck was warm in his PICS, the New Budapest Rangers were braving the elements. Ryck was getting a little touch of PICS-fever, but that was better than shivering in the cold.

The Klethos were getting closer, now less than 20 klicks away, and the group heading their way didn't look to have refused their right flank. Ryck had decided to shift the position of the Rangers to take advantage of that. Originally slated to be the task force reserve due to their lack of armor, Ryck realized that it would perhaps be better to give them a mission more to their training and tactics. If they could hit the Klethos from the flanks and take them under enfilade fire with their Kígyó missiles, they might be able to inflict some serious damage, and if the Klethos shifted to engage them, the Marine tanks could rake their forces.

Squadron Leader Hollyer, who had been chaffing at his company's previous orders, had been positively brimming with enthusiasm as Ryck and Purgatory Staff Captain Obedience, Ryck's operations officer, gave him the orders.

Despite Ryck's initial reluctance to accept a non-Marine in such an important billet, especially as he'd just started to get used to Story Hanh-de Friese, the Staff Captain Obedience had more than exceeded expectations. Ryck had known who he was, of course, as the young man was already well-published in military publications, and for once, the reality lived up to the hype.

"What do you think, Obediah?" Ryck asked as Hollyer disappeared from view.

Yes, Obediah Obedience.

His parents must have hated him, Ryck thought for the hundredth time

"I think we're about as well-positioned as possible," Obedience said. "Now we must wait and observe what the reaction of the Klethos will be."

"I think we can guess that," Sams said from behind them.

"Possibly you are correct, Master Gunnery Sergeant. But until such events actually transpire, we do not have enough data to foretell one way or the other."

Sams harrumphed loudly over the command circuit, then said "They're kicking ass while tearing through our furry friends, sir. Right, Colonel?"

"Tearing through" was an understatement, if anything. The Klethos forces were moving almost at will. In the last two days, over 4,000 capys had fallen as compared to only 18 Klethos fighters, the best the human surveillance could determine. Moving westward, six groups of Klethos, each of about 50 fighters, advanced along natural avenues, stomping on any capy resistance. Unbelievable as it might seem, about 300 Klethos seemed to be on the verge of defeating some 20,000 capys and taking the planet.

In human history, the numbers of combatants closing in battle had been constantly shrinking, from 3,000,000 Soviets and Germans facing each other in the single Battle of Kursk during World War II down to the 11,000 Fordyce Militia successfully invading and seizing the planet Quenslaw during the Interrupted War. This was taking it to new levels, however, with only 300 Klethos on their way to capture the planet. Ryck's job was to keep that from happening.

To support the 10,000 remaining capys, Ryck had 3,867 men and women on the ground, ten Davis tanks, twenty Armadillos, twenty-three fighter aircraft (Marine Osprey, Confed Aquilae and Navy Experions), five 180mm howitzers, and the might of several Navies. Pretty much every so-called expert seemed to think it was enough, but Ryck hadn't lived through so many battles by under-estimating the enemy.

If the Klethos would even be the enemy, that was.

But Ryck agreed with Sams. It looked like a clash was inevitable. And Ryck thought Obedience agreed, even if he expressed uncertainty in his formalized, somewhat stilted manner of speech.

Ryck looked around at his staff, such as it was. With only one Marine battalion in the task force, he'd been officially assigned just 32 Marines and sailors with some of the battalion staff being dual-hatted to perform brigade functions as well as battalion. Twelve of the staff had gone up north with Jorge, leaving him with 18 Marines and two sailors. However, he had four liaison officers and six action officers lent from the other militaries. Except for Obedience, however, he'd really much rather strictly have Marines. The others were just there to mark time in the snow and make sure their military could claim participation gold stars.

His hodgepodge command group was not very robust, but he had a squad from Fox, including Sergeant Jason Baker and his trusty Stinger, the same one he'd carried on Fremantle, and a Davis tank, with Sergeant Bergstrøm as the commander, for security.

Ryck checked his M77 by rote, validating the data readout. If the Klethos decided to engage, he knew that being in the command group wouldn't mean squat, and everyone would need to be able to fight.

"Lieutenant Gangun, still up with CIC?" Ryck asked over the P2P.

"Yes, sir," his naval gunfire support officer said with only a hint of condescension in his voice. "Still up."

Ryck had asked the Navy officer three times over the last 40 minutes. He knew Gangun would inform him of any changes, but nervous energy was flowing through him. He had a feeling that it could come down to the big guns in orbit, and he wanted to make sure nothing interfered with that. The capys could block all comms, so it was certainly possible that the Klethos could, too.

Ryck settled in to wait, monitoring the ragged line of Klethos as recorded by orbital cams.

"Big birds in sight," LCpl Queensbury passed on the tactical circuit some two hours later.

Everyone around him, other than Carl and the other two capys, spun around to look towards the front as if they could see anything. Ryck listened as Captain McAult recalled the OP team back to the lines, then watched on his display as the two Marines sprinted up the hill 1,500 meters to the company. There was no reaction from the Klethos. Either they had missed the two or were simply not concerned. Or possibly, they would not initiate hostilities with a new, unknown force.

To the north, the Klethos had shifted the direction of their advance, and Jorge was repositioning his forces to intercept them. Whether he would get there in time was still uncertain. Four other Klethos groups were nowhere near any of the task force positions. So if there was to be a confrontation, it was going to happen right there, in a snow-covered valley on a previously unnamed world outside the boundaries of human space. Ryck wondered if the second inter-species war for humanity was about to break out. The first war had proven to have been a needless mistake.

Is this a mistake, too? Ryck wondered.

Ryck had edged forward over the last two hours, much to Çağlar's consternation. But he didn't want to observe the first contact via a slaved cam. He wanted to see it himself, to be ready to react if even a split second quicker if need be. The Fox lines were less than 50 meters in front of him, and from the small finger on which he had positioned himself, he had a clear field of vision over the featureless snow as the two OP's came over the first rise ahead and several hundred meters to Ryck's left.

Ryck and Staff Captain Obedience had carefully picked the terrain they would hold to give them the most advantage. The task force was generally in defilade, even if only slightly so. In front of them, the slope gently fell for close to 500 meters to a slight seam, then fell again for another 700 meters to a broad valley floor. The wind was steady in their faces, so the snow was deeper in front of them, and on the reverse slope, some rocks had been swept clear. To the far-left flank, the high ground fell sharper, and this was where Ryck had sent the New Budapest company. They could stay out of the line of sight of anyone coming up the slope to face the Marines, then pop up to take the Klethos under fire.

The Klethos would be climbing in deep snow to meet the task force, and that should put them at a disadvantage. How much, Ryck didn't have a clue. After watching hours of surveillance recordings, their long legs didn't seem to have much problem no matter the conditions. But a professional soldier took any and every advantage he could, no matter how small, and by choosing the field of a potential battle, Ryck had done just that.

"Men and women of Task Force Hannah," Ryck said over the open circuit, sticking with his original name choice instead of some convoluted diminutive of Valiant Shield. "We are about to make contact with the second intelligent race of non-humans. You've been lectured about this from each of our respective governments and Admiral Parks, so I'm not going to go into the historical aspects of this. I just want to point out that as of this moment, the Klethos and humans are not at war, and we will not be the ones to instigate one. If the Klethos fight is with the Trinoculars and not us, then we will not engage. However, and this is a big however, if they start a fight, then we will end it with the most extreme prejudice. If they are a threat, then we will crush that threat."

Ryck had debated whether he should say anything at all, but in the end, history demanded it. He wasn't going to try for something notable. However, as the commander, he needed to stress that they would not start the fight, but if it came to one, they would end it. His speech might have sounded corny to him, but he wasn't some accomplished public speaker. He was just a Marine, and his job was fighting, not giving speeches.

"Well, here it goes," he said to Sergeant Major Phantawisangtong on the P2P. "Let's see what fate has in store for us."

"You and I know this is a cluster, but we've done what we could to get ready," Hecs said. "We've got the Fuzos holding the center, and I think the Budapestians and the Aussies will do fine."

"How's Sandy holding up?" Ryck asked.

"A little nervous, which is a surprise. He's been in the shit before," Hecs said.

But not as a battalion commander with so many men depending on him, Ryck thought, something he didn't say to Hecs.

Hecs was vital to the battalion as the sergeant major, and without one of his own (something he intended to rectify once they got back), as the acting task force sergeant major. But what he didn't have was the unique weight of command on his shoulders. Ryck understood that weight, and he knew what Sandy was feeling. However, he trusted that Sandy would bring it together once—*if*—a fight broke out.

"Here they come," Sams broke in.

Ryck shifted to his right so he had a better view down the slope. Two, then three beaked heads appeared below the crest, their bodies slowly coming into view as they marched up. Each was about 20 meters apart, which seemed to be their standard formation. Others started appearing along either side of the first three.

The snow didn't seem to hinder them as their naked feet plowed through it, nor did they lean into the slope as a human might have done. Even in a PICS, the internal stabilizers leaned the combat suits forward when climbing a slope.

From 200 meters away, the Klethos looked huge. Towering almost four meters high, their massive main arms were as thick as a PICS' thighs. Their visible skin was a dull, greenish-grey, and the creatures wore what appeared to be greave-like armor of almost the same color. The most prominent features of the naked head were what looked like a dull-gold toothed beak and bright red eyes.

"Steady," Major Abd Elmonim passed on the Marine battalion circuit as the first of the Klethos came to a stop.

Within a minute or so, the entire line was visible as they all stopped in the snow. It was no drill field row, nice and neat, but more of a rough, haphazard line.

Ryck had the feed from the *CS Petra* running across his display. The Confed ship was running through electronic, optic, sound, and all the other spectrums of which he wasn't even aware, ready to pick up any form of communication from the Klethos, but there was nothing. Evidently, they had nothing yet to say to the humans facing them.

"What now?" Sams asked. "Are they just going to stand there with their thumbs up their feathered asses?"

As if in response, a single Klethos strode forward some 30 meters. It stopped and swiveled its head up and down the line of the task force. Suddenly, it tilted its head back and let out a raucous shriek, surprisingly high-pitched for such a large creature. Heretofore unseen feathers around its neck flared out, forming a high, bright yellow, green, and red collar in the back of its head. Dull red feathers flared out along the backs of it upper arms as well.

It took a single exaggerated step forward, slamming its foot down in the snow, sending little mountains of flakes back up into the air. It leaned forward on that one extended leg and stared up the slope at the waiting men and women. It held that position for a few moments as if waiting for something. It then slowly pulled back up to the full upright.

"What the fuck?" Sams asked.

The Klethos screamed out once more, and then suddenly broke out into a series of jerky, almost spasmodic motions, part whirling dervish, part epileptic fit, and yes, part peacock trying to seduce a peahen.

Ryck tried to force that comparison out of his mind. The Klethos might look like a nightmare cross between a dinosaur and bird, but they were not from Earth stock, and it would be dangerous to assume they had any birdlike attributes. But hell, the dance sure reminded Ryck of a posturing bird.

These were not random movements, though. The twirling sword spun through space around it, nearly slicing off feathers on most passes, but never quite. This was a choreographed dance, Ryck was sure. It reminded him once again of the Zulu warriors at Rorke's Drift, pounding their drums and dancing with their *assengai* and *iklwa* before launching into the attack. There were far fewer Klethos in front of him than Zulus facing the British Royal Engineers and Infantry, but Ryck suddenly felt a degree of kinship with Lieutenants Chard and Bromhead despite the tremendous distance in both space and time.

The Klethos' dance continued for close to five minutes. The humans watched in silence, their comms, both from above in the observing ships and between themselves empty of chatter. Ryck knew that the recordings of this extraordinary event were being broadcast back to human space where thousands of experts would be pouring over them to determine the meaning of the dance. In his gut, though, Ryck knew what it meant. This was a call to arms, whether to challenge the humans or build up a fighting frenzy among the other Klethos, he didn't know. But it was not a simple hello, Ryck was positive.

With a final frantic twirling, the creature came to a stop, not even breathing hard the best Ryck could tell. It froze dead still, looking straight ahead to where the humans were waiting. A full thirty seconds later, it broke its pose and let out one final shriek. As if on cue, the entire line of Klethos launched into a run.

"Hold your fire!" Ryck shouted into the net.

This is it!

But he was under strict orders. Humans could not initiate. It had to be the Klethos.

And this could be a feint, he admitted. Not that he believed it for one second. The Klethos intended to fight, he knew.

Within ten seconds, the Klethos had halved the distance to the front ranks of Fox, Golf, and the Outback company.

Ryck started to repeat his order to hold when one of the Klethos, down near the Aussies, fired its weapon.

Ryck immediately changed his order to "Open fire!"

Almost immediately, a Davis opened up, simply obliterating one of the Klethos, bright red blood and feathers exploding into the frigid air. A missile shot down the line from the New Budapest company's position, hitting and taking down one of the Klethos on that side of the line.

Ryck felt a surge of confidence rush through him. These things were not invincible. They had just never run across the fighting might of humanity.

"Arty, give me some fire," he ordered his guns, waiting for their direct fire mode to rake the Klethos that were within seconds of reaching the lines.

His display started screaming alerts. It took a moment for it to register. Every single tank, every Armadillo, every arty piece, was down.

That's impossible!

He looked to his right where the *Berserker* had been a comforting presence. The hatch was being flung open, and a moment later, Sergeant Bergstrøm was flinging himself from inside to bounce down and fall in the snow. He was followed moments later by PFC Meinheim, his driver.

And then the Klethos were in among the Marines and soldiers. Ryck looked up to see a Klethos sweep its sword around, slicing right through a PICS-mounted Fox Marine, completely severing him in two. Ryck was shocked, but he pushed that back into the recesses of his consciousness. He had to act.

"Gangun, give me fire!" he shouted into his mic to his naval gunfire coordinator. "Danger close!" he added needlessly.

Orders were filling the airwaves as Marines and soldiers concentrated their fire on the Klethos. Just off to his left, Baker was firing his Stinger in long, sustained bursts. Ryck didn't have time to see if he was having any effect.

An energy beam burst through from above, ionization making it clearly visible as it incinerated a Klethos, leaving the Marine facing it from only a few meters away untouched.

That's more like it!

He waited for another shot, but nothing came as more and more Marines were being cut down. Ryck's display was flickering madly as bright blue icons switched to light blue or gray—too many to the gray.

"Gangun!"

"The *Smithfield*, she's down," the Navy officer shouted back, panic edging his voice. "The monitor, too!"

"Get them back online!"

"No, I mean she's destroyed!"

That was a body blow. Ryck didn't know how the Klethos had managed that, but he had to deal with the here and now.

Ryck didn't have the Budapestian nor Outback company on his display, but the Klethos were in among the Aussies as well. He could see that there was fighting, but it was too far to discern the details. He wanted to query Captain Hortense, but he knew the captain didn't need him interfering.

He checked on Echo, which hadn't been hit. It was still in place.

Shit Sandy! What are you waiting for?

He jumped both S3s and Sandy and went right to the company commander. "Genghis, sweep around and assault up their flank!" he ordered.

"Roger," came the relieved if anxious voice of the Echo company commander.

"I've got it," Sandy interjected. "It's my battalion."

Almost immediately, Ryck could see the Echo avatars break their positions to swing around and move up to support Fox.

From a klick or so behind Ryck, a concussion wave triggered Ryck's sensors. One of the Navy Experions had just crashed. Ryck did a quick tally. Twelve aircraft were up with Jorge, but the rest had been knocked out of the sky.

His immediate instinct was to call for those twelve remaining aircraft, but he held off just before giving the order. He tried to step back mentally for a moment to understand what was happening. The task force's man-packed energy beam weapons seemed to be pretty ineffectual. The big guns on the tanks and from above had killed Klethos, but they were knocked out. The New Budapest Kígyó missiles had worked, but Ryck had no idea if the Budapestians were still effective. Kinetic weapons were slowly wearing down the creatures, but not before Marines were falling.

A quick memory hit him, on how effective the capy shields had been against the more powerful Marine weapons, but the slower, less powerful weapons had been able to penetrate the shields and record kills.

Before he really digested this, his subconscious was shouting over the command net, "Rockets! Use your shoulder rockets!"

Immediately, salvos of rockets reached out from Marines as they struggled with the Klethos. Ryck could see some of the creatures stagger, but it still took quite a few hits for one to fall. More and more Marines were falling, though. Even with Genghis and Echo entering the fray, the Fuzos were down to 60%.

Just ahead of Ryck, a Klethos took off the left arm and shoulder of a Marine, taking his rocket pack with it. The creatures had obviously realized that the rockets were more effective against them, and they were focusing on the packs that fired them. Now, with no one between that Klethos and Ryck's command group, it had a free shot at the command group. It broke into a sprint, sword raised high.

Ryck raised his M77 and fired as he spun to sight in his own rockets. From beside him, a Marine rushed forward. Ryck thought is must be Çağlar, but his display revealed the Marine to be Staff Sergeant Kyser. The armorer was charging the Klethos as if to meet him head on a rugby pitch.

Ryck held off on the rocket; a single rocket could take out a PICS Marine.

"Kyser, to the side!" he shouted over the net.

Kyser didn't pay attention as he crashed into the Klethos, head down and hitting the creature at about waist level.

The Klethos was swinging its sword down, but Kyser's charge evidently threw off its timing, and the sword swung down over the Marine, scoring a gash in the PICS' back, but not a killing blow.

Kyser's attempted tackle staggered the Klethos, knocking it back several meters, but not sending it to the ground. Kyser was punching with abandon, and he scored on one arm, but not the correct one. He knocked the rifle out of the Klethos' hand, but he should have been concerned about the sword arm. Ryck started to yell out a warning as the sword arm swept around, cleaning taking most of Kyser's head off. Blood sprayed impossibly high as the staff sergeant fell.

He had not fallen in vain, though. By knocking the Klethos out of his charge, he'd given the rest of the command group the time they needed to aim their rockets. Çağlar stepped in front of Ryck, blocking him from engaging, but four other Marines and Doc Lewis had the thing to rights, and at least 20 rockets hit it, sending it to the ground.

One leg had been completely blown off and its other limbs were hamburger. But it wasn't done. As Ryck stepped forward, the Klethos glared at him from its prone position in the snow, as one of its little, comparatively spindly upper arms took the sword from its shattered main arm and tried to raise it to confront Ryck. The thing had just killed Kyser, and Marines were falling, but he had to respect its will to fight. Respect or not, Ryck could almost feel the alien hate directed at him.

Before he could contemplate further, Çağlar stepped back around him and fired a single rocket into the creature's head, killing it.

Get back in the game! he told himself. No *time to admire their warrior ethos!*

His eyes went back to his readouts. As a commander, the incoming data was almost overwhelming, but he'd had practice screening out the superfluous and pulling what he needed. The Fuzos were down to 50%, but as he scanned the battlefield, only a handful of Klethos were still fighting. As he watched, one more fell.

The initial frenzy that had taken over the net in the first few moments had become more professional as commanders took command and directed the swarming Marines in taking down the last of the Klethos. Ryck listened in to Sandy for a few moments as the major fought the fight. Whatever seemed to have taken his nerves before had faded, and he was back to being the Marine Ryck knew him to be.

At 16 minutes and 32 seconds, according to his display timer, after the first Klethos had fired, the last one was dead. None had surrendered, which didn't surprise Ryck in the least. Ryck pulled in the data from Hollyer and Hortense. The Budapestians had not suffered a single casualty, and they had accounted for no less than eleven Klethos kills. The Aussies had not fared so well. Out of 214 soldiers, 79 were KIA and another 51 were WIA. But they had held.

Lieutenant Grabowski, the battalion surgeon, was already swinging into action. His triage team swept over the battlefield, ziplocking the Cat 1 WIAs into stasis. KIAs would be ziplocked next where hopefully some would be zombied and saved. Ryck listened in on the mednet for a moment, but Grabowski had things well in hand, covering both the Marines and the Aussies.

He was about to switch back to the command net when HM2 Hahn came on the mednet with, "Doc, I can't get a reading on the capy! It's still alive, but I don't know for how long."

Ryck immediately keyed in Doc Hahn's heading and swung around to see where the corpsman was standing over the prone figure of one of the three capys. Bluish blood stained the snow. A quick check revealed two more capys were standing 40 meters away. Ryck couldn't see who the downed capy was, whether Carl or one of the other two.

"Did you give it the glucose?" Doc Grabowski.

"Yes, sir, but I think it'll need more than that."

"Is it going to make it?"

"I don't think so."

"Fuck it all. Ziplock the thing, and if that kills it, so be it," the surgeon said.

Ryck closed the connection. There had been quite a bit of conjecture on how to treat a wounded capy before they left, and the consensus was that human stasis might be fatal to a Trinocular. Ryck didn't know how the capys would react to one of them dying in stasis, but that was Grabowski's call, not his.

Commanding the task force was his call, though, and Ryck switched his display to the Federation forces. Eleven aircraft were destroyed, and as hard as it was to believe, possibly a Navy cruiser. Five Davis tanks and ten Armadillos were now of piles of useless junk as were ten arty tubes. But what hit Ryck hardest was the men and women. Ryck had gone into battle with 1,687 men and women. The battalion triage team had just gone into action to see who could be saved, but as of the moment, with the 79 Aussie KIAs, the total was 472 killed and 283 wounded. Facing them had been 53 Klethos. The forces of man may have won the battle, but it had been a Pyrrhic victory at best. And somewhere out there, another 200-plus of the creatures were ready to fight.

Ryck had been looking at the overall numbers. He hesitated a moment, taking in a deep breath, before looking at the KIA list. It only included the Federation forces as of yet, which were updated in real-time. Ryck scanned the names, looking, but hoping not to see certain ones. All Marines were equal, and Ryck mourned each and every loss, but he was human, and he'd know certain Marines a long, long time.

Sams' name caught his eye first, and he swallowed back the rising bile in his throat, but his friend was only WIA. He'd lost his right arm and was due for some extended regen. He continued to scan. Kyser, of course, but he'd known that. LtCol Lefevre, the Greater France liaison, had been manually entered into the database as KIA, which surprised Ryck as he hadn't seen the colonel moving forward into the teeth of the fight. Gunny Henderson from Echo. Lieutenant Vaviar from Fox. Sergeant Winston—he'd never see his little Eugenia again. Captain St. Armis.

Then a name hit him. Michael C. McAult. Hog. The broad-shouldered heavy-worlder had not made it. Ryck didn't know how he'd fallen yet. He didn't know the stories of bravery that has just transpired, he didn't know each individual fight. But he knew the losses, and they were weighing on him.

Hog!

Ryck's priority comms warning was flashing, and Ryck finally keyed it in.

"Lysander here."

"Colonel! I've been trying to reach you. What's wrong with your comms?" Admiral Parks asked, sounding more than a little peeved.

Shit, be pissed off all you want. You kept your men out of the fight, after all. Maybe not a bad idea, though, he thought.

But he said, "Sorry, sir. It's been hectic here."

"It's about to get more hectic, Colonel. The Klethos forces are gravitating to your position. We estimate that the first force will arrive within two hours."

"What about the Bravo force?" Ryck asked.

"The Klethos who had been heading that way have changed direction to head to you," he answered.

Well, at least Jorge won't be faced with this, he thought.

"You can't stand up to any more of them. We watched the battle . . ."

Yeah, I'm sure you did, safe up there in far orbit.

". . . and it's a miracle you were able to defeat them. But you can't survive another fight. You are being recalled, and all of your governments agree. Get your bump plan ready, and we'll have shuttles attempting to pick you up."

"Sir, the Klethos somehow knocked down all our aircraft. I don't think the shuttles can make it."

"You expect us to abandon you? They also destroyed the *Smithfield*, with all hands onboard. But we're going to try. There's no lack of volunteers to fly them."

That hit Ryck hard, too, but in a different way. Every fighter had been destroyed within seconds, but now men were volunteering to brave a rescue in mere shuttles. Sailors were every bit as brave and sacrificing as Marines, and this proved it.

"Roger that, sir. And we appreciate it. How much time do we have?"

"I'm not sure, to be honest. Our LSO is coordinating it now, but get your people staged. You're going first, then your Bravo force. I just wanted to give you the order face-to-face. You've got a lot to do, so I'll let you get to it. Go with God, Colonel."

Ryck signed off, then went to pass the word, but it had already bypassed him. The men and women were converging on the broad, open slope where the shuttles could land. It was chaos, but a controlled chaos as the able-bodied and walking wounded gathered the WIA, KIA, and all 53 Klethos bodies while the human armor hulks and artillery pieces were slagged. Manifests were hurriedly put together without too much regard to the bump plan, which had manifest procedures should a shuttle go down or ground forces go down. But with every piece of armor left behind, it had become more of an exercise in priority of personnel.

Along with the rest, Ryck waited apprehensively as the first shuttle came in to land, but there was no opposition. The welcomed vehicle came in gently, blowing up a small cloud of snow as it touched down. Immediately, the first stick was loaded, and the shuttle blasted up for a quick getaway.

With the first shuttle down and back up without incident, the rest landed in multiple waves. The Aussie company loaded first, followed by the New Budapest company, with the remaining effective PICS Marines providing security. Finally, it was their turn, and they quickly loaded. Ryck and Çağlar were the last two Marines to load, a Navy cargo master motioning them to hurry. The shuttle lurched into the air before the back ramp closed. Ryck's last view of Tri-30 was of blood-stained snow as the ramp closed.

FS BRANDENBURG

Chapter 18

"You need to get some sleep, sir," Jorge said as he closed up his PA.

The two Marines were in Ryck's stateroom and had just gone over the list of casualties and had worked on coming up with a plan for the return to Tarawa. A half-eaten sandwich was on Ryck's desk, but while he knew he should eat, the only thing he could get down were two slices of bacon slathered with raspberry sauce that Staff Sergeant Ekema had brought by. For all the staff sergeant's skill in the kitchen, he was well aware that the dish, which brought sickly stares by the others, was Ryck's comfort food, something Ryck had eaten since he was a kid.

Ryck knew Jorge was right. He was exhausted, both mentally and physically. But his mind was still racing, and he knew it wouldn't let him drop off to sleep. He could see Doc Grabowski, of course for a little help, but he didn't want to shut off his mind artificially. He needed the stress to run its course.

He'd been wary from the beginning of going into battle with the Klethos, but once the decision had been made, he'd allowed himself to become excited at the prospect. And now he felt a little guilty about that. It was commonly known throughout the Corps that shit seemed to follow Ryck, but what that really meant was that men tended to lose their lives when they were with him. He'd lost a lot of Marines, sailors, and Outback soldiers on the planet, and that was something to which he'd never gotten accustomed. It still ate at him.

And Hog McAult was on the butcher's bill. Ryck had hoped that Hog could be zombied like Joab Ling had been on Freemantle, but the captain had been too far gone. There had never been even a chance at a resurrection.

Ryck picked up the half-eaten pastrami sandwich, gave it a sniff, then dropped it back on his plate. He leaned back and rubbed his eyes for a moment.

"I know, but I want to talk to Sandy first," he told Jorge, eyes still closed.

"Are you sure you want to do that now? Maybe it'd be better if you do that after getting some sleep," Jorge said.

Ryck had told Jorge about Sandy's hesitation in battle and of his reaction when Ryck ordered Genghis to roll up the Klethos' flank. Ryck knew he couldn't ignore that, and while Jorge was probably right, Ryck wanted to get it over with. He'd never be able to get any decent rest if that was running through his mind.

"No, I need to get it done now. Look, why don't you get him and send him here. Then you get some rest, too. We'll go over all of this tomorrow with the staff. I want everyone to understand what is going on. If we're detaching from Quail Hunt or not, if there is even going to be a Quail Hunt, we've got a lot to cover, and that starts the moment we land."

"After you talk to him, you'll get some sleep?" Jorge asked.

"Yes, I promise."

As Jorge left, Ryck eyed the last half-piece of bacon. He reached over with his right arm—then switched to his left as a sharp twinge hit his shoulder—and with his left hand, he used the bacon to mop up the last of the raspberry sauce. Either the ship's fabricator had some exceptionally good programming, or Ekema has somehow scrounged up some real raspberries. It was a little thing, given the events of the last day, but it was easier to focus on the flavor and texture in his mouth than on the battle, even if only for a moment.

Ryck was licking his fingers clean when his hatch chimed.

"Open," Ryck ordered, sitting up in his chair.

Sandy had cleaned up and gotten into a fresh uniform. From his appearances, he might have never been in a fight just hours before.

"You wanted to see me, sir?" he asked.

"Yes. Take a seat."

Sandy sat down, back ramrod straight, his eyes almost glowering.

What? Is he pissed? At me? Ryck wondered.

Ryck ignored that and started in with, "Sandy, I want to talk about what happened today. When you hesitated."

Sandy said nothing but simply stared at his commanding officer.

"Look, I know, everyone knows, that you are a warrior, a fighter. You've proven yourself. But sometimes, as you get more men under your command, that can affect a Marine. It can make you second guess yourself," Ryck said, waiting for a response.

Sandy said nothing.

"Today, when Echo and Fox were being beaten down, why didn't you engage Golf?"

"I was going to, sir. But you jumped the chain of command. I had it under control," Sandy said with more than a little vehemence slipping into his tone.

What the fuck? That's what's got him riled up? That I stepped on his grubbing toes?

Ryck took a deep breath to calm himself before saying, "No, you didn't have it under control, Major. Your delay probably cost Marines' lives."

"I was taking into account—" Sandy started, his voice raised an octave.

"You hesitated, pure and simple. And I took action," Ryck interrupted.

"But—"

"But nothing. Listen, Major, and make sure this registers. You may be the battalion commander, but I am the task force commander. I own the Fuzos, and if I see something that needs to be done to better fight the battalion or to protect my Marines, I will do so. Failing to do that would be failing in my duty.

"You made a mistake, one that was rectified. I've made mistakes in battle, and it has cost lives as well. But as commanders, we fix our mistakes and learn from them before saluting and marching on. What we don't do is get our panties in a twist because our egos got bruised."

Sandy started to say something, but Ryck was not in the mood. He held up a hand, stopping his protégé, his friend.

"I don't want to hear it. It's done. Learn from it. Just remember that you've been given the gift of command, but you don't own the battalion. You've been granted stewardship, and you are, in effect, its servant. Not its owner. Understand?"

Visibly deflated, Sandy just nodded. Ryck knew it was time to back off.

"OK, then. We're beyond that now. Sandy, you know I think the world of you. I wanted you for command for this mission, not Lieutenant Colonel Lu Wan. I knew you were the man for the job, and I still think that. I know that. Let's take this as a learning experience.

"God knows I understand the weight of command, how it feels. I know how decisions can get harder, not easier as the units get larger, as more men rely on you. You'd think that as you get further from the men, from the personal interaction, it would get easier, but it doesn't. But you need to get beyond that. You need to think of your command as one organism and do what is best for it, nor for each component part.

"Do you know who Meister Eckhart is?" Ryck asked.

"No, sir."

"He was a 13th Century German philosopher and theologian, someone whose ideas often got him into trouble. But he said, 'The price of inaction is far greater than the cost of making a mistake.' Pretty true words, in my opinion."

Sandy seemed to contemplate this, before nodding ever so slightly. Ryck felt the slightest bit of relief.

"You did well today—the entire battalion did well. We lost some mighty good men, but we prevailed, and what we did will go a long ways in preparing us for meeting the Klethos threat, and I think they are a threat. Soon, they'll be knocking on our doors, and we need to be able to react. The price we paid was high, but probably a necessary one."

Ryck stood up and held out his hand.

"Well, I have to admit that I'm beat. I need to shower and get some rack-time. You get some sleep, too. We'll have a staff meeting in the morning where Lieutenant Colonel Simone will lay out the initial schedule after debarking. After that, it's up to the brass as to where we'll end up. OK?"

"Yes, sir," Sandy said, shaking Ryck's hand.

Sandy turned and left, not happy, but looking not quite as pissed as when he'd arrived. For now, that was good enough for Ryck. Sandy was more than another Marine. He was Ryck's friend, and coming down on him had been difficult.

Ryck eyed his shower cubicle. He knew he needed it big time, but for the moment, he was just too tired to get up and dial in a regimen. He reached over with a finger and swiped up the last trace of raspberry sauce instead, putting his finger in his mouth and letting the sweet taste fill his senses.

Anything was better than listening to the ghost voices of the 472 men and women who'd just paid the price for serving with him. Despite what he'd told Sandy, that was still something he'd never been able to shake.

TARAWA

Chapter 19

Ryck plopped down on the couch, putting his feet up on the coffee table without removing his shoes. Then, quickly realizing Hannah wouldn't approve, he bent over and took them off before stretching his feet back out.

"Daddy's home!" Ben yelled excitedly out to the rest of the house as he ran into the living room.

His young son scrambled to join him, full of a story that seemed to revolve around Lister, whoever that was, and a puppy. Ryck didn't follow much, but he simply soaked in the company.

Ryck had been back for eight days, and this was the first time he'd made it home in time for dinner. Despite her own hectic schedule, Hannah had come home to prepare a different meal each evening, one that he'd heated up each night long after the kids had gone to bed. This evening was going to be different. He'd left a pile of work back in his office, but that was going to wait until tomorrow.

The eight days had been filled with reports, medical checks (for any possible other-worldly contamination from the Klethos), debriefs, and more briefs. There'd been talk about sending him back to Earth to brief the chairman and his ministers in person, but that had been changed to a virtual brief, thank goodness. Still, that had been over five hours without a break. Ryck's bladder had been screaming for attention, but one didn't just excuse himself from the great man's presence, even virtual presence, to take something as mundane as a piss.

The long and short of all the sound and fury was that Task Force Hannah was being re-designated as the First Marine Brigade and assigned to Fleet Marine Force Alpha, or FMF-Alpha, under

Lieutenant General Bolivar, who was dual-hatted as both the Federation Marine and the Joint Ground Force Commander. Three Marine brigades made up the Federation contribution to the JGF along with a host of units from the other governments. Except for Carl—who had not been the downed capy in the battle on Tri-30—and his group of three, Ryck's brigade would consist only of Federation forces, much to Ryck's approval. All liaison personnel would be at the force level with the general's staff. The New Budapest Rangers and the Outback company had performed as well as any Marine unit, but the lack of integration had proved to be a headache and could have resulted in disaster. Ryck might be fighting alongside Brotherhood, Confed, or other human forces, but they would not be integrated at the brigade level.

And Quail Hunt was still officially on, but not for any planned offensive operations, at least in the near term. With what was learned on Tri-30, new tactics and weapons were to be introduced, and these had to become second nature to the three Marine brigades. It was taken as a fact that the Klethos would invade human space—it was just a matter of when rather than if. The data-dinkers projected that they could reach a human planet in about two years, but possibly as soon as one. That didn't give the human forces that much time to prepare.

All of human space was mustering for a protracted war. Conscription had been enacted by many governments. In the Federation, the FCDC was gearing up for home defense, as were individual planetary armies. The Marine Corps and Navy were put on an elevated alert status, but the first thrust against a Klethos incursion would be made by the three brigades in FMF-Alpha and the Navy's Fourth Fleet. Along with the rest of the Joint Task Force, they would be the reaction force to meet any threat.

"I had my doubts about this evening," Hannah said, poking her head around the door and interrupting his thoughts.

"I told you I'd be home," Ryck said.

"And you said that last night, and the night before," she said.

"I know, and I'm sorry. It's just with everything going on—"

"No need to be sorry. I understand. And after dinner, I be going back to the head shed for a conference myself," she said.

"You have to leave?" Ryck asked, disappointed.

He'd wanted to spend some time with her, and it looked liked that wasn't going to happen. Ryck might be in the spotlight, but Hannah's position outranked his, and it wasn't surprising that she'd be just as busy as he was—if not busier. R&D was a major thrust at the moment.

"The conference starts ats twenty-one-hundred. I just got home before you, and I need to get back to finish preparing. If not for Noah, we'd be eating fab food tonight."

"Noah?"

"Yes, he cooked six of the other meals you be eating the other nights. He be taking a shine to the kitchen."

"Noah cooks better than Mommy," Ben said with a sly laugh.

The meals he'd eaten each night had been good, even re-heated. He'd assumed Hannah had made them, but in retrospect, they were better than what Hannah could cook, and she wouldn't have had much time to do much cooking with her schedule. It just surprised him that he didn't know Noah had taken an interest in cooking.

There's a lot I don't know about my own kids, he thought.

"Let me help him serve up," Hannah said. "Let him know that you appreciate it."

Noah had never seemed to have much interest in anything, so if he really was into cooking, Ryck was going to encourage it. And if the other meals he'd eaten were any indication, the kid might have a talent for it. Anyone can run a fabricator, but it took something special to be able to cook from scratch.

Maybe I can hook him up with Marten Ekema, if he'd like.

Ryck put his arm around Ben. Esther was his sports star. Ben was Ben and would probably be the Chairman of the Federation someday. But it was good to know that Noah finally had something of his own.

Ryck didn't know how many evenings he'd have with his family over next few years, so he knew he had to grab each one and savor it.

Chapter 20

"It's not as effective at the Klethos blade, but it will slice through their greaves," Dr. Somebody-or-the-other said from the podium as a holo of a Klethos sword and the new "mameluke" sword floated side-by-side to his right. "We have tested it," he added.

Ryck, as one of the three brigade commanders, had a front row seat in the lecture hall. He turned his head slightly to catch Hannah's eye from where she sat at the end of the row. He raised his eyebrows and received just the tiniest hint of a smile and a cocking of her head in return. Hannah was in charge of systems R & D for the Corps, but the entirety of the Federation government, academic, and business might had turned to focus on how to defeat the Klethos. This sword was just one more effort, one probably rushed through when the Confederation of Free States introduced its own battle sword.

We're in a grubbing sword arms race, Ryck thought in resignation. *What next? Battle axes?*

The proposed Federation mameluke was patterned after the old US Marine Corps officers' sword and the British 1831 Pattern General Officers' sword. That was a very transparent attempt to appeal to the Marine Corps love of history and tradition, Ryck thought. Designed by the University of Tinto labs on Atacama, it was a fine piece of engineering and metallurgy, Ryck had to admit. But for use in combat? It might be able to slice through Klethos armor, but had anyone looked at the recordings? The Klethos were extremely fast and were undoubtedly skilled in the use of their swords. If a Marine decided to give up his other weapons and challenge a Klethos to a duel at dawn, he would get cut down in seconds.

As the worthy doctor finished his praise, he put up the specs. On the third to last line was the cost per unit. Ryck's eyes widened. At over 10,000 credits apiece, the university stood to make a killing if their offer was accepted, and Ryck had heard this already was a done deal, approved by someone high in the Federation Council.

The mameluke presentation ended, and another eager promoter took his place, this one with an aerosol compression grenade. Ryck had no idea if such a weapon could be effective. The Klethos bodies and equipment the task force had retrieved had been parceled out to the various governments for detailed examinations. None of the Klethos had been resurrected—according to official statements. Rumors swirled, though, that some had been and were now under regen. But zombied or not, they had provided a plethora of information, information that two months later was now being used to try and arm the Marines to be able to defeat them when the inevitable clash came.

Ryck glanced at his watch. He'd be stuck in the conference for the rest of the day while Jorge was in the field with the brigade. Why he had to be here was beyond him. The procurement desk-jockeys would buy what they wanted regardless of what a mere colonel thought. His presence, along with the other two brigade commanders, the CG, and the Deputy CG were mere window dressing to give the resemblance that this was driven by military requirements.

He looked to Hannah again, willing her to glance his way again. When she did, he carefully pantomimed raising his hand to his mouth to eat. She smiled and nodded, then used her face and expression to point back up to the compression grenade man, admonishing Ryck to pay attention. Ryck turned back to listen to the man wax poetic on his little weapon's capabilities.

Ryck would rather be in the field training, but at least he'd fit in a lunch with his wife. With their schedules over the last two months, that was a win no matter how he looked at it.

Chapter 21

Four Klethos strode over the rise, heading directly into the awaiting platoon from Lima 3/14.

Immediately, First Lieutenant Dandridge gave the order, and the platoon moved to encircle the creatures, pikes at the ready. The Klethos faced the Marines surrounding them, then raised their swords and jumped into the attack. Under the onslaught, the Marines pressed forward, trying to pin the creatures with their ceramochromalloy pikes, pikes that had an electrical current running to the tip at a frequency the xenobiologists thought would disrupt the Klethos' nervous systems.

As the first pikes hit home, the Klethos screamed out their rage, and instead of pressing home against the Marines, attacked the pikes. Somehow, the same swords that could slice through a PICS' armor could not cut through the pikes. But they were having some effect on the Marines' assault. On Ryck's display, he could see the current failing in pike after pike. That left them as little more than metal poles that the Klethos started to push aside and attack the Marines holding them. Marine after Marine fell as the Klethos' swords hit each one in a shower of sparks and light.

"Engage with rockets!" Lieutenant Dandridge ordered his beleaguered men.

Immediately, several salvos of shoulder rockets shot out. Two Marines fell by friendly fire as rockets flew past the Klethos and hit those on the other side. One Klethos staggered and went down, but it was too little too late. Within moments, the last of the Marines fell to the three surviving Klethos.

Fuck me, Ryck thought.

"Cease fire," Gunny DePardue passed over the training circuit.

The three Klethos, the finest simulacrums Dreamworks had probably ever made, eased back up to their default position while the platoon's PICS powered back on.

Ryck'd had high hopes for the pikes. He'd been assured that they could knock a Klethos senseless and allow the Marines to capture some of the creatures. And while the incapacitating current had seemed to have an effect, and while the pike shaft itself had withstood the Klethos swords, evidently, the transmission lines for the current had not, rendering the pikes as nothing more than long but inert metal rods.

At least Dandridge had improvised, turning the training session from a capture to a kill mission. It had been too late, but he'd done something and had even scored a kill.

"Well, back to the drawing board," Ryck remarked to the engineer from Hephaestus Foundries, SA. "I think you've got a few bugs to work out."

"I'm not sure what happened, sir. But trust us, we'll fix it."

Ryck ignored the engineer as the man started going over possible fixes. The engineering was beyond Ryck anyway. He as a fighter, not an engineer. Just give him a weapon and tell him how to use it. He didn't need to know how it worked, just how to work it.

He looked up at the three upright and one prone Klethos simulacrums. Now those were amazingly complex—and amazingly expensive—pieces of gear. Dreamworks had long been the leader of making fake dinosaurs and fantastic creatures for flicks, amusement parks, and even museums. They had quickly made up a life-size Klethos for display, and almost immediately, a master sergeant in one of the battalions attached to the Second Marine Brigade tried to rent one for training. It was one of those "duh" moments when everyone else realized this should have been done immediately and not waited for a battalion staff member to think of it.

To really be effective, though, the simulacrum should be more than a static display to get Marines used to a Klethos' size and movement patterns. It should be able to interact with the Marines and Marine weapons. Cybogen, the AI company, had already developed a computer program that weapons companies could use to simulate the efficacy of new weapons against the Klethos. Marrying up two unique sets of capabilities, Dreamworks teamed up with Cybogen, and together they poured countless manpower and hours to create the Klethos Interactive Training Unit. The KITUs had proven to be invaluable with five units going to each brigade and more planned to be delivered as they got off the manufacturing line.

The KITUs simulated weapons, both the gun and sword, were connected to the Marines' AI control, so when a ghost sword, for example, swung through a PICS, the AI shut that PICS down. It was easily as good as the RECT systems back on base, but these allowed Marines far more realistic training scenarios. The RECTs had also been reprogrammed, but as more KITUs were delivered, larger units would be able to go force-on-force with the simulacrums.

One of the Dreamworks engineers moved forward to reset the downed KITU. The contracted support teams had been very protective of the units, especially since one had been knocked out by a very energetic group of 2/3 Marines, who, led by Sergeant Wayne Miller, a former street kid from Piaster who was being noticed as an up-and-comer, had physically mauled the unit and knocked it out of action.

Ryck and Sandy had both been called on the carpet for that by Major General Sergovich, the Deputy CG, who in no uncertain terms told both of them that a single KITU was worth more than any number of Marines. New ROIs were enacted, with intensive SNCO supervision, that eliminated any physical contact between a PICS and KITU.

Ryck wished he'd had that fifth KITU online, but he couldn't—wouldn't—fault Marines for being aggressive. When the real shit hit the fan, they'd need all Sergeant Millers they could find and all the aggression they could raise.

Chapter 22

Ryck sat in the waiting room, his nerves on edge. He was pretty sure he knew what he was going to hear. He'd spent enough time on the net researching, and Marines were always aware of the risks. Still, he needed a doctor's confirmation.

He held out his right arm, slowly rotating the wrist back and forth. The twinges of pain were there, subtle and weak, but there. This was not his imagination working overtime. It had been almost 13 months since his golf injury—that still sounded crazy to him: "golf injury"—and there should be no trace of it anymore. But it was still there, and then there was the incident of getting into his PICS on the *Brandenburg*. No, something was wrong, and Ryck thought he knew what it was. He *feared* he knew what it was.

"Mr. Stilicho, the doctor will see you now," the receptionist said from her desk.

"Mr. Stilicho! The doctor will see you," she said again, looking straight at Ryck.

Oh, shit, that's me, Ryck thought as he hurriedly got to his feet. *I need to remember that!*

He went through the indicated door where a nurse waited for him. The nurse, a rather large, slightly overweight young man, smiled broadly, putting his hand on Ryck's shoulder and ushering him down the hall.

"Right this way, sir. I'm Gefflin. Dr. Patterson will be with you in a moment. Can I get you anything? Tea? Coffee? Zoom?"

"Uh, no thanks. I'm fine," Ryck said.

"OK, if you need anything, just let me know," Gefflin said, waving open a door that slid silently on its tracks. "Please, take a seat."

"Th . . . thanks," Ryck said, his voice catching.

"I know you're nervous, Mr. Stilicho. But rest assured, Dr. Patterson is the best, simply the best."

"Yes, I know he is. I've read the reviews. It's just, well, I've never, I mean—"

"I understand," Gefflin said, patting Ryck's arm. "Don't worry. We'll take good care of you."

As the nurse left, he murmured something, and a moment later, soft classical music filled the room. It was a pretty obvious ploy, but it did lower Ryck's anxiety a bit.

Ryck had not been to a civilian doctor since he was 18 and still in high school. He trusted Navy doctors, and he wasn't sure if he had that same degree of trust in mainstream medicine. That was irrational, he knew. Medicine was medicine, and the Hope Clinic of Jorneytown was highly rated. But the overt, well, *commercial-ness* of the clinic was a little unsettling to him. It was like they were trying too hard, trying to awe the patients. This waiting room, with the soft, muted colors, art on the walls, and very comfortable furniture was a far cry from the Spartan, yet professional-feeling treatment rooms of the Navy.

Ryck had gotten up at 0515 that morning, telling Hannah he was going to play golf at 0700 at Thunder Bay, a civilian course some 110 km north of the city. He'd loaded his clubs, but instead of heading north, he drove to the maglev station and bought a ticket to Jorneytown for his appointment. At 0930, he'd been ushered in for his scan, and now, an hour after that, he was waiting for the news.

Ryck jumped when the hatch opened five minutes later and the doctor came in, dressed in a light blue high-neck, sleeveless T and khaki bongo pants. His smile and outstretched hand, along with his dress, conveyed the obvious corporate philosophy of a caring group of friends, but Ryck didn't resonate too well with the image. He wasn't here to find a friend; he wanted a professional, competent doctor.

Ryck pushed that thought away and stood up to shake the doctor's hand.

"Hi, Mr. Stilicho, or can I call you Sandy?" he said, his teeth gleaming impossibly white.

"Uh, sure. Sandy is fine," Ryck said.

"I'm Gregori, Sandy. Good to meet you. Please, take a seat," the doctor said as he sat down, not behind his desk, but in the chair next to Ryck's.

"Well, I'm sure you want to get your results," the doctor said, looking at his PA for a few moments.

Ryck was sure that was just for show. The doctor had to have already seen the results before coming into the room.

"Sandy, we've done the scan, and the results are pretty conclusive. It's not good news, but we can almost certainly take care of you."

Get to the grubbing point!

"I can confirm that you have BRC, but still in the early stages," the doctor said without a change in his cheery voice.

BRC! The Brick! Boosted Regeneration Cancer, Ryck thought, his heart falling.

He already knew that is what he had. It made the most sense. But still, to hear it was a blow to the gut.

". . . get you into your first treatment on Friday. I'll have Gefflin brief you on the procedures—"

"Aren't I a little young for the Brick?" Ryck asked, interrupting the doctor.

Ryck had been sure he had it, but he still wanted to know why.

"Well, yes, you're 46, and we generally don't see too many people before they are in their 60's, but it isn't that rare. How old were you when you had regen?" he asked, looking at his PA in earnest this time.

Ryck hadn't given any health data, so the doctor would be looking in vain.

"When I was 19," Ryck said. "A full limb regen."

"So, 27 years ago. Not too surprising then. Rare, but reasonable."

"But I know people who've had five regens, and they haven't caught the Brick," Ryck protested.

Why he was protesting, he wasn't sure. It wasn't the doctor who put him in this position. But Ryck hadn't been able to talk to anyone about it, and he needed the catharsis.

"Sandy, you know what causes BRC, right?"

Ryck nodded, but the doctor went on, "Cancer is caused by cancer stem cells. Most cancer cells, cells that everyone has in their bodies, can't reproduce any more than your own heart or brain cells can reproduce. However, through the process of epithelial-to-mesenchymal transition, or EMT, a normal cancer cell is changed to a stem cell, which not only can develop into many different kinds of cancer, but through an elongation process, can form metastases by using the blood stream as sort of an expressway to distant sites in the body, where they can then establish new, malignant tumors."

He looked at Ryck expectantly.

"Look, what I mean is picture these inert cancer cells as square blocks, which is a fair depiction. EMT changes these cancer cells to stem cancer cells, and by stretching them out, they can slide through the bloodstream like eels, migrating to anywhere" the doctor said.

"But I have the cancer killer nanos, like everyone else," Ryck said.

"Yes, but you've also had regen. You know, right, that people cannot just grow a new arm when they want to."

"Of course, I do. That's why we use stem cells in regen."

"Well, what regen does is use its own form of EMT to create viable stem cells from what your body has."

"I didn't lose my testes," Ryck protested. "They got the stem cells there."

"True, but you were not an embryo. And while testes-harvested stem cells are much easier to work with than regular cells harvested elsewhere, they still need to know where to go and what to do. So, through our own EMT process, they are given their marching orders and put to work. But we also boost them. How long did it take for you to grow a new arm?"

"About eight months," Ryck said.

"And how long for you to grow that arm in the first place? To its full size?"

"Well, I don't know. Eighteen years?"

"Exactly. So, you have not-so-efficient stem cells and not so much time, so we boost the regen process," the doctor said, his eyes brimming with the excitement of someone immersed in the process. "We give the orders, and in eight months, you have a new arm."

"OK, and so?" Ryck asked.

"Don't you see? We boost the stem cells, make them super stems. But that same process boosts the cancer stems cells at the same time, or at least gives them the foundation. They lie quiet for a time, for reasons we still don't understand," he said, his eyes furrowing together as he seemed to contemplate the universal unfairness of the lack of complete mastery over the process. "Then something, an injury, a sickness, even stress triggers the metastases process."

Like a golf injury? Grubbing hell. I've got this now because I was determined to outdrive Sams?

"But the good thing is that we can defeat this. It is not too late for you by a longshot. Basically, we just repeat the process, regening your blood, lymphatic system—where your BRC is primarily located at the moment—and anywhere the BRC resides. You'll need better monitoring as you have proven yourself to be susceptible, but there's no reason that you won't live a long and productive life."

Ryck sat back, letting the words sink in. He'd known most of what the doc said, of course. BRC was an occupational hazard for Marines. Twenty percent of all regen patients contracted it at some time in their lives.

"If I don't start treatment, how long, I mean, well, how long before it's untreatable?" he asked.

"Oh, if you can't start treatment on Friday? Don't worry, it's not that urgent yet. I'd say from the readings that you have nine, maybe ten months before it gets to the point of no return."

"And how long is the treatment?"

"For your type of cancer? Unless it metastasizes elsewhere, you've got about six months of regen," the doctor told him.

"So I can wait awhile?" Ryck asked.

"Sure, but I don't see why you'd want . . . uh, do you have a financial concern? I see you don't have Prime, T1, or private insurance."

Ryck was covered by the Navy, and his wife and kids were under Prime, the federal health insurance given to government employees and both military and government dependents. T1 was the Tarawa health plan.

"You know, if you received regen through military or FCDC service, you are still covered, even if you have no other insurance. It doesn't matter if you have money or not. Show us proof that your regen was service-related, and we can start the treatment now. We'll bill the Federation directly. You won't hear from our bookkeeping at all."

"No, I have insurance," Ryck said, standing up. "I just have a few things I need to get done before I take the time for regen. Business matters. But don't worry, I'll be in soon, long before it gets too late."

"Well, if you're sure," the doctor said, his eyes expressing doubt.

"I'll be back, and I'll get the treatment. What am I, an idiot?" Ryck asked.

"No, of course not. Just, well, just keep in touch, and if you do need anything, like if your business encounters some money-flow issues, we'll work with you. OK?"

"Sure thing, doc. I will," Ryck said, taking the doctor's hand in a firm grip. "I'm sure you've got other patients waiting for you, so I'll just let myself out. I'll check out with the receptionist before leaving, though."

Ryck could tell that the doctor was truly concerned for him, and given Ryck's haircut and the fact that the military was a big part of Tarawa, he'd guessed, and guessed correctly, that Ryck's regen was done by the Navy. What he didn't guess correctly was why Ryck was hesitant.

It was the same reason that Ryck had taken the maglev to Jorneytown. It was the same reason why he'd checked into the clinic as Sandy Stilicho. He didn't want the Marine Corps to know. The rules were pretty straight forward. A Marine in regen had to give up his command. General Papadakis hadn't been able to fight that iron-clad regulation, and he was the commandant. If Ryck went into treatment, he was done, and given his previous resignation and the unique reason for his reinstatement, he might be done for good.

Ryck wasn't done, though. There was still a fight to fight. The Klethos were still out there, and they were a threat to humankind. His brigade was getting ready to embark once again, and they needed him. They needed his leadership.

At least that was what he kept telling himself.

Chapter 23

Ryck was immersed in the after-action reports for Bold Tender, the first full-scale Joint Ground Task Force training operation since its formation when Hannah stuck her head into his office. Ryck smiled and put down his secured reader, his mind going back to when Hannah made an appearance before he last deployed. That smile faded as he saw the expression on her face.

"You've got your PA turned off," she stated.

"Yeah, I was going over the after-action report, and I didn't want any interruptions. Sorry if I missed your call. What's up?"

Ryck's PA, while Level 3 Secure, was not authorized for the after-action report, which requited a Level 2 security certificate. So, he'd turned it off after drawing a Level 2 reader.

"You need to turn it on and check the news feed," she said.

Can't you just tell me? he wondered. *What's the big deal?*

He secured the reader and turned on his PA. His homepage was FNF, and immediately, the main news feed caught his attention.

Holy fuck! was all he could think.

The FCDC, backed by a battalion of Marines, had just taken over the government of Ellison, the homeworld of his parents and his long-lost brother, Myke. Ryck had never felt much of an affinity for the planet; Prophesy was his homeworld, and his parents had never said much about Ellison and their reason for emigrating, but still, the news hit Ryck hard. There had been an unreported number of casualties, and the reason for the takeover was not explained.

Ryck switched the channel to Truthtellers. FNF was not officially affiliated with the Federation government, but it was known to be quite friendly to government desires. Truthtellers was an independent news agency from Indigo, and while it tended to be slanted against the Federation (and the Brotherhood and Confederation), it also tended to have more details, especially when covering controversial issues.

The "invasion" was the lead story on Truthtellers. According to them, the Federation had gotten tired of the impasse with the two main unions on Ellison and had invaded to break the unions' stranglehold on the planetary government. Initial accounts were that over 10,000 people were killed, almost all on Ellison side.

Truthtellers labeled the action as a Marine invasion, but reading between the lines, Ryck could see that Third Battalion, Ninth Marines had secured the two main spaceports for the FCDC to land unopposed. It was the fuckdicks who were taking over and breaking the protests.

So much for always telling the truth, Truthtellers, Ryck thought to himself, but as an aside.

While he was relieved that the Marines were not out there killing citizens, the fact that any Federation troops were there made him sick to his stomach. He'd been aware that there had been increased disillusionment on Ellison (and other worlds) as the Federation declared martial law in response to the Klethos threat, and that there had been protests. But he had not been aware that it was this bad.

"What do you think?" Hannah asked, sitting down on one of the chairs.

"I don't know. I . . . I just . . . Hell, what the heck's going on? We've got the Klethos on our doorstep, and we're doing this?"

"The government says they had to move in *because* of the Klethos threat," she countered. "They say we cannot have any interruption to the war effort."

"And you believe that?"

"No, not really. I think they be taking advantage of the situation," she relented. "Ellison has always been a thorn in their side."

Which was putting it mildly. The Marines themselves had landed on Ellison not 60 years before, and the carnage was one of the darkest blotches on the history of the Corps. Ellison had never forgotten that history, and while still a member of the Federation, the planet took pride in being a voice of opposition to the central government. The central government was not welcomed, nor were most of the big multi-system corporations.

The Truthteller feed just updated, changing the casualty count to 15,000. Ryck placed his PA on his desk, face down. He didn't want to see it anymore.

Despite his bloodlines, Ryck didn't have much of a connection with Ellison. He didn't know many people from the planet. His brother, who had abandoned Lysa and him after their father died, might be alive out there somewhere. David Kyser, who had attacked the Klethos on Tri-30, earning a posthumous Navy Cross, had been one of the few Ellison natives that Ryck had known who had enlisted in the Marines.

There was one Ellison native who still haunted his dreams, though. Caporal-chef Coltrain Meyers, the Legionnaire who on Weyerhaeuser 23 had invited Ryck to share a beer with him sometime and who Ryck had killed with his bare hands the next day, had evolved over the years from an accusing spirit to almost a kindred one.

If only for Meyers' memory, Ryck felt deflated and depressed. He didn't know if whatever had been taking place on Ellison had really been affecting the ramp-up for war, but he did know that he was ashamed of the Federation, his Federation, the government for whom he worked and to whom he'd sworn an oath. For a moment, it almost overwhelmed him, and he felt a sudden urge to chuck it all, to resign.

"You be OK?" Hannah's question cut through his thoughts.

He looked up at his wife, gathering himself. As much as he hated to admit it, whatever was happening on Ellison was a minor blip on what was facing mankind. The Klethos could be the single most dangerous threat ever experienced by the human race. Given what was happening to the capys, mankind could be facing extermination. It was that serious.

If Ryck resigned, then what? What good what that do? Someone else would step in and take over the brigade, someone who was not as capable of leading it into battle.

He wasn't even sure they would let him resign. There was the little issue of the capys insisting on Ryck being their point of contact. The *Mathis* had evolved into a naval command post, with capys and humans on board, but for ground operations, Ryck was still the focal point between the two races.

"Yes, I'm OK," he told her. "Let me get back to my after-action report. I'll be late again, but I'll see you at home around 2000, OK?"

She looked at him for a moment, then nodded and left the office.

He watched her go. Then, with a silent apology to his parents, to David Kyser, and to Coltrain, he simply turned back to his task at hand.

GREATER PIEDMONT

Chapter 24

Lieutenant Colonel Bryce Fukoka was on the podium, extolling the history of the Gregorian Marines, the patron unit of his Third Battalion, Fourteenth Marines.

The Gregorian Marines were the junior-most patron of the Federation Marine Corps, having been formed only 14 years before the formation of the Federation. They had fought exactly one engagement during their short existence, but of course, it was one of the pivotal moments in time, where if not for the efforts of a few brave men and women, history would be changed.

During the Consolidation, the "Peacekeepers" not only managed to take over the Bastion Army's nuclear armory, they also held it against the full and furious New Day onslaught for four days until the combined Russian, British, Indian, and Kiplinger forces could relieve them. Six-hundred-and-twelve Gregorian Marines assaulted the armory. Twenty-two Marines emerged from the rubble when the Earth forces broke the counterattack and rescued them.

When the New Day was defeated, the rest of humanity discovered that the intent of their assault on the Bastion Armory was to seize the six planet buster bombs there, bombs that no one—other than the Bastian government—even knew existed. The target for those bombs had been Mother Earth itself.

The fallout from all of this formed the very system in place to this day. Earth had come close to being destroyed, and no one had realized the threat until it was almost too late. The Federation was formed so that could never happen again. It was a too pat solution, though, given the vast diversity of humanity. The Confederation of Free States soon broke away, followed by the Brotherhood and Greater France. There were more shifts to and from until the muddied mess that now ruled human space evolved. But none of that would have happened without the Gregorian Marines and the Battle of The Bastion Armory.

It was a good story, one every modern Marine knew by heart, but Bryce was doing a credible job of retelling it. Ryck sat back in his folding chair, letting it just sink in. It was not lost on him that possibly soon, there would be another one of those pivotal moments in history, and this time, he could be part of it.

Ryck looked out over the field where the brigade was gathered, and pride filled his soul. These were good men, and together they formed a magnificent fighting team. They'd been sent to Greater Piedmont, a mostly empty world in the Confederation, to continue to train. Clouds were gathering on the horizon, and it looked like a conflict was imminent.

And it was about time. Ryck did not wish for a fight with the Klethos. There was too much unknown about them, and that could spell disaster for humanity. But if a fight was coming, he wanted it soon. His brigade, and the other two brigades as well, were finely tuned and ready to go. Any more delay and that degree of sharpness would begin to fade. They would lose their edge. At some point, the entire cycle would have to begin again, training up new forces to take their place.

And for a personal reason, if Ryck was going to be involved, that had to happen soon. He was running out of time. Still unbeknownst to anyone else, his cancer was spreading. He'd bought a bio-scanner on the black market, then gotten it hacked and shielded so it was pretty much undetectable to anyone not specifically searching for it. His nanos were fighting a losing battle, and if he was going to get treatment, it really had to begin within a few weeks.

He knew what he had to do. He didn't think anyone was ready to take over for him. But if he were incapacitated, he couldn't command. It was that simple.

Having the patron day celebration was a godsend. It gave all the Marines in the brigade, not just those in 3/14, a chance to unwind. And when Sergeant Major Ullovitch and Lieutenant Colonel Fukoka had approached him with the idea of having the patron day celebration in the field, in their skins and immediately following a 30 km hump, Ryck had readily agreed, making it a brigade function, not just a battalion one.

Ryck leaned back in his folding chair, the legs digging into the soft soil and almost tipping over.

"Easy, there, Colonel," Hecs said, reaching out to keep him from falling.

Hecs was now the brigade sergeant major, having left the Fuzos. With Hecs on one side, Jorge on the other, and with Çağlar's ever-protective eyes on him, Ryck felt at ease, surrounded by friends. It was with a twinge of regret that he looked to his left where the Fuzos were assembled, Lieutenant Colonel Sandy Peletier-Aswad commanding. The deep friendship between the two Marines had suffered. There was no difference on the surface. Sandy was as professional as ever, and in social occasions, he made polite with remarks about Hannah and the kids or sports gossip. But something was missing, and that caused a rift in Ryck's heart. Their friendship had suffered due to their command relationship.

Sandy had become a better commander, though. That was obvious. And that was the important thing. Maybe, after all of this was over, the friendship could be re-kindled. He hoped so.

Lieutenant Colonel Fukoka finished his speech to the loud and thunderous "ooh-rahs" from the gathered Marines and sailors. More than a few of the men were probably a bit drunk. Breaking tradition, the bar had been opened before the ceremonies were completed. But this was not a normal Patron Day celebration. There were no civilian guests, and Ryck was the senior officer present. Instead of a fine meal, the same ghost shit Marines ate while in a PICS was served. They weren't even inside a building, but out in a grassy field. So the bar had been opened before the cake, before the toasts. And if a few Marines were already in their cups, if a few had taken to relieving themselves under the table and onto the grass, no one bothered to notice.

Some traditions could not be broken, though. Martin Ekema, now a gunny, who Ryck had snatched into the brigade headquarters from 2/3, had somehow come up with a tremendous birthday cake. An honor guard of Marines marched the cake up to the head table, and Master Gunnery Sergeant Silas Brightness and Private Yancy Eithan were called forward as the oldest and youngest Marines in 3/14. Brightness was given the first piece of cake while Eithan the second. Ryck, as the guest of honor, got the third, but as the senior Marine, he felt uncomfortable taking a bite until all the Marines and sailors were served, so he just placed it on the table to wait.

With an entire brigade to feed and no civilian staff, Ekema was hopping, having drafted some 50 Marines to assist. In the meantime, Lieutenant Colonel Fukoka called for the Drum Corps commander to begin the beating.

Ryck sat up higher in his chair, which was sinking unevenly into the loam. He wanted to see this. As was becoming more and more common, Drum Corps beatings were employing Marines in PICS for both drumming and the accompanying dancing. Ryck had first seen this on Sierra Dorado as the company commander with Charlie 1/11. That was still his all-time favorite Patron Day celebration, but he enjoyed all of them, and he eagerly looked forward to seeing what 3/14 had in store for them.

And he wasn't disappointed. If the beat of the drums were not as loud out in the open air, that didn't matter. The corps made up for that with exuberance, and the PICS, the PICS! They were amazing. Ryck liked to occasionally—and secretly—practice in his PICS, trying to master some of the moves he'd seen before, but these Marines (and one sailor) went beyond what he thought a combat suit could do. Twirling, jumping, even a straight-legged somersault, they took Ryck's breath away. When they finally finished with a crescendo of drums and intricate moves, Ryck jumped up, cheering himself hoarse.

As he thrust his fist into the air, the sharp stab of pain in his shoulder brought him back down to earth, though. He quickly looked around to see if anyone had noticed him flinch, but everyone was cheering, even the taciturn Çağlar.

An unwelcome thought forced itself into his consciousness. Would this be Ryck's last such celebration? What if the cancer won? But more than that. Would it be everyone's last celebration? A year from now, would there be a Marine Corps to celebrate!

"Some show, huh?" Hecs asked, hands clapping.

"Yeah, Hecs, some show."

Chapter 25

"Well, we could try our old reliable," Hecs said.

"Reliable?" Jorge asked.

"He's referring to a field day. Let the men burn off some steam with battleball and a barbecue, if Ekema can pull the food part of it off," Ryck answered.

The Marines were ready, and Ryck was even more concerned about them losing their edge. There was only so much they could do at this tempo in a training environment. Every day, fights were breaking out, the majority of them for the most picayune of reasons.

Both Lieutenant Colonels Fukoka and Lu Wan, who had been given 3/5 when Sandy had been confirmed as the permanent commanding officer for 2/3 (and who had been assigned to the brigade in what Ryck was sure was a pissed off colonel's monitor in a snit directed at Ryck) had asked to cut back on the training tempo. But less time training also meant more time sitting around camp, and that mean more bored Marines who could get into more trouble.

The brigade had been scheduled to return to Tarawa two weeks earlier, but they had been extended on Great Piedmont twice now, which could be a sign of impending action. Ryck had given himself a deadline of ten days ago to give up his command to get treatment, but the knowledge that they could deploy any moment now held his hand.

"I could do it," a voice said from the tent flap.

"As I live and breathe, Master Gunnery Sergeant Samuelson!" Hecs said. "They let you out of the brig?"

"I promised good behavior, Sergeant Major," Sams said, stepping in to hug and pound Hecs' shoulders.

"Good to see you, Sams," Ryck said, hand out to shake. "I thought you were waiting back on Tarawa."

Sams' regen, his second, had a few hiccups and had taken longer to complete. Ryck had pulled his usual strings to get Sams assigned to the brigade staff, and his regen done, Sams had been waiting for the brigade to return. With the brigade delayed on Greater Piedmont, evidently Sams had taken matters into his own hand.

"I couldn't leave you all alone out here, so I hitched a ride with General Mbanefo," Sams said as calmly as if he was talking about catching an autocab.

"The commandant's here? On Piedmont?" Ryck and Jorge said, both men jumping up.

"Yeah, I figured you knew that. He's with General Bolivar at Camp Fauston or Faxton or whatever you call it."

"Fauxon," Ryck corrected automatically. "And no, we didn't know."

Camp Fauxon was the name of the temporary bivouac for the ground force commander and the Second Marine Brigade. It was located some 120 km to the northwest of Camp Kyser, the temporary bivouac for the First Marine Brigade. Ryck knew the commandant could be just making the rounds, but his warrior sense told him that something was up. He wanted to call up Hasting Johns, the Second Brigade CO to see if he had any scoop. But he withheld, knowing Hasting was probably shitting bricks with the commandant there. He'd find out soon enough.

As if on cue, his PA buzzed. He looked down at the message before turning to the other three.

"Sams, welcome aboard, and get your kit. Jorge, get the commanders ready for a brief when I get back. Hecs, you and I are being summoned. Let's go see what's up."

Chapter 26

Ryck and Hecs were rushed into the briefing tent by an armed corporal. More armed Marines and a handful of civilians with that bodyguard look were inside, which struck Ryck as odd. That the civilians physically searched him seemed even odder and more than a bit insulting, to be honest.

Both Marines took their places in the front row. Ryck nodded to Hasting and Kjartan Snæbjörnsson, his old operations officer in 2/11 and now a fellow brigade commander. On either side of them were commanders of no less than half of the ground force, all the units who had been training on the planet.

"Do you know what's up?" Ryck whispered to Hastings.

"It's go time," Hasting whispered back, before hushing Ryck from asking anything else as the commandant and ground force commander walked in, preceded by yet four more mean-looking, no-nonsense civilians.

Have things deteriorated so much that the commandant needs civvie bodyguards? Ryck wondered before the commandant began his address to the assembled men.

"Gentlemen . . . and lady," he said, belatedly including the single female in the tent, a liaison major from New Budapest. "Two hours ago, just before we arrived in what was simply to be a quick visit and look at the troops, we received word of a Klethos landing on Roggeri's World."

There was a collective intake of breath from the gathered people.

"For those of you who are not familiar with it, Roggeri's World is in the Confederation. Confederation pickets were in position, but they did not detect the manner of the Klethos arrival. All we know is that the Klethos have landed in force. There is a division of the Confederation Army in place to supplement two divisions of the local militia, but as of the moment, there has been no outbreak of fighting.

"Colonel Dryson," the commandant said, looking straight at the senior Confederation officer serving on Lieutenant General Bolivar's staff, "let me assure you that this is not a Klethos assault on the Confederation of Free States. This is an assault on mankind, and our chairman has ordered me to pass to you that we in the Federation will honor our pledge to you, to all of mankind, to join in rebuffing the Klethos invasion.

"The order to kick off Quail Hunt will be issued momentarily from Admiral Parks as soon as all the governments officially authorize it. But we don't have to wait. The Federation Navy has just deployed and will move capital ships into Confederation space as soon as Admiral Parks gives the order, but the Confed government has authorized the troop transports to begin embarking those of the task force here on Greater Piedmont. Needless to say, time is of the essence. All of your commands are being given the orders now, and you will be released to join your units soon. First, though, Lieutenant General Bolivar has a few things to pass. General?"

Ryck wanted to leave right then, to get back to his brigade. He wasn't sure why this meeting had to be in person, or what the task force CG had to say that hadn't been said already. The holo cams in the back of the room manned by more civilians might be the answer, Ryck realized, to his disgust. When politics interfered with military necessity, the Marines on the ground usually suffered.

Aware, though, that the cams could be looking at him due to his status as a Nova holder, he tried to look interested as the CG attempted to speed through an atta-boy, we-are-all-in-this-together, ooh-rah speech. Finally, they were dismissed, and Ryck and Hecs rushed out to their waiting lift to fly back to Camp Kyser.

"This is it, Hecs," Ryck said as they strapped in. "Let's get it done!"

ROGGERI'S WORLD

Chapter 27

"Get the reserve up now!" Ryck shouted into his throat mic to Lieutenant Colonel Lu Wan.

A reserve was supposed to exploit success, usually with the counterattack, not get thrown into failure, but Ryck was out of options. 2/3 and 3/14 were firmly engaged and could not withdraw, and Major General Sergovich had ordered Ryck to put pressure on the Klethos attacking the Third Brigade.

Sergovich was screaming down Ryck's ass, and Ryck was on Lu Wan's. In his heart, Ryck didn't think that 3/5 would be able to do much to stem the tide, but orders were orders, and even if strategically unsound, Ryck couldn't bear to see Marines die in droves.

So far, Operation Quail Hunt was an unmitigated disaster. The Roggeri's World militia and most of the Confederation Division had been wiped out almost before the Joint Ground Task Force had landed. The ferocity of the Klethos attack was nothing like what Ryck had seen on either that first capy world or on Tri-30.

Initially, the Klethos tactics seemed much the same. They appeared on the planet without spacecraft, at least those that the Confed systems had picked up. Once on the ground, they started with the same deliberate movement to contact, ignoring buildings and even the scattered civilians who fled before them. A militia regiment had hastily formed up a defensive line between the Klethos and Sundale, a city of 600,000 people on the confluence of two rivers. Ryck had watched the overhead surveillance recording of that meeting. As before on Tri-30, the Klethos line had stopped a klick or so beyond the front lines of the defense. One Klethos started forward, only to be immediately incinerated by a huge defensive plasma gun. The power of the gun had to have been immense as it smashed through the Klethos' shielding and left only a few vapors of the creature's component atoms to wisp away in the wind.

Immediately, all hell broke loose. The Klethos line broke into a charge as the big militia gun simply exploded, taking out a full city block. Weapons of an unknown nature swept the militia lines, and militiamen either fell still, or more horribly, seemed to come apart, leaving red, messy, piles of organic material on the ground. Replays showed that the militia lasted no more than fifteen seconds.

Fifteen seconds! For more than 1,800 men and women to simply cease to exist!

Humans had weapons that could kill in the multitudes in an instant. A planet buster could do that, for example. But whatever the Klethos deployed swept through the militia like the grim reaper's scythe. The 200 or so Klethos swept through what had been the city's defenses, and this time, instead of ignoring the civilians, they started in on a slaughter, killing everyone that moved.

A Confederation frigate moved in to provide fire support, but it hadn't even gotten off one shot before it was a lifeless hulk, spinning out of control. An unmanned monitor was sent in, and it, too, was knocked out.

The Klethos were on a rampage, and the slaughter was mindboggling. Energy readings were making surveillance monitors light up, but the data made no sense to the human observers. The Klethos were using weapons other than their swords and personal sidearms, but just what they were, no one knew yet.

Ryck watched all of this on his display as the shuttle took him down to the planet's surface. By the time he'd landed and married up with the rest of his staff, the battle for Sundale was essentially over. Somehow, 200 Klethos had killed over 600,000 humans. It simply did not seem physically possible, but the feeds were pretty clear.

Six-hundred-thousand people should have been able to bum rush 200 Klethos, no matter how strong the creatures were, and simply smothered them by the weight of their bodies. Instead, the people panicked and ran—and died as the Klethos slaughtered them.

With the city lost, possibly 95% of the population killed, and the local government under pressure from the Confederation and the Combined Task Force, the Roggeri's World government pulled the Zero Sum Option. A thermonuclear device that had been staged at the local library was triggered. Sundale disappeared in a fireball, taking with it almost the entire Klethos force.

Ryck wasn't sure what horrified him most: the fact that the government had just killed several thousand men, women, and children, or that it had staged the device in the city in the first place. Using it looked to have wiped out almost all of the attacking force, but at a tremendous cost, and Ryck didn't envy the men or women who had made that decision and then pushed the button.

All around the planet, the Confeds threw everything they had at the Klethos groups in a furious assault. They had some success with large numbers of Klethos fighters being killed. But the weapons used against the Klethos were quickly eliminated, and thee Klethos who had survived the initial Confederation fury went into rampage mode. Score after score of Confed soldiers were wiped out, and civilians, who tried to flee before the onslaught in panic-mode met the same fate.

Several more cities were nuked, sacrificed to kill Klethos, but still, the creatures pushed forward from expanding circles of control. And by the time the first wave of the Joint Ground Task Force had landed and been deployed, what was left of the planet's defenses was in full retreat.

Only half of the task force had landed, however. The rest, with the Brotherhood host being the largest unit, was still in transit. The half on the planet had already been in Confederation space, and so had been able to transit and land quickly—but not quickly enough to save the lost cities.

Facing an unknown number of Klethos were close to 35,000 Marines, soldiers, and sailors. The Federation Marines component of the task force, FMF-Alpha, some 10,000 strong, moved into position in a broad valley, the main avenue of land approach to the capital. With the city to their rear and an ocean behind that, the Marines had to hold. There was no room for retreat.

First Brigade held the right flank of the defense. The hills to the north were not very steep, and the Klethos should be able to navigate them. That concerned Ryck, but the Klethos had so far shown no sign of maneuver other than frontal assaults. Still, Ryck sent his attached recon teams and a platoon of Marine up the slopes as OPs, to warn him if the Klethos departed from their usual modus operandi.

The xenobiologists had many different theories as to the purpose of the Klethos' ritualistic-seeming dance before closing into battle, but when the Roggeri's World militia had interrupted that dance, all hell had broken loose. General Bolivar ordered all units of the task force not to engage until the Klethos did first, something with which Ryck heartedly agreed. The Klethos seemed to have some sort of alien chivalry thing going on, and it seemed to revolve around that dance. Ryck didn't want to see the berserker Klethos in battle with whatever weapons that entailed being brought to bear.

The Marines had almost a completely new arsenal with which to fight the Klethos, and those weapons were based on the fight on Tri-30. With tanks and air evidently on some sort of verboten list, the Marines had reverted to older-style weaponry. While the M77 flechette rifles were still part of Weapons Pack 1 and the HGL 20 mm grenade launchers part of Weapons Pack 2, neither weapon was a Marine's primary weapon. That was the new rocket pistol, in which the 7.5 mm rocket pack on the PICS' shoulder had been exchanged for a single shot pistol that fired a modified version of the rocket.

The pike that Ryck had been introduced had been improved and widely issued. It wasn't intended to be a kill weapon, but more of something with which to immobilize a Klethos.

With a nod to Ryck's use of a grappling hook against the capys, a much sleeker—and meaner—version had been developed with an intent to not only hurt a Klethos, but to lasso it in place so it could be dispatched.

Their most powerful weapon was the new remotely-controlled snap gun. The Klethos had been vulnerable to high-powered energy weapons, so these squat guns were all power and a sighting system. The sights were close cousins to those on the Davis tanks, so it made sense that tankers be used to control them, much to the general disgust of most tankers. It was hoped that the snapguns would be able to inflict some significant casualties among the Klethos before their ultimate destruction, but as remote-controlled weapons, that destruction would not cost Marine lives.

Not all changes were in offensive weaponry, though. There were several R & D types with the command. Thiago Florence was a stereotypical nerd with a ferret-shaped head on an impossible skinny neck and equally skinny body, but one in whom Hannah had great confidence. She had stuck up for the man when Ryck had indicated his lack of enthusiasm for having to babysit a non-Marine in a combat situation. With Hannah's endorsement, though, Ryck had called the young man in to discuss what he could contribute to the cause. And Ryck had to admit that the Thiago had a very bright and inquisitive mind. Together, they had come up with a number of possible improvements to a defense.

Part of a defense is called "shaping" the battlefield. That meant using any means to fool or change the enemy's use of it. The Klethos didn't seem to be too vulnerable to classical subterfuge, but Thiago had gone way back in history for a suggestion. Borrowing from the Romans, he suggested caltrops, those multi-pointed spiked devices originally designed to stop cavalry advances. Thaigo had a blueprint for some light-weight and easily deployable caltrops that would not hinder a PICS Marine but which should at least bother the bare-footed Klethos. He even had a mechanical deployment device planned that used a stored energy spring to fling the caltrops forward in a desired pattern.

Depending on the patterns, these caltrops could either hinder the Klethos or at least canalize them to where Ryck wanted them. He gave the go-ahead to Thaigo, using his discretionary funds to get them made. After the initial testing, Hasting Johns had gotten onboard, getting some made for Second Brigade. Kjartan Snæbjörnsson, though, had not seen their potential and refused to use his funds to get any made for Third Brigade.

With the snapgun, the caltrops, and by mining the AO, Ryck hoped to get an advantage that his Marines could exploit.

When the Klethos arrived, they sent out one in front of Third Brigade to do the dance. The dancer was too far away from first brigade's position to see, but Ryck watched it on his display where it was being broadcast. Within moments of the dance's conclusion, the Klethos was advancing into the attack. The initial wave hit Third and hit it hard, but it wasn't long before the flanks advanced on First Brigade.

The snapguns never got off a shot. They simply melted in their dug-in fighting holes. Only one of the mines went off, taking the legs off of a Klethos fighter. But the rest were somehow neutralized. The caltrops proved to be very effective, though. The first Klethos to reach them actually hopped up and down, backing and then stopping in its place. The Klethos seemed to notice the dull metal spikes for the first time, and when they recommenced their advance, they moved much more cautiously, even submitting to being canalized. This made a big difference when the two forces clashed. The Marines, pikes, pistols, and tridents at the ready, met them with ten or more Marines to each single Klethos.

The tridents did nothing, but the well-trained pikemen were able to isolate and hold the Klethos while the pistoleers finished them off.

Marines were dying in greater numbers than the Klethos, but there were far, far more Marines on the battlefield, and they were fearless in their attacks.

Ryck was more than pleased with First Brigade's initial performance. Second was holding well, if not as well as First, but Third was getting devastated. They had borne the brunt of the assault, and with only trenches dug and mines laid in front of their positions, the Klethos advanced where they would, and the Third Brigade Marines were not able to mass as many Marines to face each of the enemy. The Klethos cut right through them, and when the command icon switched to Major General Sergovich, Ryck knew General Bolivar was dead as well and the Force command overrun.

Sergovich quickly stepped in, and his first order was to Ryck to get Marines over to support Third Brigade. Lieutenant Colonel

Lu Wan was a little slow in reacting, and Sergovich was hot on Ryck's ass.

"Jorge, take charge of the reaction force," Ryck ordered his deputy on the P2P, careful to use the phrase "reaction force" instead of "3/5."

If he'd used the battalion's designation, that would essentially mean he was relieving Lu Wan, something he was not willing to do in the midst of battle. Lu Wan was a capable commander, even if he was not moving fast enough.

Ryck's plan was for 3/14 and 2/3 to stop the Klethos advance with firepower and lances, with 3/14 pushing the Klethos to the side and forming a gap in the enemy's advance. Lieutenant Colonel Lu Wan had been ready to fall into place inside that gap and then orient 3/5 to join with 3/14 and roll up the line, bringing an overwhelming concentration of force on small groups of Klethos at a time. This had been rehearsed over and over back on Tarawa and Greater Piedmont, and Ryck had been moderately optimistic that this technique could work.

Now, 3/5 was going to do essentially the same thing, but in support of Third Brigade, which was on the brink of collapse. But the two brigades had never rehearsed this together, and Ryck wasn't sure they could maximize the potential. They had to try, however.

"Roger that," Jorge responded as he issued a series of orders to Lu Wan.

He'd been ready for the command, Ryck realized, and had formed a plan to implement it. Ryck should have given him the mission five minutes ago, but better late than never.

Leaving the reaction force to Jorge, Ryck pulled up his display. 2/3 and 3/14 were still online, facing some 150 or so Klethos. Fifty were in 2/3's AO with the rest in 3/14's. Marines were falling—too many—but they seemed to be holding well. Between the surprisingly effective caltrops and the pikes, the Klethos were being surrounded by Marines and isolated from each other, easier targets for the pistoleers and tridentmen. Ryck wished he still had 3/5's Marines, but he was confident now that his plan was workable.

"Sandy, bring down the OP platoon to reinforce your flank. And I want full caltrop coverage now if you have any more."

"Roger, I have six more loads," Sandy replied.

"Get them out and surround your targets. Then break off Golf to start sweeping 3/14's line. Can you handle that?"

"Roger, we can. Give me a moment," Sandy replied.

With 3/5 now committed to Third Brigade, Ryck didn't have a reserve. It was all well and good to bring in the OP platoon and to get Golf Company to start to run up the Klethos line, but it was standard operating procedure to assign a new reserve when the old one was committed, and Ryck was running out of bodies. But there was one last group, he knew.

"Hecs, I want the headquarters and the gunners ready to move, to support either battalion as soon as we see which way it goes," Ryck passed to the sergeant major.

Ryck's headquarters was only 24 Marines and a sailor—23 Marines with Jorge leading 3/5 now—and three capys, but with the 25 now out-of-work remote gunners, that was a sizable-enough force that it could turn a localized fight. Ryck was also well aware of what had just happened to General Bolivar and his headquarters, and he was damned if he'd go down without fighting. Given the gap he was creating in the brigade's lines, it was certainly plausible that some Klethos would exploit that gap and hit them.

"About friggin time," Hecs replied as he rushed to ready the men.

Ryck put his attention back on his two battalions. Casualties were mounting, but it looked like the Marines would outlast the Klethos facing 2/3. The numbers were not so sure for 3/14, even with Golf now joining them. Ryck's AI kept giving new and sometimes conflicting projections based on the changing data.

He took a quick look at Jorge and 3/5. Jorge had them moving, and the first of them were pouring over the boundary and into Third Brigade's AO. The situation gelled in Ryck's brain, and almost before he knew it, he had a course of action and was on the hook with Hecs.

"I want our headquarters force to follow in trace of 3/5. When we hit the FEBA, we'll go right, though, through 3/14's lines. We're taking over the counterattack."

Hecs immediately passed the message on the command circuit, and almost immediately, loud "ooh-rahs" sounded over 50 external speakers. Ryck had been absorbed with his tasks and fighting the overall battle, but most of the other HQ and gunners had been doing nothing except following the battle, watching as Marines fell. All they wanted was to join in the fight and support their brothers, and now their constraints were being taken off.

Release the Kraken! Ryck thought to himself.

Ryck switched his display to focus on the Fuzos for a moment. More Marines had fallen, but the Klethos force was down to an even dozen. Sandy and his men were putting up a good fight, with the tactics and teamwork being the deciding factor. Ryck felt a surge of pride, not only because of their performance, but a little selfishly, because the tactics had been mostly his. They had been shaped with input from many people, but the concept was his.

"Sir, we need to go," Çağlar interrupted him.

Ryck looked around. It had only been a minute or so since he passed to Hecs the order to move out, but already, the small hill where he'd had his command post was emptying. Any longer, and he had Çağlar would be alone.

"Sorry, right you are. Let's move it."

Trusting Çağlar to keep an eye out for any Klethos that might break through the defenses, Ryck focused on his displays, only taking the time to respond to General Sergovich's demand for an update. The general's voice bordered on panic, Ryck thought disgustedly, but that might just be his style. Still, he was Ryck's commanding general now, and he pushed any misgivings out of his head.

The defensive frontage for a PICS-mounted brigade was about 30 km per SOP. However, the entire valley was only 42 km wide, and their defense was predicated on how the Klethos advanced, so it was only about four km from the hill to the boundary with Third Brigade. The scattered trees and the one small stream were no impediments to the PICS, and his new reaction force reached the brigade's flank in less than six minutes—and were immediately thrown into the fight. Jorge and 3/5 had created a gap between the two brigades, but 3/14 was heavily engaged. Twenty or so Marines, led by Gunny Larry Williams and Sergeant Bergstrøm, who had been mightily upset at being separated from his Davis and assigned to the remote-gunner crews, flew into contact with Marines from Fox Company as they surrounded two Klethos, fighting back-to-back. Ryck had a quick glance of a Marine going down to one of the Klethos' sidearm as a flurry of rockets hit the creatures before he rushed past the small group. Major Freebottom, who Ryck had pulled onto his staff, led the assault on the next Klethos, where five Marines were trying to isolate it with their staffs. The bodies of three Marines, two pistoleers and a pikeman, were underfoot as the big Klethos swiped at the pikes.

This was Ryck's first eyewitness look at the new tactics. He'd watched on slaved cams, but when 15 meters away, the action took on a far greater urgency, and Ryck's tactics, which had seemed so reasonable and logical in the simulations and training session, looked a little less certain in reality.

Six Marines, all pikemen, had the Klethos surrounded. The Klethos looked at them in what Ryck assumed to be a wary manner. The Klethos suddenly darted forward to swipe at a pike with its sword, knocking it aside, but the two Marines adjacent stepped in, jamming their pikes into the chest of the creatures, bringing it to a stop and almost knocking it off its feet while the first pikeman recovered. On the other side of the Klethos, one of the Marines had out his mameluke and was holding it alongside his pike.

The pikes were holding against the Klethos, but not penetrating its armor, and the debilitating current was not proving effective (something already reported to Ryck). Ryck knew the mameluke would slice through that armor, but a Marine had to close in to use it, and from the looks of one of the bodies, unsheathed mameluke at his side, that had cost a Marine his life.

As the Marines in the Ryck's headquarters ran up, the Klethos snapped off a shot with its sidearm, a blue haze enveloping Çağlar. The sergeant kept advancing, though. The Brotherhood scientists, after examining the captured Klethos weapons, had come up with a tweak to shielding that they had shared with the rest of humanity. It had really been a fairly simple thing to make the adjustments in the PICS to provide added protection.

Shielding aside, going against an alien in today's age with weapons more akin to a thousand years ago was still surreal to Ryck, but as the remote guns indicated, for whatever reason, more advanced weaponry was not accepted without a huge reaction. The Klethos were willing to forgo technology to fight, however, and as their technology seemed more advanced than humanity's, that was fortuitous. Their warrior ethos was giving the humans a chance.

The rocket pistols didn't seem to cross that magic line where the Klethos would retaliate with either berserker fury or more advanced weaponry, though. Çağlar tried to step in front of him, but Ryck sidestepped the sergeant and joined several other Marines in drawing his pistol and firing between the pikeman at the Klethos.

The pistol had been in reaction to the less-than-refined aiming of the PICS 7.5mm shoulder rockets, which had proven on Tri-30 to have some effect on the Klethos. It took quite a few to take down one of the creatures, but enough would do the trick. But several Marines had been killed by friendly fire given the salvo method of launching the rockets. R & D had come up with a simple solution—taking a Navy signaling gun and modifying it to fire a rocket. The rocket itself was modified to fly slower, as counterintuitive as that might sound, and the warhead was refined, and so far, the pistol had proven to be a valuable addition to the Marines' armory.

Ryck fired his pistol from 15 meters away. He could see it arch despite the short distance, but it hit the Klethos high in the chest. Whether it was Ryck's shot or any of the other four or five that affected it, the Klethos staggered, only stopping its fall by extending its arm and using the muzzle of its sidearm against the ground to keep it upright. From behind it, the Marine who had unsheathed his mameluke lunged forward, dropping his pike and swinging at the extended left leg of the Klethos, nearly severing it at the knee.

Unbelievably fast, the Klethos bent back on itself, swinging its own sword and cutting through the juncture of the Marine's shoulder and neck. Blood fountained up through the PICS.

That move was its undoing. Its sword stuck for a moment, embedded in the PICS' armor. That was all the time the Marines needed. Ryck joined five others in drawing their mamelukes and lunging to swing their swords down as the Klethos struggled to dart out of the way.

It was fast, but not that fast. Three blades, including Ryck's hit the creature, one taking off an arm, but two almost cutting the thing in half.

Ryck was breathing hard, not from exertion, but from adrenaline. He'd never been a proponent of the mameluke and had resented it being forced on them, but there had been something visceral, something that resonated deep in his psyche and reveled in the feel of metal slicing through flesh. He knew they could have stood off and poured more rockets into the wounded Klethos, and the mad rush had resulted in a self-inflicted gash in the thigh of one of the other Marines, but the kill had been somehow more fulfilling.

Doc Lewis was already in action, hitting the emergency molt on PFC Ermine Roary's PICS, pulling out the Marine who'd scored the first hit on the Klethos leg. It looked like the Marine had almost been cut in two from shoulder to belly, but he was surprisingly conscious and even bragging, if in obvious shock, about what he'd done. Ryck made a note to commend Roary, punching it into the ethersphere should something befall him before he could act on it. Doc was already deploying a zipperbag as Ryck turned away to continue the fight.

He knew he should step back a moment and look at the big picture, but with a greatly diminished reaction force, he knew every swinging dick mattered. He could command the brigade and still fight if needed. That was what he told himself, at least, and almost convinced himself as to its veracity.

Sandy and 2/3 eliminated the last Klethos in their AO, and Ryck ordered them to start working down 3/14's defensive line. More and more Klethos were being eliminated. Ryck joined in two more fights. Çağlar physically kept him from drawing his mameluke again and getting in close, but he did fire his rocket pistol, scoring a hit on one.

With each Klethos killed, the surviving Marines facing it were freed to swarm to the next one. Before too long, 30 or even 40 Marines faced each of the creatures. Ryck kept half-expecting the remaining Klethos to revert to their more powerful weapons to stem the tide, but they didn't. Ryck didn't understand why, but he was not going to argue with them about it.

The tide of Marines was just too much, and one by one, the Klethos was swarmed over. Within 20 minutes, there was not a living Klethos in the brigade's AO.

Even before the last one fell, Ryck let Çağlar pull him out of the fight, and he focused his attention back on the rest of the task force.

Jorge was a maniac, rallying the beaten Third Brigade into a killing frenzy. With Colonel Snæbjörnsson killed, Jorge had taken command not only of the reaction force, but of the entire brigade. Ryck knew this was Jorge's first experience in combat, and it seemed that he had 18 years of pent up plans upon plans that were suddenly released. Within a few moments of review, Ryck was surprised and mightily impressed with how Jorge was changing plans on the fly and meeting the threat with what was a seriously depleted force.

Brilliant or not, Third Brigade was still undermanned, so Ryck asked General Sergovich permission to abandon their AO and move to shore up Third. The general didn't even hesitate but granted permission. Ryck would be leaving his AO undefended, but the Klethos had never shown any indication of subterfuge, so that was a pretty safe bet. At this stage of the battle, the mission was to kill the enemy, not protect territory.

Leaving behind only enough Marines and sailors to recover the dead and wounded, Ryck swung around his brigade, at only 55% of its initial fighting strength, but still a pretty powerful force, and crossed the boundary into Third's AO and essentially put the brigade under Jorge's tactical control. It was Jorge's fight now, and Ryck didn't want to interrupt the genius at work. He asked Jorge what he wanted First Brigade to do, then he followed those orders.

With General Sergovich rallying Second Brigade and Ryck's First Brigade supporting Third, slowly but surely, the Klethos were worn down and killed. They had to have known what was happening, but they never broke from their mano-y-mano style of fighting.

Almost three hours after the first shot fired, the last Klethos fell. Something like 700 of them had died, but at the cost of over 6,000 Marines. At half strength, Ryck's First Brigade was the largest Marine unit left on the planet. Third Brigade was down to less than 1,000 Marines.

The "Berserker" Klethos, the ones facing the Confeds some 4,500 kms away were still on their rampage, using unknown and more powerful weaponry, and most of the Confederation units and a good portion of the planetary militia had been wiped out by them. One militia regiment had yet to engage and was nervously asking for reinforcements.

Just 50 km to the north, the Combined Ground Force, made up of some of the forces of the smaller planets and governments, had held off some 300 Klethos, but at a steep cost. The New Budapest Ranger company that had served with Ryck on Tri-30 without a single casualty had been wiped out to the man, and as a whole, the force was down to 30% effective.

The Joint Ground Task Force had prevailed in two out of three theaters, but it was beaten and battered, its Commanding General killed along with much of the leadership. The remainder of the ground task force just about to arrive in-system was now to land where the rampaging Klethos were heading, with command shifting to the Brotherhood forces. That gave command of both the naval and the ground forces to the Brotherhood, but there wasn't much the battered Federation forces could reasonably do about it, and to Ryck's surprise, the Federation government ignored politics to go with common sense.

Ryck met with General Sergovich, who confirmed command of Third Brigade to Jorge and then ordered a stand-down to evacuate the wounded and dead and replenish ammunition, exchange coldpacks, and consolidate forces. No one knew what would be coming down the pike, but he wanted the Marines to be ready. Then, leaving Colonel Tyrell Smith, the former chief of staff and now assistant commander, in charge, he took off in a shuttle to meet with the Combined Ground Force.

Ryck returned to the brigade to assess the unit. Nine-hundred and sixty-three Marines and sailors had been killed in the fight. Many of those would be resurrected, but that number wouldn't be known for some time yet. Six-hundred and two were wounded, with five-hundred and seventy-eight of those needing evacuation.

Ryck was out two commanding officers: Bryce Fukoka was KIA and Clarance Lu Wan was already ziplocked and in stasis. Sandy's sergeant major had been killed. Six company commanders and seven first sergeants were KIA or WIA. Joab Ling, who had managed to get a company in 3/14 only four months previous (over the objections to the PA folks who feared that two of the Marine Nova holders could be lost on the same mission) had been hurt with a gash that had shattered his PICS face shield and cut off a good chunk of his nose, was one of the walking wounded.

With Jorge reassigned, Ryck gave Lieutenant Colonel Story Hanh-de Friese the additional duty as his chief of staff. With Hecs and Sams, the four of them came up with a plan for getting all the cold-packs exchanged and the PICS recharged. Ryck sent Hecs and Sams off to get it done, then sat down with Story and Justice Freebottom to start discussing how to reallocate the weapons. The trident had proven to be pretty useless, and the remotely-controlled snapguns had been slagged somehow by the Klethos. That left the pikes and rocket pistols as their most effective weapons. Several toads had been used as well, with only one hitting and sticking long enough to burn through the Klethos' shielding or armor.

With so many killed or wounded, there were more than enough weapons to reconfigure the remaining men of the brigade, Ryck realized soberly.

The three officers hashed things out before Sams had come to insist they recharge and exchange coldpacks as well. Ryck was surprised that five hours had passed, and it would soon be dark. He dutifully ate his ghost shit, something he'd really never learned to like despite years of his life inside a PICS.

He and Story had just got back to planning when Çağlar interrupted him with, "Sir, you need to look at this."

Ryck looked up, noticing that all the Marines around him were staring at the sky. Ryck elevated his gaze as a meteor streaked through the sky. Then another, and another.

Are we in some sort of meteor belt? he wondered.

Then two more, then five, then ten. Before long, hundreds of meteors were falling through the sky, all in a pattern too organized to be natural. Not meteors, though. Meteorites. It was evident they were reaching the ground out there, maybe 50 or 100 km away.

The circuits became abuzz with chatter. The orbiting ships could see the meteorites, but nothing was registering on any of their instruments. A Navy Experion flew into investigate and was destroyed in a burst of flames.

Ryck knew what they were. More Klethos. This is how they landed. They didn't use ships but rather some sort of personal containment bubbles or vessels. And even though the Klethos didn't use any cloaking while on the ground, they evidently had pretty effective cloaking while in space. Ryck's assertion was confirmed when other Navy instruments picked up the telltale readings of Klethos fighters where the "meteorites" had landed.

Ryck watched for two minutes in which his AI counted 1,212 incoming Klethos—if it was one Klethos per entry. And more were coming.

Seven hundred Klethos has fought 10,000 Marines almost to a standstill. The Marines had carried the day, but while losing over half of their forces. Now, over a thousand and probably many more Klethos were landing.

Ryck immediately called in his commanders and staff. If the Klethos were landing only 50 km away, they didn't have much time. Ryck didn't know how the Marines could withstand a couple thousand or more of the creatures, but he wasn't going to stand there with his thumb up his ass in defeat.

If the Klethos wanted to wipe out the Marines, it was going to cost them, and cost them dearly.

Chapter 28

Ryck watched on his display as the avatars for the ten Marines who had voluntarily and on their own formed a rear guard went gray one after the other. Led by Gunny Miller, the men had been fighting a delaying battle, trying to give the rest of the Marine Ground Force a chance to get to the evacuation sites. Ryck had been about to order someone to fall back, but Gunny Miller and the others took that difficult decision out of his hands, and he just hoped their sacrifice would not be in vain.

"Semper fi," he whispered, out of breath as he ran with several Marines of his command party through the almost-deserted streets of Knoferee, the Roggeri's World capital.

Navy surveillance had confirmed over 7,000 Klethos had landed about 70 km to the east of the Marine positions. With about twice that many human forces to confront them, the top brass dithered as to the response until word reached them of similar passage traces that the Klethos had made in landing—just analyzed and now recognized by the fleet's AIs—had just been picked up outside of Yakima 4, a Federation world. The Federation immediately gave the recall order, and the Brotherhood-led remainder of the ground task force was turned back, never landing on the planet.

Despite half-hearted protests from the Confederation, Ruggeri's World was essentially being ceded to the Klethos. The Marines and the Combined Ground Task Force were ordered to evacuate, the Marines to the harbor at the capital and the rest to the mouth of the Rugged Flow River.

As the most robust of the Federation forces left, First Brigade held its position while First and Third started their mad dash to the capital and transport off the planet. The delay in receiving the evacuation order meant that the Klethos were within kilometers by the time First Brigade started their withdrawal.

The Klethos were ungodly fast, though, so what started as an orderly, bounding overwatch—the by-the-book method of a retreat where one unit covered the movement of the other two until one of those stopped and covered first unit's retreat, each unit taking a turn in covering as the entire force hopscotched back—quickly changed to an all-out race as Ryck ordered speed over security. Second Brigade was already boarding the shuttles and other atmospheric vessels when the first of the Klethos reached the rear of Ryck's Marines. Several localized fights broke out, and each fight resulted in slowing down the Marines involved as more Klethos reached them. Over a hundred Marines had fallen to only a few Klethos.

Ryck's instincts were to turn the brigade and fight to recover those Marines, but with so many of the Klethos in pursuit, he knew that would only result in the total destruction of the brigade, with every Marine and sailor lost. Instead, he urged his men on, telling them to ignore redlining PICS as each Marine pushed the combat suits past the max sustained pace and into sprint mode, which was supposed to be limited to five minutes or less.

Ryck, with Çağlar on his ass, ran through the eerily quiet city. A few civilians peering from doorways and out windows watched them run by with empty eyes, but most of the population had fled to the harbor and had boarded boats, planes, and shuttles—anything to get away. Third Brigade, now boarding the fleet of craft sent down by the Navy, reported that the docks, gangways, and the sports complex on the shore were packed, and fights were breaking out.

The task force had been sent to save them, but now Marines in PICS were physically shoving the people out of the way as they cleared landing zones. This wasn't how it was supposed to be.

Ryck was huffing far more than he should be in his PICS. The combat suit was merely taking his own musculature impulses and transferring them to the suit's mechanical "muscles," so Ryck shouldn't be winded. But he didn't need to pull his unauthorized monitor online to know why. He'd known the Brick had metastasized into his lungs already, and now it had to be pretty entrenched.

Ryck, Çağlar, Staff Sergeant Baptiste, and Doc Lewis ran together down a broad, tree-lined boulevard. Other groups of Marines ran within sight as the AIs frantically ran calculations, adjusting them according to the situation, in order to give each Marine an embark point. Ryck may still have been in command, but the retreat had devolved into a personal effort, with the AIs directing each one individually. Ryck could still take over and issue orders if he deemed fit, even to order the brigade to hold and fight. He'd considered that for a moment. He'd "run" from the capys on GenAg 13 to get civilians evacuated, and while the cause had been just, that still ate at him. By long tradition, Marines did not run from a fight.

But to stop and fight now would accomplish nothing other than getting his brigade wiped out, and to what avail? The Navy craft coming in to pick them up would not be rescuing civilians, so while an additional handful of the civilians might have time to flee if Ryck turned the brigade, it would be at a tremendous cost in Marine lives, lives that were now needed to defend Yakima 4. Ryck's orders were firm: get off the planet. It tore him apart that the he was abandoning the people he'd been sent to save, but there wasn't a tactically sound reason for him to disobey his orders and turn the brigade.

Ryck tried to filter his display to monitor to where his men were being directed. It was almost impossible, but he felt he had to be doing something.

"Sir, you're slowing down," Çağlar said over his externals, moving up to take the right arm of Ryck's PICS in his as if he was going to pull him along. "Are you OK?"

"Default display," Ryck ordered his AI, then, "Yes, I'm fine. I just got caught up in trying to monitor everything. I'm with you now, Hans."

Without the data overload, Ryck could concentrate on keeping moving. The four of them had been being directed to the sports complex, but as they came within 600 meters, they were redirected to the Knoferee Pier, a kilometer-long tourist destination dotted with small food stands and shops.

Ryck pulled up an overhead view of the harbor area. The last of Third Brigade was lifting out of the sports complex, and the hordes of civilians were mobbing the fields, obviously hoping for more shuttles. With the mass of humanity, the shuttles couldn't land, and Ryck doubted the Marines could clear either of the two playing fields before the Klethos arrived.

Marines from 3/14 had been directed to the harbor's edge and into the water. Within moments, a huge ore hauler floated down from the sky to land some 20 meters offshore, sending a little tsunami that knocked down a few PICS Marines and more than a few civilians who had followed the Marines into the water. So far, the Klethos had left shuttles alone, but this was the largest vessel to test the Klethos. Ryck knew the Navy didn't have any ore haulers, so the civilian pilot must have had a large set of gonads to bring the big ship in.

The ore hauler was one of the largest vessels that could transit space as well as land on a planet. Most, like this one, were not capable of deep space travel, but between planets within a system, they were work horses. And if the Klethos allowed it, the ship could certainly haul Marines up to the waiting Navy vessels. It could haul a *lot* of Marines.

What it didn't have was an enclosed and pressurized cargo bay. Ore didn't need oxygen. Ore was typically loaded into the open hauling bay and kept in place with short-reach tractor beams.

Ryck had to acknowledge the quick-thinker who had sent the ore-hauler. A Marine in a PICS could survive a vacuum until the oxygen inside the suit ran out, which might be in ten or twelve hours. And what was a PICS but metal ore, if rather refined and worked ore? The tractor beams would hold them just as well as raw ore, and with the Marines stacked like layers of sardines, Ryck thought the entire depleted battalion could be loaded on board.

Ryck watched long enough to see the Marines start to clamber aboard. A few civilians tried to get on as well, only to be thrown off by the Marines and into the water. That saved their lives, as least for the moment. They would have died as soon as the hauler left the planet's atmosphere.

Ryck's PICS' navigator shunted him off the main boulevard and to a smaller road leading down the pier's entrance. Some of the

2/3 Marines were already moving onto the pier, but more and more civilians were also streaming on and clogging the route.

"Sandy, I want a team to close off the entrance to the pier," he passed on the P2P.

Sandy's avatar showed him to be about 200 meters ahead of him, out of Ryck's view what with the people and other Marines between them.

"Roger. I'm on it," Sandy replied.

Ryck pushed closer, but was slowed down by the need to avoid crushing the civilians.

"Please, sir, help us," a woman cried out as she ran up to him, one hand reaching up to touch his chest carapace, the other holding a baby.

Ryck's heart broke as he used one arm to gently push her aside as he twisted his PICS to slide past her. He didn't know what her fate would be, what any of these people's fate would be. At some point, he was pretty sure Knoferee would be nuked, and they had to get out of the city before then. They needed to be gone before the Klethos arrived.

He turned to look back, half-expecting to see the first of the creatures running down the road. There was just no way the people were going to be gone before the Klethos were among them.

More and more Marines converged at on the traffic circle in front of the pier entrance. Ryck was trying to be careful, but several bleeding people, pushed up against the storefront and with others tending them, were a testament that not all of the PICS Marines had been able to avoid stepping on or otherwise hurting them. One teenage boy lay in the gutter, his neck and half of his face crushed, the crowd ignoring him. His "Sneering Eagles" white t-shirt was stained bright red.

It took the four of them almost five minutes to make the 200 meters to the pier. Ryck checked his schedule. He'd previously instructed his AI to get him on one of the last shuttles. Someone from above had countermanded that order, but Ryck had reinstated it. He understood that the high command wanted him off first, to make sure he was around to lead the brigade on Yakima 4, but he just couldn't do it. He had to watch out for his men.

Twenty Marines stood guard at the entrance, keeping the civilians at bay while letting other Marines through. Along the length of the pier, shuttles, returning from the first lift, were slowly maneuvering, some of the smaller ones landing on the pier itself while the larger ones hovered just off the pier, their ramps lowered so the leading edges crushed the guardrails and were flush on the pier's surface.

A quick scan showed that 12 of the Marines forming the guard were scheduled to embark on a shuttle that was already in place. The AIs would adjust as necessary, but time was of an essence.

"Lieutenant diCarlo, get your men on the shuttle," he ordered.

"But—"

"But nothing. We can't screw this up."

Ryck turned to face the crowd as more Marines made their way onto the pier. He looked up and down the beach from his vantage point, seeking any sign of the Klethos. All he saw was a mass of bodies, thousands of them, and the ore hauler, a good klick away. There was a dwindling number of Marines in the water and climbing onboard. A quick query, and he could see that almost the entire battalion, those who had survived the battle, would be able to make it. Within a minute or two, the hauler would take off to rendezvous with a Navy ship above.

Panicked screams from down the road alerted Ryck. He swung back and caught the unmistakable sight of the beaked, crested head of a Klethos 300 meters away. Another joined it. There was no dancing now. The battle had already been joined. Ryck could almost feel the glare of the creatures as they seemed to lock onto him.

Directly in front of Ryck, civilians heard the screams, and they twisted around to see the cause. The rest of the people blocked the Marines' views though, but they had to be able to guess what was happening.

"Get moving!" Ryck shouted needlessly into the command circuit to the 30 or 40 Marines still out on the street. "Now!"

The Marines pushed against the crowd, heedless if they were hurting anyone. It still took a precious minute or two for the Marines to get onto the pier. A number of civilians squeezed through the Marine cordon as well, but they were ignored.

"Scatter!" a Marine shouted over his externals, his PICS boosting the amplitude. "Get off the street if you want to live!"

If there had been any doubt in the minds of those nearest the pier entrance, that shout dispelled it. People started screaming as they pushed, some onto the pier, most to the sides and even down into the water.

The two Klethos were halfway to the pier. There were just too many people in the way, people they slashed with their swords. It wasn't as if they were attacking them; it was more like an old-time farmer scything the wheat or an explorer using a machete to make his way through the jungle. They just wanted the people out of the way so they could reach their target, which Ryck knew was them.

He asked his AI for an embark report. As impossibly quick as the embark was going, the Klethos would reach them before the rest of the Marines boarded.

The huge ore hauler lifted out of the water, its cargo of Marines aboard. Ryck risked a glance and caught sight of Klethos rushing the beach, too late to reach the hauler. Some turned to look up at the pier and started to this new target.

"Sir, you need to go now," Çağlar insisted, pulling on his arm.

Ryck shook free of his nanny and turned back to the two oncoming Klethos. Çağlar was probably right, but if they let the two creatures onto the pier, Ryck wouldn't have had time to make it to his shuttle, and he'd be damned if he was going to be cut down from behind. No, their best chance was to hold them off right at the entrance, a natural choke point. It had been designed to keep out the non-paying customers, and it should work just as well against some jumped up bird-creature.

This was Horatio-at-the-Bridge time.

"Form up," he passed to the 20-odd Marines. "They don't get through no matter what."

"I've got this, sir," Sandy said on the P2P, moving up alongside him.

"I know. But I'm here, too," Ryck said, a sense of satisfaction coming over him.

Sandy was his friend, even if their relationship had become a little strained. So it felt good to have him on one side, Hans Çağlar on the other. If he were going to Valhalla today, he'd be going with friends.

The first Klethos cut down two civilian men in the front ranks, severing one totally in half. It then vaulted over the dead bodies, lifted its head to scream, and charged. Four rockets slammed into it, one a lucky shot right into it leathery beak. The head was almost taken off as the creature's body slid to a halt not two meters from the Marines. That had been a very, very lucky shot.

The second Klethos burst into the traffic circle as people cowered, trying to push out of its way. Its attention was strictly on the Marines formed up in front of it, however. It glanced at its dead comrade, then with sword raised, started to step up to meet them. Twenty-to-one was probably too much to overcome, but it never hesitated.

Only one of the Marines still had a pike, and one pike was not enough to corral one of them. Still, the Marine raised his pike, hitting it in the chest just at the creature lunged. The pike tip skittered off of its armor, but that had been just enough to throw the Klethos off balance, and its foot slid in its comrade's blood. Several rockets were fired with minimal effect, and a Marine darted forward to slash at it with his mameluke. The Marine scored a hit, but with unbelievable speed, the Klethos twisted and slashed through him, scoring deeply through his belly.

Ryck tried to move forward, but several more Marines beat him to it, blocking him. They repeatedly slashed down, animal frenzy overcoming rudimentary swordplay, shouting inarticulately. Sometimes, though, animal frenzy wins out. Several Marines were cut, one losing his forearm, but the Klethos was chopped to pieces.

"Recover!" Sandy shouted. "Recover, Marines!"

Discipline kicked in, overcoming the frenzy. The Marines fell back into line.

Ryck stepped back, checking the embark progress. Then he looked forward again. Down the road, several more Klethos made their appearance. Along the beach, a dozen or more were slashing their way through the people. Ryck figured they had a minute, two at the most.

"Time to embark?" he queried his AI.

His display flashed 85 seconds. They had to move.

"Take our wounded and move it now!" he ordered. "Get on the shuttles!"

Marines broke the formation to comply. The Marine almost cut in half was not even molted—he was picked up, PICS and all, by two Marines and dragged away. The one who had lost an arm was mobile, but already under anti-shock drugs. Another Marine took him by the other arm and helped him back.

All along the pier, shuttles were lifting. It was amazing that there were no collisions in the mass confusion. Four shuttles were left, then three, then two.

Ryck took one quick look back off the pier to see if they had left anyone. The civilians were creeping hesitantly forward. Suddenly, they broke into a run, charging the pier.

With Çağlar at his side, Ryck turned to run as well. His AI redirected him to the last remaining shuttle some 60 meters away. In a surprisingly calm train of thought, he noted that it was an AED class, a smaller shuttle that could carry maybe 30 PICS Marines. It hovered over the water, ramp on the edge of the pier. Ryck could clearly see the pilot through the front canopy, hand on the controls as he looked back down the pier at the oncoming Marines.

Ryck pounded down the pier. When he was 20 meters away, the pilot pointed behind him. Ryck flipped to his rearview screen to see three Klethos on the pier and pushing forward through the people.

"Get onboard now!" he screamed at his Marines.

The Navy crew chief was standing on the ramp, a small riot blaster in his hand and pointed at the Klethos. He looked ready to use it as he leaned forward, almost out of the craft, one arm hooked on the ramp strut to keep him inside.

The Marines hit the ramp at about the same time. Ryck and Çağlar turned to face the oncoming Klethos, rocket pistols out and ready. As Ryck turned, a tall, rugged-looking man threw something at him. Ryck instinctively caught it. To his surprise, it was a small, crying girl, who was now clinging to his arm like a baby monkey clinging to its mother. Ryck looked back up just in time to see the man mouth "Please" as one of the Klethos stepped on him, crushing him to the deck.

Something pulled Ryck back, and with the child on his arm, he turned and dove onto the ramp just as it was lifting from the pier. Careful not to crush the girl, he scrambled up, turning to look back as the shuttle lifted off.

One of the Klethos ran to the edge of the pier and launched itself up at the shuttle, amazingly jumping far enough to grab the edge of the ramp. The back of the shuttle dipped momentarily.

Shouts came over the open net. The crew chief leaned forward and blasted the Klethos in the face with its riot blaster. It didn't knock the creature off of the ramp, but it had to have hurt it. The Klethos screamed as it scrambled up and grabbed the crew chief, tearing him through the safety harness and throwing the broken body overboard.

Marines struggled to orient themselves and pull out their weapons as the Klethos stood up, if hunched over. It almost seemed to smile as it pulled out its sidearm with one hand and the sword with the other.

The Marines were too jumbled together, lying on top of each other, to immediately do much. The Klethos could take down the shuttle, Ryck realized and he tried to get up and unsheathe his mameluke. He shook off the girl, heedless of her screams just as a shape knocked him aside. He fell to the deck and looked up in time to see Sergeant Hans Çağlar hit the Klethos low on the thighs, arms wrapped around it in a classic rugby tackle.

"Hans!" Ryck shouted as the two tumbled out of the shuttle to disappear from sight.

"Pilot, we have to turn back!" he passed on the command circuit, and then the open circuit.

There was no answer as the shuttle climbed higher, picking up speed. The ramp closed, and Ryck's view was cut off.

Ryck slumped back, eyes closed as it all hit him.

When he opened them again, a small pair of eyes was looking at him.

"What's your name," he passed on his circuit.

"She can't hear you, sir," some passed to him.

Marines were untangling themselves from each other, and several were looking in his direction.

Of course, she can't hear me.

"What's your name," he asked again, this time on his externals.

"Esther," she answered cautiously.

Something hit his stomach hard, and he gasped for breath.

Esther? Like my Ester?

"Come here, Esther," he said, holding out an arm.

Hesitantly, like a little mouse creeping out of a hole, the little girl crawled forward and crept into his lap.

Ryck put an armored arm around her and said, "You're going to be OK, Esther. Your daddy loves you, and he made sure of that."

He turned off his externals as a tear slid down his face.

FS OMAHA BEACH

Chapter 29

"You are one lucky motherfucker," Sams said in awe as they stood in Ryck's stateroom.

Çağlar just shrugged and said something unintelligible.

Ryck had been amazed and thrilled when he'd gotten word that Çağlar had been brought on board, by a Navy Experion, no less. And he'd had company that could have made the entire fight on Roggeri's World worthwhile. He'd watched the recording, of course, which as it was taken from orbit, had not provided much in the way of a clear view.

"So, what did you think? I mean, come on, Hans, you have to admit that's a little, well, unique," Ryck said.

"Freaking copacetic," Sams said.

Çağlar looked uncomfortable, but with Ryck, Jorge, Hecs, and Sams leaning in eagerly, he didn't have much choice.

"Well, I, uh, I knew that if the Klethos got into us, he could take the shuttle down, so I just thought I'd knocked him overboard, sort of. But when I did, me and him, we sort of went together."

"Sort of," Ryck said, rolling his eyes.

"Yeah, I mean yes, sir. Me and him, we hit the water, and like I don't think the birds can swim too good. I sank like a rock, so I hits my buoyancy compensators, and I'm shooting to the surface, and I feels his arm on my leg, and me and him, we come up together," he stopped, looking uncomfortable.

"And?" Hecs asked. "Go on."

Çağlar looked to Ryck, who nodded, so the sergeant went on, "Well, I'm looking at him, sort of, and he's looking at me. I tried to push him off me, but he's real strong like, you know? And then he takes his sword and holds it over me, but not swings it. So, I take the hint and stop."

"And?" Hecs prompted again.

"Well, then the Navy fighter swoops down and uses its tractor beam to grab me, and 'cause he's leeching to me, we both go up to the ship," he said, seemingly relieved to be finished.

Ryck knew the fighter had not used a "tractor beam" to pull Çağlar out of the water. All Navy fighters had parking pads that held them fast to a ship deck while the ship was under maneuvers or in Zero G. The used a molecular attraction similar to magnetism, but they were nowhere near as powerful as a tractor beam. The Navy pilot had witnessed Çağlar's fall, which had been broadcast on more than a few channels, and ignoring the fact that other Experions had been blown out of the sky, he'd swooped in to snatch the sergeant, unintentionally snatching Çağlar's "guest."

"That's it?" Sams complained. "What about when it tried to fly away? You don't think that's important?"

"Oh, yeah, Master Guns. About that. Well, like were flying up, and the bird's just hanging on to me for dear life. When we get up high, I think it's going to pass out, and then we're surrounded by a fuzzy bubble."

"Fuzzy bubble?" Ryck asked.

"I don't know, sir," Çağlar said, looking miserable. "That's what it seemed like. The fighter starts to wobble, like. And the bird, he lets go of me and it's like we are all going together in the other way. The Navy pilot puts on his afterburners and fights it, but we're moving away. Then I'm pinned and can't move. And me, the fighter, and the bird, we all get pulled into the ship. We're there in the hangar and can't move, and a million squids come and look at us. Finally, they send in one of those little mule things. It ties up the Klethos guy, and then we can move. Then I told them I need to get back, so they brought me here."

Ryck shook his head in amazement. That was probably the most Ryck had ever heard his sergeant speak at one time, and while he hadn't been the most eloquent man around, he'd covered the gist of it.

Ryck had already read the report while Çağlar was enroute to the *Omaha Beach*. The Klethos had waited until the Experion had taken it into orbit, then activated what was undoubtedly its personal spaceship, which was more of a force field than a physical ship. It had tried to pull the Experion and Çağlar with it, and it was winning the tug-of-war with the Navy fighter when a quick-thinking crewman on the *FS Barcelona* captured the fighter with a focused tractor beam and reeled it in. While the Klethos space-conveyance might have been more powerful than an Experion, it was no match for a Federation cruiser.

Once on board and realizing the importance of their prisoner, the Barcelona's crew had to come up with a way to separate the Klethos from the Experion and Çağlar without letting it fight or escape. So they had sent in a simple cargo mule that was impervious to tractor beams as part of its purpose. It had tied up the Klethos, as simple as that. The Klethos was secured in the ship's brig, and with xenobiologists onboard, the cruiser was dispatched for an unknown solar system—but not before Çağlar was returned to the brigade.

Ryck stared at his sergeant. If this had been in a flick, he'd have jumped all over it as being complete and unbelievable BS. But it had just happened. And Çağlar just stood there looking sheepish as if he was embarrassed about the whole thing, as if he'd done something wrong. They kid was a hero, and with a live Klethos to poke and prod, the science types just might come up with ways to defeat them.

Ryck looked at his watch. Time was getting short, so he had to cut this off, as fascinating as it had been.

"OK, Sergeant. That's pretty amazing, and I'm proud of you. But we've got about five hours before we're in orbit. Go get some chow and accelerated shuteye. You need to be ready to go."

Sergeant Çağlar came to attention, then stepped out the hatch.

The other four Marines looked at each other for a moment before simultaneously breaking out into laughter.

"Holy fucking shit!" Sams said.

"I've, never . . ." Jorge added. "I mean, have you?"

"No, and I still can't believe it," Ryck agreed. "But what I told him is true. We've still got more to do, but I need you alert and capable. So all of you, back to your racks, and accelerated sleep. That's an order."

The three Marines nodded, still laughing over Çağlar's little adventure, and got up and left. Ryck took a moment to check on the refit. The Navy and Marine armorers were working frantically to refit and replenish each of the PICS. Satisfied that all was being done that could be done, Ryck got up and moved to his rack, laid down, and put the AS armband over his left bicep. Dialing in three hours, he hesitated. Accelerated sleep was painless, but no one liked it. Vague, uncomfortable dreams filled AS, dreams that faded as soon as the person woke up, but dreams that still left an unsettled feeling.

With a sigh, he pushed the enter button, and within moments, had fallen into the dark, troubled reaches of AS.

YAKIMA 4

Chapter 30

Ryck watched the tall conifers sweep by as the surface effect craft whisked them up the Skykomish River. It was frankly beautiful. Yakima 4 had been terraformed for over 400 years, so the forest was mature, rivaling any of the few pockets of old growth left on Earth itself. In another time, he could imagine taking his family here, camping and fishing for the huge runs of salmon that migrated up the stream.

As if on cue, the craft crossed a series of shallows, and the bright red humped backs of sockeyes stood out against the graveled river bottom as they swam upstream. Klethos had landed and had engaged with FCDC troops only 120 kms away, yet the salmon ignored that, following the call of their DNA, on a world far from where they evolved. Nature worked its way as she willed.

The FCDC troops, using tactics developed by the Marines, had tried to interdict the advancing Klethos. Most of the planet was still free of the threat, but if the 4,000 or Klethos were allowed to continue, and especially if they were reinforced, there was little doubt that the planet's 9.5 billion people would be exterminated. Evacuation plans were already in progress, but 9.5 billion was a huge number.

As on Ruggeri's World, the sheer mass of people could crush 4,000 or 40,000 Klethos. But Ryck knew it wouldn't happen. No one wanted to be the first to sacrifice himself, preferring to let the trained fighters take the creatures on. Even when the Marines were overrun and the planet lost, the civilians would still flee rather than fight. Regrettable, but a fact of life.

If we're overrun, Ryck reminded himself, trying not to be pessimistic.

The top brass wanted the initial wave of Klethos to be stopped before they reached Spokane, a city of over 10 million, and where the Marines had landed. Heavily populated, the planet hosted close to a million FCDC troops. Some 20,000 of them had been in Suquamish, the state for which Spokane was the capital, and they had deployed up the Skykomish to try and stop the Klethos before they had even begun their advance.

The FCDC troops had fought hard, but they had been readily defeated with only a handful of troopers escaping into the deep forest. Very few of the Klethos has been killed, but what the troopers had succeeded in doing was to delay the Klethos long enough for the Marines to land. Now, they were being rushed up river to the Green Canyon Gorge, a bottleneck where they hoped to stop the Klethos advance.

Once in the gorge, the Klethos could very easily bypass them, but no one expected that. The Klethos seemed to seek confrontation rather than capture land or strategic points.

First Brigade was the Marine point of main effort. Ryck had demanded it of the general, and as the most robust unit left in the force, it made sense. That and their success on Roggeri's World made them the logical choice. If they could stop the advance, then several million Marines and FCDC troopers would have time to deploy to the world. Humans may not be able to match Klethos one-on-one, but there were a lot of humans to throw into a fight.

Ryck had another reason that he wanted to be thrown into the breach, a reason his subconscious just couldn't quite seem to release. As he watched the river flow underneath him as he leaned over the rail, whatever it was seemed to hover just out of reach, almost there, but not quite. He hoped whatever it was would surface before the fight.

As a warrior, he'd learned to trust his gut, but at the moment, he just had a whole lot of nothing.

"You ready for this?" Hecs asked, coming up to lean on the rail alongside or Ryck.

"I think so," Ryck said, watching a heron take off in flight, frightened by the big surface effect craft zipping up the river.

"We've come a long ways, you and me," Hecs said.

"Yeah, we have, Sergeant Major Phantawisangtong, that we have. But if you're going to get maudlin on me now, I think I'll just have to toss you over the rail here and feed the fishes."

Hecs laughed, but it wasn't a very enthusiastic effort.

"Yeah, I know. I just wanted to say, sir, that it's been an honor."

"Fuck you, King Tong," Ryck said, embarrassed.

This time Hecs laughed with more emotion.

"And you were that skinny, selfish kid, always me, me, me," Hecs said lightly.

"Hey, I wasn't skinny!" Ryck protested.

"But you were me, me, me," Hecs said more soberly. "Remember that inspection?"

"The junk-on-the-bunk? With Calderón?" Ryck asked.

"Yeppir. That one. You were so pissed to lose your recruit stripes. I knew then that was your what-if moment."

"Huh?"

"That was when you were either going to become a Marine or become a shitbird," Hecs said.

"And?"

"And I think we can safely say you became a Marine. And I'm damned proud to have been one of those who helped you become one."

Ryck said nothing, but he felt a warm glow sweep over his body. More than his medals, more than that damned movie, this was what made him want to be a Marine. He wanted, no he *needed* the respect of those who he respected. With that, if this were going to be the end of the road, he couldn't complain.

Even if they got through this, however, he was pretty sure his cancer was too far advanced. He'd regret leaving Hannah and the kids, but given the choice, he'd do it again.

"Calderón, huh? I wonder what happened to him," Ryck said, more to change the subject than anything else.

"You never heard? He's retired, now. He made gunny, married, and has a couple dozen kids or so."

"No shit? A gunny?" Ryck asked, surprised.

They stood silently, watching the river for a few moments before Ryck asked, "As long as we're in the reminiscing mood, you remember Recruit MacPruit?"

"The MMA champion?"

"Well, planetary champion, but yeah. You know what we did to him at boot?"

"You beat the shit out of him," Hecs answered. "In the showers."

Ryck felt a wave of guilt wash over him as if he'd just been caught with his hand in the cookie jar. "You knew that?"

"We'd have been pretty shitty DIs if we hadn't, right? Besides, the little shit needed it."

"You know, he saved my life," Ryck said after a few moments.

That seemed to take the sergeant major by surprise.

"He did?"

"Not in that way," Ryck said. "Not in combat. But in MCMA[16]. He broke my arm, you know. On purpose."

"And that saved your life."

"Sort of, yeah. He taught me that in a fight, everything is legal. Eye-gouging, ball kicking, whatever. If you're going to fight, do it for real."

"Good advice, but that saved your life?"

"When I fought the capys on GenAg 13, the hand-to-hand stuff, I was remembering what he taught me, and without it, I don't think I would have won. I knew I had to do what needed to be done, and I just did it."

"Hmph," Hecs grunted. "Well, I guess the little shit had some value after all."

"We've known a lot of Marines, you and me, Hector, and all have had value. All of them," Ryck said.

"Ain't that the truth, sir. Ain't that the truth."

---

[16] Marine Corps Martial Arts

"And we're going to know a lot more. It isn't ending now," Ryck said, but without the conviction he wished he'd felt.

The two friends fell back into a companionable silence. Sometimes simply not talking was the best form of communications.

"Sir, the pilot says we'll be landing in a few," Çağlar said, coming up and interrupting their thoughts.

"Well, Sergeant Major, it's time to earn those big bucks. You ready?"

"Ready and able, sir. Let's kick some avian ass."

"Let's get this show on the road," he bellowed out, turning to face the bulk of the Marines in the craft. "Hop to it Marines!"

Once a DI, always a DI, Ryck thought with a smile on his face.

The line of eight surface effect craft followed the lead craft out of the river and onto the shore. The Marines had landed.

Chapter 31

The Rugged Flow River ran generally east to west. The river fell some 70 meters through the Green Canyon Gorge with a tall, vertical cliff to the south, and as the river had meandered over the eons, a wide valley stretching to the not-quite-as-steep hills to the north. The gorge was as wide as 30 km as the river flowed out into the forested land below, but the Marines were stationed at The Throat, a constricted point that was still three kilometers across. For a brigade of Marines, even one so depleted, this was incredibly tight quarters, but it would limit the forward wave of Klethos, who seemed pretty much wedded to a 30-meter interval between fighters. Just as the Marines had been able to hold the pier against two Klethos with 20 Marines, the general hoped that more Marines in depth would be able to hold The Throat.

Ryck wasn't so sure. He had no doubt that his Marines were learning how to engage the creatures, and they should be able to defeat the first wave, but with 10,000 Klethos now confirmed on the deck, they would be able to keep advancing, wearing down the brigade until it was no more. Then it would be Second in the breach, followed by the remnants of Third with Jorge in command. As he ran through numbers in his head, asking his AI to crunch them, he just didn't see the force being able to hold off the Klethos long enough for reinforcements to reach them.

Ryck positioned himself just to the north of the river along the most logical avenue of advance. Something told him that he needed to be on the lines, in amongst the Fuzos. Hecs and Sams had tried to talk him out of it, and Çağlar was beside himself, but some instinct told Ryck he had to be at the tip of the spear. He knew he had a plan, but it was buried in his mind, refusing to come out. The more Ryck tried to concentrate, the further that plan sunk into the recesses.

A wave of dizziness swept over him, and he put his arm out against an old fir tree to steady himself. He refused to activate his sensor. He knew the cancer was winning. One way or the other, his time was limited.

As the dizziness passed, he decided to relax. His "plan" could just be his synapses misfiring as the cancer took a stronger grip on his body. Better to focus on the mission. His men were trained, and they would make him proud. He just hoped his body would hold up long enough to join the fight as a warrior should.

Well, I guess it will, he thought to himself as the recon team station above them on the cliff reported that the Klethos were coming down the slope and were two klicks out.

Ryck looked up to where he knew the recon team was. He didn't even know their identity, but he wished them well. They might very well be the only Marine survivors of the coming battle.

At least they had full comms. With the capys, comms were usually blocked. The Klethos didn't seem to give a shit about that.

At the thought of the capys, Ryck looked over to Carl and his two shadows. Ryck had lost contact with the three capys during the retreat to Knoferee, and given their slow, deliberate pace, he'd been sure they'd been overrun by the pursuing Klethos. On the *Omaha Beach*, though, he'd found out that Marines in 3/5 had picked up the protesting capys and carried them under their arms to the pier and onto one of the shuttles.

Neither Carl or either of the other two had offered any kind of thanks. They'd merely tracked down Ryck to find out what was next as if nothing had happened. The capys looked more Earthlike than the Klethos, but they were far more alien, to Ryck's way of thinking. He thought humans were far more like the Klethos, who at least acted in a somewhat understandable manner.

While he didn't want to admit it, he had a degree of respect for the dinosaur-birds. He would do his best to kill every one of them, but there was a code of the warrior that he thought they followed.

Shit, now they are knights of chivalry? he derided himself. *Is the cancer eating out my brain?*

Ryck edged forward. The 2/3 Marine to his left looked over, then edged towards him a few steps, as if to be better placed to protect him. Ryck appreciated that, but he didn't want anyone putting himself in danger by trying to keep him alive.

The trees to the front of Ryck were young, only a meter or so tall. When the Klethos emerged from the forest, they strode among the trees, stopping only 200 meters from the Marine lines. As expected, one Klethos stepped forward, looked at the Marines facing it, then launched into its dance.

It looked pretty magnificent, Ryck acknowledged. Its feathered collar flashed in the sun, the bright yellow and red tinted with some other iridescent, almost lilac color. Ryck remembered the report about the necropsies the xenobiologists had performed on the dead Klethos the brigade had recovered, and they found out that the feathers had densely packed nerve bundles that branched directly into their brains. Some of the xenobiologists thought the feathers were sensing appendages of some sort, some thought they had a sexual purpose.

Why am I thinking about that? Ryck wondered. *Feathers or no feather, we've got about three minutes until all hell breaks loose. Their sexual organs don't really matter much.*

This Klethos seemed to jump higher and spin faster than any Ryck had seen before. The other Klethos seemed enthralled as well, if he was reading alien posture correctly. This was more than a Zulu warrior beating his shield. This was a pure celebration of the warrior ethos, of what a warrior was, Ryck was sure. This was a physical celebration of what made a Klethos a Klethos.

With a final flurry, pieces of small trees flying into the air as they were torn up, he lifted his head in a screech as he spun to a stop, facing the Marines in the now-familiar lunge pose.

Ryck almost laughed, wanting to shout out "ta-da!"

Now he's going to slap me with his glove and call me out at dawn, he thought, actually laughing at loud.

And with a thundering explosion that almost stunned him, the dam in his subconscious broke, and his "plan" boiled to the surface.

Grubbing hell, he thought, suddenly sure of himself.

The Klethos pulled back from its lunge and half turned to the others who seemed to gather themselves.

Ryck stepped forward, rammed his externals to the max, and shouted out "Ooh-rah" as loud as he could.

And almost broke down coughing,

The lead Klethos stopped, uncertainty evident in its posture as it turned to look back at Ryck.

"Sir!" Çağlar shouted, stepping forward.

"Hold, Hans! That's an order!"

Ryck started forward, walking straight at the Klethos.

"All hands, hold your position. Do not fire," Ryck passed on the open circuit.

Am I fucking out of my head? he wondered, as second thoughts started to chip away at his determination. *Shit, I'm almost dead as it is. In for a penny.*

None of the Klethos moved as Ryck marched deliberately forward. All had their eyes locked on him. The Klethos looked impossible tall as Ryck stopped ten meters in front of it.

"I challenge you!" Ryck shouted, knowing the thing wouldn't understand the words, but he hoped it would understand the tone.

The blast of his externals caused ripples in the thing's feathers, and Ryck was pleased to see it flinch before it stood back taller, the feathers around its neck standing straighter.

Carefully, Ryck took out his rocket pistol and dropped in on the ground.

"Sir!" Çağlar shouted over the P2P.

Ryck turned off his comms. With his right arm, he grabbed his M77, and with a wrench, tore it off his arm, hydroconnector fluid spurting from torn lines. Then, and most important, he slowly took out his mameluke, dropping it to the ground.

He stared up at the Klethos, unarmed and at its mercy.

The Klethos stared back down at Ryck for a long ten seconds, the longest ten seconds of Ryck's life. Then, Ryck swore it nodded at him. It dropped its rifle, then held out its sword horizontally at shoulder height before dropping it.

A wave of relief swept through Ryck. He'd been right, and he'd known it for a long time. He just hadn't realized he'd known it.

The Klethos did have their own code of chivalry. They were warriors, and they fought, not for land, but for the glory of the battle. Before each battle, though, a champion was offered to fight. If the challenge was not accepted, the other side was slaughtered. And that explained their berserker reaction on Ruggeri's World. Their champion, leader, or whatever had been cut down before the challenge had been made. The code had been broken, and the transgressor had to be punished.

Ryck was as sure of this as of anything he'd ever known in the past. More than that, he understood it—and accepted it.

Ryck weighed his chances. The Klethos was much larger than Ryck and much, much faster. Ryck was in a PICS. With the sword, Ryck wouldn't have had a chance. Without weapons, he thought he might. He flexed his left arm, which was still balky as the suit's nanos tried to reroute the hydroconnector fluids Ryck had torn out.

Afraid of breaking some unknown code, Ryck moved into a modified en garde, waiting for the Klethos to move. And without warning, the Klethos struck. Ryck barely had time to raise one arm as the warrior hit him like a freight train. Both of them crashed to the ground, flattening the small seedlings around them. Instinctively, Ryck put one foot under the Klethos' crotch as they hit, and kicking out, he sent the big guy flying over him.

Ryck scrambled back to his feet as the Klethos got up as well, facing him. Ryck didn't recognize the position it was in, but it sure had the feel of a type of martial art. As it darted forward, Ryck spun around on one leg in a move he'd practiced not for combat, but for the patron day's dance.   Converting it mid-swing into a spinning back kick, his armored boot hit the Klethos high on the shoulder as it came forward, driving it into the dirt. Before Ryck recovered, though, to exploit the situation, the Klethos scrambled forward and out of the way. It seemed to Ryck slightly dazed and favoring its left side, raising his hopes.

"MacPruitt, help me here," he called out, scoring a jab to the warrior's chest and bringing an uppercut that strained the PICS' servos.

Only the uppercut never connected. Incredibly, the Klethos stopped the swing with its own hand. Hans had said his Klethos was too strong for him to peel its grip off of him, something Ryck should have remembered. And now he'd closed in.

Stupid!

Ryck brought up his knee, ramming it into the Klethos' belly, but the knee glanced off with no discernable effect. He stomped down on the unprotected claws of its feet, hurting it, he knew, but it leaned forward, pushing its feet out of Ryck's reach. It started pushing Ryck back, bending the left arm as if could sense the damage Ryck had done to it. Ryck struggled to resist, his AI calling out a warning. Ryck thought he could smell something burning inside his combat suit.

With a force of will more than anything else, he stopped the arm, right at what he was sure was its breaking point. His back was arched, his feet couldn't reach anything, one arm was pinned, and the other was about to break. Ryck was in the shit.

The Klethos shifted, and it let go of Ryck's right arm to apply more pressure to his left. Immediately, instinctively, Ryck hopped up with his legs and ducked down with shoulder, relieving some of the pressure on his left arm. His right arm flailed for purchase as he tried to keep from falling, pain lancing through his cancer-eaten shoulder.

His hand closed over the Klethos shoulder, over its left small arm. He couldn't see it given his arched back, but his biofeedbacks left no doubt. Ryck raised his right arm and brought it down as hard as he could, once, twice, three times, each blow a jolt of agony from his shoulder. He felt the Klethos small arm give, and while the Klethos screeched something, it never let up, bending Ryck's left arm farther and farther. When it snapped, as it would, Ryck knew it would be over. He'd have lost.

He reached for the Klethos neck, but it was leaning out of the way, as only his fingertips touched it. Something lighter touched his gauntlet: the neck feathers.

"Go for the balls if you have to," Seth MacPruitt's voice reached him from across time and space.

Ryck couldn't reach the Klethos' crotch, even if it had balls. And he wasn't sure if the feathers-have-a-sexual-function faction was right, but it was all he had. He closed his fingers around the feathers and pulled with all his might.

And had an immediate reaction.

The Klethos went ballistic. It screeched and shook Ryck like a terrier on a rat, all the time trying desperately to break Ryck's left arm. Ryck managed to grab another handful of feathers and pull them out.

Ryck landed with a thump on the ground. He jumped back up, flexing his left arm. In front of him, the Klethos staggered before righting itself. It seemed out of balance to Ryck. Unless it was faking, it was hurt and hurt badly.

Ryck circled his opponent warily. It might be unsteady, but those arms were too strong for him. He could not afford to be caught again. He had to keep his distance.

Glad for his MCMA training, glad for all the hours he'd spent practicing PICS dance moves in the hopes of performing at a patron day celebration, he married the two, darting in and out with kicks that rained upon the Klethos body. If it had been whole, Ryck knew he'd have been caught and drawn in like a fish on the line. But the Klethos was not whole. It was damaged. It had almost no balance, and it was much, much slower.

But it never gave up. It kept swinging for the fences, twice connecting with thunderous blows that cracked Ryck's display panel and almost knocked him down. But it couldn't take the beating the smaller Marine was giving it. Ryck attacked the legs. One snapped gruesomely, yet it still stood erect. When Ryck connected to the other leg's knee, it toppled to the ground where it glared at Ryck.

A wave of weariness washed over him as adrenaline faded. He asked his AI for a boost, but his suit had taken too much damage. All power was shunted to keep it working.

Ryck looked back at the line of silently waiting Klethos. He knew in his heart this was a fight to the death. The question was if this was it, or if another champion would be sent out to face him.

Ryck staggered as he was hit by dizziness.

Not grubbing now, he told himself. *Keep it together.*

His cracked display was still trying to post suit failure warnings. Several of his systems had redlined. He needed to end it now.

The Klethos had one good arm, and it held that up, palm flared. Ryck had to get past that. In the end, he just fell forward, the hand catching his throat as he broke out the ground and pound, fists pummeling the Klethos head.

The Klethos' good arm tried to find a purchase on Ryck, but the blows were coming in too thick and powerful. It took ten or fifteen seconds, but the Klethos' arm fell away. Ryck's display plate was covered in blood, the too-scarlet blood of his opponent. Ryck stopped hitting.

Slowly, he pushed his way upright and turned to the Klethos, expecting another champion to come forward. If it did, so be it. Another Marine could challenge it after it killed him, and on down the line it would go, Marine and Klethos, Klethos and Marine, delaying the Klethos long enough for reinforcements to reach them.

There was movement in the line, and Ryck tried to wipe the blood off of his display plate so he could see. If he was going to die, he wanted to look his executioner in the eye.

But he began to realize that today was not going to be his day to die. The Klethos were turning around. They were giving up the field of battle. Ryck watched them disappear back into the forest. Slowly he turned around back to the Marines. A groundswell rose in volume as almost 2,000 Marines shouted his name at the top of their voices. A horde, with Çağlar at the head, rushed forward just as things went black and Ryck collapsed into the welcome embrace of the dark.

TARAWA

Chapter 32

Ryck opened his eyes to a soft white light. He was in a bed, not his bed, and he wasn't sure why. His mind was fuzzy, like it was coming out of regen, but that didn't make any sense. He was on Yakima 4, right?

Yakima 4 or not, he was in a hospital, he realized, looking down past his feet at the white room, holoscreen up in the corner, and too cheerful print of daises on the wall. Shifting his gaze, he saw Hannah in a stuffed chair, head back and eyes closed.

Shit, what happened to me there? he wondered. *I wasn't hurt that bad. Is it the Brick?*

"Hannah?"

His wife startled, then looked up, catching his eye. She rushed over with a relieved look on her face and put her arms around his neck, squeezing tight.

"What happened?" he asked.

Hannah pulled back, the relieved look being replaced by something harder, something angrier.

"What happened? How can you be asking me that? You almost killed yourself!" she said, grabbing the lobe of his right ear and pinching it hard, her Torritite accent getting stronger as she became more stressed.

"What?" he asked, trying to pull away.

"Your BRC! You knew you had it. You had to as advanced as it be. Yet you go off and fight, and that almost be your end. You knew it, right?"

"I . . . I . . ."

"I knew it! So, you be willing to leave your children, your wife, because only the great Ryck Lysander be good enough to save the world. And so you kill yourself!" she shouted at him, tears welling in her eyes.

"I'm. . . I'm dying?" he asked.

He'd already come to terms with that, but seeing Hannah cry sank home just what that meant. His kids would grow up without him. He'd never see them mature, marry, have their own kids. His grandchildren.

"No, you not be dying," Hannah, said, pinching his ear lobe once more. "But no thanks to you. If you were not put into stasis when you were, you would be dead. When you got here, and by the time the doctors realized you had BRC, it was almost too late. Even then, we almost lost you. Doctor Brennan said another twelve hours, and it would have been too late."

As she calmed down, her accent faded back to normal for her. She squeezed his hand so tightly that he had to adjust its position.

"Twelve hours?" he asked, more to himself that to her.

"Twelve grubbing hours," she responded, the first time Ryck had ever heard her use his most common expletive.

"And now I'm cured?"

"No, you know better. You be in remission, but you're always going to have to be checked. This regen just increases the rate of the BRC coming back. It be when more than if. But that be OK if we just catch it early."

Ryck knew that, but with so much to take in, his mind was in a muddle.

"What happened on Yakima?" he asked, suddenly remembering why he'd delayed treatment.

"Yakima? Oh, the great Ryck Lysander did save the world," she said sarcastically, but she couldn't keep a hint of pride out of her voice.

"Is it still in human control?"

"Yes. The Klethos left when you defeated their *d'relle*, and they'll hold to that for over 17 years," she said.

"Their what? Dulla?"

"D'relle. Something like a battle leader. You accepted her challenge, and you defeated her. So now they have to cede the planet to us for 17 years. Sixteen years now."

Ryck's mind was reeling. *"D'relle?"* "Her?" SIXTEEN grubbing years?"

"How long have I been in regen?" Ryck asked.

"Honey, you were as close to death as possible. The regen was very, very extensive. You've been under for 15 months. You've got therapy coming, but the docs decided it was finally time to bring out of your coma."

"Fifteen months? How are the kids? What's with this ceding the planet? Are we at war?" he asked in a hurried muddle.

"At least you put the kids first. They're fine, and mighty proud of you. They'll be by later today if you're up to it."

"I'm up to it," Ryck said assuredly.

"As far as the Klethos, you've got a lot of catching up to do. We are at war, but not at war. They took three planets with huge losses of life before communications were initiated. That's when we learned about their rules, which I think you figured out before anyone. Since then, one more planet has been lost, but two were saved."

Ryck wasn't sure he'd figured out any "rules." He'd been acting on his gut without really analyzing why. But he was beginning to see the picture.

"So they want one of our planets, they issue a challenge, and we can defend it. If we win, they keep their hands off for 17 years. If we don't accept the challenge, it's war? And we accept that?"

"We have to accept it. They be far more advanced that we. If it be total war, then we're gone like the Trinoculars."

"The capys are gone?"

"They will be soon enough. No Trinocular champion is strong enough to challenge a *d'relle*, and to be frank, we don't think they really grasp the concept."

"Ah, General Lysander, how are we feeling today," a man in a white lab coat and the assured manner of a doctor came in, ignoring Ryck but looking at Ryck's bioreadouts.

"I'm fine," he started before exclaiming *"General* Lysander?"

"Oh, I didn't tell you yet. You were promoted to Brigadier General almost a year ago," Hannah casually said as if she was mentioning what she had for dinner the night before.

"But, I just got my permanent colonel's grade," he protested.

"That be almost two years ago. And now you be promoted again."

"Did you tell him about the, you know?" the doctor asked.

"What? Tell me what?"

"Oh, you were awarded a second Federation Nova. When you be ready, we be going to Earth for the ceremony."

"I meant the flick," the doctor said, "but yes, the Nova is pretty big. Do you know you are the first living recipient of two Novas? They said that in the flick."

Ryck felt dizzy and overwhelmed. There was too much data overload. They were dueling with Klethos? He was a general now? He'd been awarded a second Nova? And now there was a second flick about him?"

"So, you know they used the real footage of your duel with the *d'relle*? It was the bomb!" the doctor said, excitement in his voice. "Oh, of course you don't know. You've been induced for the last 15 months. But you need to see it. Copacetic plus!"

"I was there," Ryck said for lack of anything else to say.

"Hah! 'I was there!' Priceless! I'm going to repeat that, if you don't mind. 'I was there!'" the doctor said, obviously delighted.

"Well," the doctor started, getting back to physician mode. "We've got FCN news waiting outside. They'd like an interview with the Hero of Yakima 4, if you feel up to it. If you don't, though, tell me. I'll send them packing until another day. I'm here for you to help you speed up your recovery."

"FCN?" Ryck repeated.

He was repeating quite a bit of what was being said to him. He hoped the Brick had not damaged his cognitive abilities, because he was sounding like a blooming idiot.

"Honey, things have changed while you have been under. We're in Star City now," she said, referring to the neighborhood at Headquarters where the flag officers were given housing. ". . . and, well, Doctor Brennan is right. You're the Hero of Yakima 4 now. I even sort of signed a contract for your action figure," she said, suddenly looking unsure of herself.

Hannah was always confident and assured, and this view of her like a shy teenager made him smile. He hesitated a moment, wondering if he dared string her along, and she mistook his silence for disapproval.

"I can cancel it, but General Mbanefo thought it would be good for the Corps, and Ben, Ben was so excited. Half of the fees are going to the families of those who fell," she quickly said, running her words together.

Ryck laughed and grabbed her hand. "It's OK. If you thought it was a good idea, I agree.

"Tell me, though, does it look like me?" he asked, suddenly curious.

"Turn around, General," Doctor Brennan said.

Ryck twisted his neck. On the shelf beside the bed, a 25 cm tall action figure stood in its stand, awaiting activation. And it did look like him—a 25-year-old him, a him with a Mr. Universe physique, but him none-the-less.

Ryck had a lot to digest, but he knew Hannah was right. His life had changed when he'd been awarded this first Nova. If what Hannah and Dr. Brennan had said was even 50% accurate, his life was going to change even more.

"Well, Doctor, about the news crew. Sending them away isn't going to do much, so let's get that out of the way. But nothing more after that until I see my kids. Agreed?"

"Yes, sir, General. I'm on it," he said as he left the room, calling for a nurse.

General Lysander. It has a nice ring to it, he thought as he let Hannah smooth his hair and straighten out the sheets around him.

Epilogue

With a clean bill of health and as the new Director of Public Affairs, Brigadier General Ryck Lysander thanked his driver, telling him to be back at 2200 to pick him up. His life had turned topsy-turvy since he left regen and rehabilitation, but having a driver was one of the most jarring things for him to accept.

Ryck liked to drive, and with his new Fratelli Scorpion sitting in the garage, he wished he had more of an opportunity to drive it. But in the flag officer's finishing school, he was told in no uncertain terms that generals were driven, especially when they were generals with strong public recognition. Sergeant Theodore was not only his driver, but he was also a deadly bodyguard.

Staff Sergeant Hans Çağlar had requested the position, begging Ryck for it, to be clear. Ryck refused. Çağlar needed to get some time in the fleet. He'd never been a squad leader, and Ryck was not going to let him get further out-of-touch with what it meant to be a Marine. Besides, as a fellow Federation Nova holder, it just didn't seem right to relegate him to being a driver. Ryck would be more than pleased to serve with Hans again, but the staff sergeant needed to get some leadership time under his belt.

For most of Ryck's career as an officer, he'd been one of two living Marine Nova holders. With Joab Ling and Max Zachary, there had been four. Now, after the first battles of the Klethos War, there were seven living Marine holders, and one of the 22 living Navy holders was a corpsman serving with the Marines. It was getting so that you couldn't swing a dead cat at headquarters without hitting one, as Bert Nidischii', also a brigadier general, was fond of saying. Of course, only Ryck had two of them.

Today was not about the medal, though. Today was a different ceremony, a different celebration, one that had been delayed, but was finally about to take place.

Two paparazzi were waiting, cams recording as Ryck strode up the walk into the Globe and Laurel. At least the numbers were down from the swarms that had followed his every movement after his release from the hospital. He hoped that as the routine of his new job became the norm, even the last diehards would abandon the chase and focus on the newest boy band members or crystal stars.

The front hatch of the pub swung open before Ryck could reach for it, and Mr. Geiland said, "Welcome, General Lysander. Your party is in the back."

Ryck stopped and held out his hand. Mr. Geiland had been part of the pub since Ryck first stepped in. He was a civilian, but he was part of the very essence of the Corps.

"I'd be honored if you would join us, Mr. Geiland, for the toast."

A slight smile creased the old man's wrinkled face as he said, "It is I who would be honored.

Marines, sailors, civilian friends, and more than a few politicos stood up as Ryck walked in. A few gave out shouts of welcome, and Ryck nodded and shook hands. General Mbanefo and his wife sat with Hannah in the corner, a pitcher of beer on the table. Lieutenant General Ukiah sat next to them. Ryck blew Hannah a kiss as he pushed his way to the back of the pub. He'd be out later to mix and mingle, but the raison d'être of the evening was in the back room.

He'd been given a time to arrive, and as he pushed through the heavy wooden doors, 53 men stood up and clapped.

"Welcome, sir," Colonel Jorge Simone said, motioning to a seat near the podium. As the second senior Marine in the room, he was once again the master of ceremony.

Jorge clinked on his glass with a fork in the time-honored tradition for silence, and the men in the room quieted down.

"Friends," he began, "and I will call all of you friends. We are gathered here for a joyous ceremony. The last time we met, it was to bid farewell to Major Donte Ward, the first of our class to fall."

"Here, here!" several of the others called out, lifting glasses.

"Since that time, three more of us have made the voyage to the beyond: Major Elijah Temperance, in battle against the Gionva Faction; Major Crispin Volaire, in the disappearance of the *FS Dubai*; and Mr. Liam Xu, to complications of Crispen's Disease. I would like to lift a toast to our fallen comrades."

Mr. Geiland had slipped a stein of Corona in front of Ryck, so he had something to lift in the toast.

Jorge waited a few moments before he resumed speaking, "But today is not for solemn reflection. Today is a celebration. Today we open that bottle of champagne and toast in honor of our most illustrious classmate, a man whom I am proud to call friend. . ." he paused, then dramatically added, "SIR!"

The gathered men broke out into laughter.

"Brigadier General Ryck Lysander!"

More cheers broke out.

Jorge nodded at Mr. Geiland, who brought out the tray of tulip glasses and set them down. Solemnly, he walked up to the class box, punching in the code to trigger the release, and carefully took down the bottle of Krug Clos d'Ambonnay.

Almost regally, he took off the lead foil, and with his thumbs, applied pressure until the cork popped, flying across the room and almost hitting Gervis Smith in the head, to everyone's amusement. Mr. Geiland quickly raised the bottle, minimizing the amount of champagne that foamed out to fall on the floor.

He wiped off the bottle with the towel he'd had hanging from his belt, and then handed the bottle to Jorge.

Jorge poured just a swallow of champagne into each fluted glass. The bottle was a full magnum, but with 55 glasses, that still didn't go a long ways.

When he was finished, he turned to Ryck and said, "Traditionally, the senior Marine present is the last to be served. In this case, tradition is reversed. After the toast, if you would lead us, sir?"

"Classmates, in celebration!" Jorge shouted out as all 55 men, Mr. Geiland included, raised their glasses.

Ryck felt a wave of warmth sweep over him. The men around him were the ones he'd been commissioned with. He'd lost touch with some, even most of them, but they had still shared a connection. They were his brothers.

He raised the glass to his lips and took a swallow, the bubbly effervescence tickling his throat.

"I declare this fit for human consumption!" he shouted, not really part of this ceremony, but welcomed if the response from the others was any indication. Within seconds, all the glasses had been drained.

"Friends, brothers, I am in awe of all of you. Things happen to swing my way, but anyone of you could be in my place today had circumstances been any different."

"No!" a few men responded.

Maybe not all of them, Ryck acknowledged, being frank, *but certainly some.*

He looked to Jorge, the man Ryck thought would earn his stars first. He'd been too competent for his own good, and had been constantly yanked out of the billets he'd needed to advance quickly. Even his chest told the story. Instead of the stacks of ribbons Ryck wore, or any number of the others wore, Jorge had four ribbons: the combat ribbon with three battle stars for Tri-30, Ruggeri's World, and Yakima 4, two low level staff achievement ribbons, and the Navy Cross. Once given a chance, he'd proven himself. Given more of a chance, and he'd have made general first, Ryck was sure.

"It's true," Ryck said. "I've just been in the right time at the right place. And for that I am grateful. But more than that, I am grateful for the brotherhood and support you have shown me.

"Prince," he said, singling out his old friend. "Without you, I would never have made it through MOTC in the first place. I was ready to bilge out, and you got me over that hump. So I owe you."

Major Prince Jellico raised his empty glass in acknowledgement as those standing next to him clapped him on his shoulders.

"You, John, Curt—I see you hiding there. Jorge," he added, turning to his friend. "All of you, I thank you. And I thank you for coming. "Derrick Ohu, you came from where, from Dryer? All that way?'

"Wouldn't have missed it, sir!" Derrick shouted out.

"Well, I'm glad you made it. It means a lot to me."

Ryck looked down at his glass, then made a show of turning it upside down.

"Looks like we're dry. So before I break down like a baby, what say we move into the main pub? I had to take out a second mortgage to buy enough booze for you—"

"You're in Star City now!" a voice called out to general laughter. "It's free housing!"

"Well, true. So, I had to sign over my firstborn, whatever. But let's get out there before everyone else drinks me dry."

There was a cheer, and each man came up to congratulate him before wending out to the main pub.

"Thanks, Jorge," Ryck said as only the two of them were left. "I appreciate it. I really thought it would be you, though."

"Ah, I knew it would be you, sir. There was no doubt in my mind."

"I think you're next."

"Maybe, or maybe Travis. Or Zeke. Or me, I'll admit. But I don't think I'd even have a chance if it weren't for you. You gave me the opportunity," Jorge said.

"Which you took and ran with. You did an amazing job," Ryck said, flipping a finger to point at Jorge's Navy Cross.

"And I know you put in the good word for me with General Nidischii'."

"I can think of no one better to be on the Klethos Response Council," Ryck responded.

With the "war" with the Klethos, the Federation, and the Marines in particular, were trying to come to grips with the new paradigm. Marines and sailors were no longer dying in battle with them. Only four champions had been killed, in fact. But it was still a war, and the Klethos wanted to take over human planets.

The Klethos has wiped out the capys, with fewer than 20 million of the Trinoculars left alive, refugees on two Brotherhood worlds and now under human protection. The Klethos may not wipe out humanity, if the war continued to be played by the same rules, but humanity needed to make sure they understood those rules. Jorge and Bert Nidischii' were two of the men who were going to make sure of that.

"Hell, Jorge, let's go get something to drink," Ryck said, putting his arm around the broad shoulders of the heavy-worlder.

The two Marines stepped out into the pub to the cheers of the gathered crowd. Ryck caught sight of Hecs, Sams, Joab Ling, Bert Nidischii', Çağlar, Gunny Bergstrøm, "Genghis" Bayarsaikhan, Martin Ekema, Doc Adams, Fearless uKhiwa—Marines and sailors with whom he served. Men who he'd do anything for.

He intended to thank each and every one of them, not just for coming, but for serving alongside him. But there was something he had to do first.

"Drink up, people!" he called out as he made his way to the table in the corner. "The bar is still open, and food will be out in a few minutes."

The Commandant of the Marine Corps stood up to accept Ryck's greeting, but Ryck brushed by the outstretched hand and took Hannah's, lifting her to her feet. He pulled her into his embrace, giving her a bear hug, squeezing for all he was worth.

"Thank you, Hannah," he whispered into her ear. "We've been through so much, and I never would have made it without you."

Hot tears fell onto his uniform blouse, soaking into his shoulder.

"I love you, too, Ryck," she whispered back as cheers filled the pub again.

And Ryck was at peace.

Thank you for reading *Colonel*. I hope you enjoyed it, and I welcome a review on Amazon, Goodreads, or any other outlet. Please, continue with Ryck's story in the next books of the series, *Commandant*.

If you would like updates on new books releases, news, or special offers, please consider signing up for my mailing list. Your email will not be sold, rented, or in any other way disseminated. If you are interested, please sign up at the link below:

http://eepurl.com/bnFSHH

Other Books by Jonathan Brazee

The United Federation Marine Corps
Recruit
Sergeant
Lieutenant
Captain
Major
Lieutenant Colonel
Colonel
Commandant

Rebel (Set in the UFMC universe.)
Behind Enemy Lines (A UFMC Prequel)
The Accidental War (A Ryck Lysander Short Story Published in *BOB's Bar: Tales from the Multiverse*)

The United Federation Marine Corps' Lysander Twins
Legacy Marines
Esther's Story: Recon Marine
Noah's Story: Marine Tanker
Esther's Story: Special Duty
Blood United

Coda

Women of the United Federation Marines
Gladiator
Sniper
Corpsman

High Value Target (A Gracie Medicine Crow Short Story)
BOLO Mission (A Gracie Medicine Crow Short Story)
Weaponized Math (A Gracie Medicine Crow Novelette, Published in
The Expanding Universe 3, a 2017 Nebula Award Finalist)

The Navy of Humankind: Wasp Squadron
Fire Ant (2018 Nebula Award Finalist)
Crystals
Ace
Fortitude

Ghost Marines
Integration (2018 Dragon Award Finalist)
Unification
Fusion

The Return of the Marines Trilogy
The Few
The Proud
The Marines

The Al Anbar Chronicles: First Marine Expeditionary Force--Iraq
Prisoner of Fallujah
Combat Corpsman
Sniper

Werewolf of Marines
Werewolf of Marines: Semper Lycanus
Werewolf of Marines: Patria Lycanus
Werewolf of Marines: Pax Lycanus

To the Shores of Tripoli

Wererat

Darwin's Quest: The Search for the Ultimate Survivor

Venus: A Paleolithic Short Story

Duty

Semper Fidelis

Checkmate (Originally Published in The Expanding Universe 4)

THE BOHICA WARRIORS
(with Michael Anderle and C. J. Fawcett)
Reprobates
Degenerates

SEEDS OF WAR
(With Lawrence Schoen)
Invasion
Scorched Earth
Bitter Harvest

<u>Non-Fiction</u>

Exercise for a Longer Life

The Effects of Environmental Activism on the Yellowfin Tuna
Industry

Author Website
http://www.jonathanbrazee.com

Made in the USA
San Bernardino,
CA